Dr Ribero's Agency of the Supernatural:

The Case of the Green-Dressed Ghost

Lucy Banks

Amberjack Publishing
New York, New York

Amberjack Publishing

Amberjack Publishing
228 Park Avenue S #89611
New York, NY 10003-1502
http://amberjackpublishing.com

Publisher's Cataloging-in-Publication data
Names: Banks, Lucy, author.
Title: Dr. Ribero's Agency of the Supernatural : the case of the green dressed ghost / by Lucy Banks.
Description: New York, NY: Amberjack Publishing, 2017.
Identifiers: ISBN 978-1-944995-04-1 (pbk.) | 978-1-944995-12-6 (ebook) | LCCN 2016947703
Subjects: LCSH Ghosts--Fiction. | Supernatural--Fiction. | Fathers and sons--Fiction. | Private Investigators--Fiction. | Mystery and detective stories. | Exeter (England)--Fiction. | London (England)--Fiction. | BISAC FICTION / Occult & Supernatural | FICTION / Mystery & Detective / Private Investigators.
Classification: LCC PS3602.A641 2017 | DDC 813.6--dc23

Cover Design: Emma Graves

Printed in the United States of America

To my amazing boys, who helped make this happen.

CHAPTER 1: THE DOOR

Kester Lanner had never liked doors. As a small boy, wide-eyed and duvet-wrapped, he refused sleep until his mother opened his bedroom door with a sigh. The thunder of the school toilet cubicle doors forced his skittish heart into arrhythmia, and the mere sight of his mother's closed bedroom door threw him into an immediate state of loneliness. Fortunately, as he swelled into rotund young adulthood, fear deflated to scanty wariness, as he realised that doors were disappointingly mundane.

However, he'd never come across a door like this before. It was truly remarkable, and for all the wrong reasons.

More relic than modern business entrance, its surface was coal-smudged and splintered, with a tinge of odious decay. Its grubby demeanour, combined with a whiff of mildew, rendered it vaguely organic—as though sprouted from seedling instead of hinged by human hands. The surrounding alleyway was stagnant, simmering in the still afternoon air, and the silence steeped it in secrecy.

Kester surveyed it nervously, trying not to look too closely at the details. If he squinted, it looked just about acceptable. Quaint even, if he took off his spectacles and let astigmatism do its work. But, on close inspection, the spidery cracks, pockmarks, and gritty, crumbly bits were a bit too much to take in. He especially protested at the sight of the moss blossoming from the unspeakably greasy crannies. Bright against the gloomy wood, they were like tiny, mouldy limes, luridly acidic and indecently bold. All in all, it was not a door that he liked at all.

This can't be right, he thought, tugging the letter out of his satchel. The gold-embossed letterhead glinted in the dusty light. *Dr Ribero's Agency, 99 Mirabel Street.* And this was certainly that street. The mottled Victorian road sign on the red-brick wall confirmed it.

The letter had implied something grander, something with a bit more style. He'd imagined a stained glass affair, complete with polished brass letterbox and neoclassical pillars. Instead, a tumble-down building confronted him, without even a mounted plaque to announce the name of the business. It was unceremoniously wedged between a barber shop and a boutique selling voluminous hippy skirts, and had a shifty look about it, as though trying to squeeze surreptitiously between the two.

"Well, this is strange," he muttered, looking around him. "Very strange indeed."

He'd never even heard of Dr Ribero until two weeks ago. The name had been one of the last words his mother had said, as the disease pulled the final moments of life from her body. He remembered the night well. It was unlikely he'd ever forget it. It had been ten to midnight, and the moon, unnaturally bright, had sent a trail of milk-whiteness across the bedspread to his mother's upturned head.

"You must find Dr Ribero," she had said, eyes urgent-bright, clutching his hand in hers. "I ask nothing else of you, my boy. Only that you find him. Find him and tell him who you are."

Who this mysterious man was, or why his mother had insisted that he be found, remained an enigma. She had died only a few moments later, her wheezes subsiding to hollow silence. All was quiet, and the room the more dreadful for it. Kester had not wept; only remained at her side, still holding on to her hand, which gradually turned icy as the next day rose behind him.

In the solitude following her death, he forgot her final words, submerged in the grief of losing his only parent. However, a few days after, when he had a chance to compose himself, he found himself recollecting that strange, foreign-sounding name. In his practical way, he had immediately set about searching for her leather-bound address book.

He located Ribero's name straight away—the only "R" in the book. There was no phone number beside it, only a tightly folded, official-looking letter tucked into the page. It was a strange note, indicating a level of intimacy between sender and recipient, but beyond that he couldn't discern much, only the name and address of the mysterious agency. A search on the internet revealed nothing. Likewise, a visit to the library and a flick through the business directories drew another dead end. *Who is this strange man?* he wondered. *And how had Mother known him?* In spite of his grief, which was still raw, his interest was piqued.

And so it was that he found himself here, a fortnight later, armed with nothing more than his toothbrush, a change of clothes, and a book, standing outside the curious door.

It doesn't look like much of a business, he thought. He peered through the window of the shop next door, hoping to see a member of staff to whom he could ask a few questions. However, he couldn't see a soul through the tie-dyed blouses and velvet waistcoats, only his own owlish reflection staring back at him.

Kester was only twenty-two, but his image suggested older;

wispy hair already starting to thin, watery eyes floating behind thick spectacles, not to mention the paunch tucked uncomfortably into his ironed slacks. He was the very epitome of middle-aged academic, squeezed inexpertly into a younger man's body. He turned away, refusing to dwell on his appearance, and focusing instead on the problem at hand. He'd travelled a long way. Should he simply retreat, board the train, and go home again? Exeter was nicer than he'd expected, with its squat cathedral and swarming streets. Its people bobbed along pavements like contented honey bees, and, in spite of his melancholic mood, he was reluctant to leave it so quickly. The city's blend of traditionalism and modernity soothed his spirit in a manner that he hadn't enjoyed for many months, making him feel a bit more like his former self.

However, this forgotten alleyway reeked of an earlier era. The twenty-first century hadn't touched its cobbled streets. The atmosphere of the Dickensian era still roamed unabated, uninterrupted by modern glass frontages or neon signs. It hung from the wrought-iron lamp posts and the dark beams overhead. It pressed against him in the very weight of those red-bricked walls.

Edging forwards, he studied the door more intently and pondered what to do. There was no intercom, no bell, no buzzer to alert the people inside of his presence. It went against every ingrained rule of etiquette to rap upon such an uninviting entrance. But rap he must, if he was going to solve the mystery of the strange Dr Ribero. Delicately, he knocked. The door felt oddly spongy underneath his fist, like brine-soaked wood that had dried out in the sun. Kester decided unreservedly that this was the most unpleasant door he had ever encountered in his twenty-two years of life.

There was no answer. The alleyway lingered with the echo of his fist. Somewhere nearby, a bird cawed, taking off in a clatter of feathers. He shivered, in spite of the afternoon's warmth.

So, what am I supposed to do now? he wondered. *I've spent fifty quid on a train ticket, forty pounds for a room for the night, and it doesn't even look like the building's occupied.* It was frustrating, but also a relief. The whole experience thus far had been far too surreal for his liking, and now he felt that he had licence to depart with a clear conscience.

I tried my best, Mother, Kester thought. He smoothed his sweaty fringe and gave the door a final once-over. *Obviously it just wasn't meant to be.* He turned to leave.

A strange feature in the centre of the door caught his attention, and he narrowed his eyes, surprised. A perfectly circular knot sat roughly at eye level, darker than the surrounding wood, indeed, almost ebony in appearance. He could have sworn it hadn't been there before, though now, he doubted his own senses. After all, it had been a long journey from Cambridge, and he was exhausted, both mentally and physically. Perhaps it had been there all along, and he had simply missed it? It was unlike him not to notice a prominent detail like that, he took pride in his observational skills. *My little Kestrel,* his mother used to call him. *Always scanning the surroundings like a bird of prey.*

Instinctively, he brushed it with his index finger, noting its peculiar glassy smoothness. It felt warm and glowed a little, as though lit from within by a lightbulb. Feeling a little foolish, he pulled his finger away furtively, like a child caught with his hand in a biscuit barrel. To his amazement, the door swung open, revealing nothing but darkness beyond.

Blimey, Kester thought, peering in. *Now what do I do?*

The meagre light of the alleyway revealed the beginnings of a narrow corridor, and not a lot else. A threadbare Persian rug formed a burgundy road into the blackness; a blood-red path into a rather eerie hallway.

"Hello?"

His voice wavered in the silence. It was tempting to turn away. After all, he had tried. He had travelled for hours to find this blessed business, and now, no one was in; if indeed anyone had ever been here. The place looked as though it had lain empty for years, decades perhaps. It had the cobwebby look of something long since forgotten, neglected and left to crumble away in the sombre hands of time.

The emptiness of the narrow corridor unsettled him, even spooked him a little. It was all rather strange, and as a general rule, Kester didn't like strangeness. He preferred the predictable, the reliable, and the well-established. Anything that stepped outside those parameters he tried to ignore as best as possible. It was as his mother had always advised, when he'd awoken from nightmares as a child, "Turn your mind from it, Kester my love. Then, you'll find that it's simply not there anymore." It was very tempting to follow that wise advice now, and return to the train station, go home, and forget all about it.

The smell of age wafted from the enclosed space with the musty scent of air that had spent too long sealed up in darkness. He glanced over his shoulder. The alleyway was still empty. Even the neighbouring shops appeared deserted. It was worryingly silent, as though someone had pressed a pause button, sealing everything into stasis.

"Oh, this is ridiculous," he muttered. Shunting his black-rimmed spectacles up the bridge of his nose, and trying not to dwell on the darkness too much, he stepped over the threshold.

It was noticeably stuffier inside, and sweat prickled at the back of his neck. Beside him, remnants of parchment-dry wallpaper peeled and curled like dead ferns. The ceiling was low, so low that if he were to extend his arm, he would be able to place his palm easily on its surface. It was an unpleasant space, hot, dusty, and stale—and it reminded him of a tomb.

The dead end at the back of the passageway loomed in the shadows, confusing him. Instead of the expected door leading to offices, there was the vague outline of a spiral staircase, coiling snake-like in the corner. *It looks like something waiting to pounce,* he thought, tugging at his collar. *I don't like this one little bit.* He felt as though he'd stepped into the underworld itself.

He crept along the Persian rug, tiptoeing deliberately over the places where footsteps had already worn holes through to the floorboards.

"Hello?" he called out again, louder this time.

There was still no answer. He scarcely knew what to do. Nerves and a sense of impropriety stopped him in his tracks, and he looked uncertainly at the staircase, unsure how to proceed. *What in god's name am I meant to do?* he wondered, fiddling anxiously with the straps of his satchel. *I don't want to burst in on this Dr Ribero uninvited. If indeed he's actually here, which I seriously doubt.*

And, in truth, he was feeling more than a little uncomfortable. The narrow corridor was oppressive, the walls seemed ready to squash him like a bluebottle, and his heart was beating faster. It was an unfamiliar sensation. Normally, Kester had his late mother's calm demeanour, combined with a quite remarkable lack of imagination. Fear of the unknown was not an emotion that generally troubled him, as he seldom ever thought about it. Superstition and the supernatural were only fanciful concepts for him, nothing more, nothing less. However, the events of the last fortnight had shaken his sensible foundations, leaving him more sensitive than usual. His normally sturdy brain had been shaken, rocked like a ship lost at sea.

Right, he thought firmly, straightening his spine and staring at the stairs. *I've come this far, I'm inside the building now, so I may as well carry on. After all, what would Mother think if she could see me now?* As a matter of fact, he knew perfectly well what she would say. He could almost hear her soft voice now, gently urging him to continue, to find that bravery deep within him. She had always had such faith in him, even when he had none in himself.

Kester gulped, suddenly lost in the memory of her. She had always been his most devoted supporter: giving him a standing ovation when he wheezed in last in every school sports day race, and whooping with delight when he was given his degree certificate at Cambridge, in spite of the sombre silence. A strong sense of her presence came to him now, lingering behind him and shooing him tenderly into the darkness. It made his heart heavy with her loss once again.

Do it for her, if not yourself, he thought. *After all, it was her last wish. She said to find Dr Ribero. And now you're here, you'd best go and find him, whoever he may be. Judging by the state of this place, you're not likely to find him unless he's a skeleton, propped up in the rooms upstairs.*

With that unpleasant thought in mind, he began to climb. The first step of the spiral staircase clanged under his polished shoe, echoing into the blackness above. Unnervingly, the stairs simply disappeared into utter blackness. He had no idea what might be lurking up there, if indeed there was anything up there at all. Still, he knew that the only way of finding out was to venture upwards, despite the fact that every part of him really didn't want to. He ascended, setting off a discordant din of metallic bangs and leaving the last of the light behind him.

Who is this peculiar man, and why on earth does he choose to work in such a hovel? he wondered as he climbed. The building was obviously ancient, at least three or four hundred years old, and, Victorian staircase aside, didn't look as though much had been altered since the time it was built. Many old buildings had charm and personality—this wasn't one of them. So far, all he could detect about this crumbling monstrosity was that it looked ready to be condemned and demolished. Kester wasn't particularly sensitive to atmosphere, but even he could detect something hostile, watchful, and downright eerie about the place. Had he not made a solemn promise to his mother, he'd have walked straight out again.

At last, Kester arrived at the final stair. Panicking, he groped for a wall—anything to provide him with clues about his surroundings. Aside from a dim semi-circle of light coming from the stairwell, he was lost in blackness; he couldn't even begin to work out where he was, or for that matter, who was up here in the dark with him. He shivered at the thought.

"Is anyone there?" he called. "I'm looking for Dr Ribero, am I in the right place?"

Once again, silence was the resounding response. *It's rather like one of those horror films,* he fretted, not that he had much taste for the genre. *I suppose this is the point where the unseen monster leaps out of the shadows and starts doing dreadful things to my person. Well, that's a nice thought, isn't it?*

Fighting to remain calm, he squinted around him. Somewhere in the dense darkness, he could make out the tiniest line of light running along the floor. *Aha, a door,* he thought, with a sense of triumph. *So someone is here after all. I wonder why on earth they didn't come out to greet me when I called out?*

He marched towards the glimmer of light, and pushed at the hard surface that met his outstretched fingers. To his surprise, it immediately gave way under his touch, swinging open into the room beyond.

Kester blinked in the sudden light and gawped. He wasn't sure what he had been expecting, but this certainly wasn't it.

"Hello?" he stammered, eyes widening. His greeting was met with only silence.

CHAPTER 2: THE OFFICE

Kester looked from face to face, scanning the room with disbelief.

Four pairs of eyes returned his scrutiny, staring at him in bafflement, curiosity, and vague annoyance. They peered from behind their desktop computers as though a creature from another world had just stumbled into their lair.

The room itself was airy and fresh, and clearly a professional office space. It was as shockingly different from the hallway below as could be imagined, and it astounded him into slack-mouthed silence.

There was an indeterminable pause, as Kester surveyed his surroundings, and was surveyed in return. There was something about the collective glares that made him feel like a field mouse under the glare of a flock of falcons, and he didn't much like it. He was unsure how to proceed, how to protect himself against such an appalling lack of social finesse. It certainly wasn't what he was used to at Cambridge.

Finally, for want of anything better to do, Kester coughed. The silence and staring continued. He coughed again and smoothed down his shirt for good measure, waiting for at least one person to smile. Then he waited for a few seconds more. His cheeks, normally ruddy at the best of times, reddened to a deep shade of puce.

The eldest person, a severe-looking woman perched behind the largest of the leather-topped desks, raised a steel-grey eyebrow.

"Can we help you?" she said eventually, ice dripping from every syllable.

Her fingers pressed against one another, forming a sharp triangle of disapproval. She looked as though she was surveying something a passing dog might have deposited onto the carpet, and her quivering nostrils suggested that she disapproved of every inch of his person.

He read the brass plaque standing at the front of her desk. *Miss J. Wellbeloved, BA, MA, MPhil.* Kester looked up again. Then down. Then up once more, just to double-check. If it had been a different situation, a different place and time, he would have laughed out loud. He'd never seen a surname so ill-suited to its owner. The name suggested warmth and gentleness. Cuddliness, even. In stark contrast, this woman had all the natural warmth and gentleness of an over-sharpened pencil.

"I . . . I did actually call out several times," he stuttered. "I knocked too, but no one answered."

"I see," Miss Wellbeloved said. Her lips tautened to a thin line, and she leant back, glowering over half-rimmed spectacles.

He cleared his throat. The room was so much at odds with the rest of the building that it had completely thrown him off guard, leaving him as confused as a hook-caught fish hauled from the water. Why they chose to leave the downstairs corridor in such a horrendous state when their actual office was pleasant was completely beyond him. It was as though they didn't want visitors, and were using the horrible entrance to discourage entry. *But what sort of a business would operate like that?* he wondered, feeling more perplexed by the second. *How on earth do they get any customers?*

Unlike the ancient hallway downstairs, the office was clean and spacious, with fresh paint, high ceilings, and elegant panelled walls, lending it a sense of gravitas. The faintest hint of a summer breeze drifted in from an open window, and four computers hummed quietly, each with a person behind them. Their modernity was a stark contrast to the rest of the setting, which was austere, timeless. At the end of the room, there were two simple wooden doors, leading to goodness knows where. *Ugh, more doors,* he thought, feeling his stomach lurch. Kester felt thoroughly displaced, an astronaut exploring alien territory. The sensation was an unsettling one.

"Oh Christ, I don't bloody believe it," one of the other occupants growled, a series of burly consonants slicing through the quiet.

Kester looked over to the source of the sound, just in time to spot a flurry of sparks erupting from one of the desks like a miniature volcano. He grimaced, surprised to see what looked like two large car batteries perching squarely in front of a bearded, baseball-capped man. The man glared at Kester, all hair, bristles, and sheer bulk. Kester shrivelled, wishing that he could somehow creep back out of the office without any of them noticing him.

"Mike, you shouldn't be doing that at the desk, you'll start a fire one of these days," Miss Wellbeloved tutted with a disapproving shake of the head.

"That's why I treated my desk with fire-retardant paint," Mike retorted. His desk was a wild sea of electrical contraptions and wires. Jabbing a screwdriver in Kester's direction, he continued, "Anyway, it was his fault for distracting me."

A younger woman with a sharp black bob, and an even

sharper chin, rolled her eyes from the neighbouring desk. "According to you, everything's a distraction," she scowled. "A sneeze is a distraction. Me itching my neck is a distraction. Someone breathing too heavily is a distraction. We should get you some earplugs."

"Well, your neck scratching is a bloody distraction, it's like an ape searching for fleas," Mike barked back, folding his arms across his sizeable check-shirted chest.

Kester coughed again, feeling uncomfortably as though his presence had already been completely forgotten. "Erm," he started, then stopped. At once, all eyes were on him again.

"Yes?" Miss Wellbeloved said. Her eyes narrowed to granite slits.

"Look, I'm terribly sorry to disturb you," Kester continued, fumbling for his letter. "But I'm looking for someone, someone who I don't think is here actually, judging by . . . well, judging by all of you. But perhaps you know where he might be? I presume he once worked here?"

A plump woman sitting in the furthest corner peeped over the top of her computer monitor. She had been so well concealed by her enormous computer that he hadn't really noticed her before. Now he had the chance to study her more closely. Her face was doughy and mottled, giving her the general appearance of an overcooked dumpling. However, she looked slightly less annoyed by his presence than the others, which was a certainly a start.

"Well," she said, in a voice that was almost kind, "why don't you tell us his name? Then we might be able to solve the mystery for you."

Kester smiled gratefully, tugging the letter open. He wafted it in her direction, a pointless gesture given that she couldn't possibly read it from that distance.

"My mother," he began, then stopped. "Well, you see, my mother, when she died, she told me to come and find this man. Only she didn't give me any other information. So I did some research, and I drew a complete blank, but I did find this address. It took me a while to decide to come here, I really wasn't sure what the point was initially—"

"How about *getting* to the point?" the black-bobbed woman snapped, rapping a biro in a staccato of ill-concealed irritation. "Just a suggestion?" She frowned, plucked eyebrows forming a sharp V above her weasel-sharp eyes.

Kester shrank under the weight of her contempt. He felt as though one glare of those bright green eyes might be enough to deflate him, puncturing his flaccid body with a single needle-sharp stare. It was something he was used to. Most girls found him rather an unappealing prospect. Attractive women, like this one, even more so. And they generally weren't afraid to let him know how they felt, in no uncertain terms.

"Serena, be kind," the plump woman said with a frown. Turning back to him, she nodded, encouraging him to continue. Kester pulled at his collar, trying to ignore the audible tutting from across the other side of the room.

"Of course, I appreciate I'm wasting your time here," he said stiffly. "I don't even know why I came up really. I should have realised from the start that you weren't the type of business to welcome visitors. And it's now obvious to me that there's no one called Dr Ribero here. Please excuse me for interrupting you."

He turned, the blush still firing his cheeks. *What a pompous group of people,* he raged silently. *And I've wasted all that money coming down here for nothing.* He felt like a fool. He hadn't managed to get a job since graduating and money was tight, too tight to waste on pointless trips to the West Country, regardless of how pretty the landscape might be.

"Wait!" an imperious voice commanded. Kester paused. He peered reluctantly over his shoulder.

Miss Wellbeloved had risen from her seat, erect as an obelisk. "Dr Ribero, you say?"

Kester nodded. She clicked her fingers impatiently at his letter, which he obediently handed over. Like a schoolboy in front of a headmistress, he waited, twiddling his thumbs together as she scanned the paper.

"Where did you get this?" she asked eventually.

"I just found it in my mother's address book."

Miss Wellbeloved reached over, shaking the letter in the plump woman's direction. "Read this, Pamela," she said, ignoring Kester. Silence descended as the larger woman scanned the contents of the paper.

"Goodness me, how on earth did you come by this?" she said finally, handing the letter back to her colleague.

Kester shrugged with confusion. "Well, I suppose it was sent to my mother. It is addressed to her. I don't understand it though; it made no sense at all."

"Your mother was Gretchen Lanner?" Miss Wellbeloved asked.

Kester nodded. The woman gasped, iron composure shaken. She slumped forward, pressing her palms against the desk, and breathed heavily.

"My goodness, does that mean Gretchen is dead?" Pamela said. She covered her mouth, eyes widening.

"She died two weeks ago," Kester said quietly. He still hated saying it aloud. He wondered if he would ever get used to saying it. Right now, faced with these strange people, he realised with an even greater pang of pain that she had been his only real friend in the world.

"My goodness," Miss Wellbeloved murmured, closing her eyes. Her face had gone remarkably pale.

"Hang on a minute," Serena said, striding the room and seizing the paper. "Are we talking the about famous Gretchen Lanner here?" She looked at Kester, pursing her lips in disbelief. "And you're her son? Are you serious?"

"Serena, there's no need to be unkind," Pamela said,

squeezing out of her chair. She padded over to Miss Wellbe-loved, giving Kester a sympathetic look. "I'm so sorry for your loss. We knew your mother a long time ago." She paused, and a look passed between her and Miss Wellbeloved that Kester couldn't decipher. "She was a wonderful woman," she concluded, nodding.

"You knew her?" Kester said incredulously. His mother, like himself, hadn't been one for socialising. To the best of his knowl-edge, she had only had two friends. Only one, if you didn't include Mildew the cat. The other was their elderly next door neighbour, Mrs Winterbottom, who popped round for the occa-sional chat about the garden. Aside from that, he and his mother had simply enjoyed one another's company, and had never really needed anyone else in their lives. She had never mentioned these people. He was sure he would have remembered her talking about such a strange cluster of individuals.

"Your mother was . . . a friend of mine," Miss Wellbeloved muttered, looking out the window. "Though we have not spoken in many years. Decades, in fact. And now it seems, we never shall again. Or at least, not in the conventional manner."

Kester raised an eyebrow, but was distracted by Pamela placing a bundle of kindly, sausagey fingers on his arm. "I didn't know your mother so well," she explained to him. "I had only been here about a year or so when she left. But she always seemed very friendly." She glanced at Miss Wellbeloved, who nodded. "She was very kind to me when I arrived; she really helped me to settle in. You must miss her terribly."

"I do," Kester said, clearing his throat. He felt strange discussing his mother with these people. Who were they exactly? And why had his mother never talked about them? It was all most mysterious, given how open she had been about every other aspect of her life.

The young woman with the black bob sighed. "Look, I didn't mean to be nasty," she said. Leaning over, she extended a hand with cat-like grace, albeit with a lingering air of hostility. "I'm Serena. I didn't know your mother at all, but heard some impressive things about her. She was great at her job, from what these ladies used to tell me. It's rough luck, you losing her. Sorry about that."

Kester duly accepted the slender hand. He looked up, observing her pointy chin, wide cheekbones, and bright green eyes, which gave her the look of a cunning, but very pretty, pixie.

"My mother never talked about any of this," he replied. "I feel a little confused, to be honest."

Miss Wellbeloved and Pamela shared another meaningful look.

"Why don't you sit down?" Pamela suggested, gesturing to a worn leather sofa tucked snugly against the wall behind him. "I'll make you a cup of coffee."

"I don't drink coffee, but thank you anyway."

"Tea? Everybody drinks tea."

"I'll have a cup of tea if you're brewing, Pam," Mike shouted from behind his desk.

Pamela sighed, giving Kester a conspiratorial look, as if to say, *see what I have to put up with?* He felt himself brighten at the show of comradery, in spite of the circumstances. "Milk and sugar?" she asked, with a flash of a dimple.

"Yes, three sugars please."

"Three sugars? Blimey," Mike commented. "Fast track to a heart attack, that is."

"Oh Mike, do put a sock in it, will you?" Serena chided. Lowering herself onto Miss Wellbeloved's desk, she added, "Though it is bad for you. You should consider cutting back. Sugar does terrible things to your body." She nodded at his generous waistline. Kester folded his arms over his stomach, trying to breathe in as much as possible.

"Goodness, leave the poor boy alone!" Pamela exclaimed, scuttling through one of the doors at the back. Her voice echoed back through the office. "Last thing he needs is a lecture."

"Might we ask what your name is?" Miss Wellbeloved asked, after allowing him a minute or so to get settled on the sofa.

"It's Kester, Kester Lanner," he replied. "I take it yours is Miss Wellbeloved?"

"Wellbelov-ed," she corrected, emphasising the final syllable. "That is indeed correct. Serena Flynn has already introduced herself, I believe, and Pamela Tompkin is the final member of the team."

"Oh, don't I exist then?" Mike boomed indignantly from his cluttered corner, like a disgruntled thunderstorm.

"Mike's just the IT guy," Serena explained.

"There's no 'just' about what I do," Mike retorted. "It's an integral part of this company, as you well know." He scraped his chair back along the floorboards, ambling good-naturedly over to join them. "Sorry I snapped at you earlier," he said, shaking Kester's hand with a bear-like grip.

Kester noted the contrast to his own pale hands, complete with his unsightly patches of psoriasis. Up close, he could now see that Mike's baseball hat was from Legoland, a strange choice of style given that he looked almost exactly like a muscular lumberjack who had never stepped foot outside the Canadian Rockies.

"That bloody machine has been driving me mad all morning," Mike continued to explain. "I just can't make it capture the right frequency. It needs to be so sensitive to capture spirit noises, and—"

"Spirit noises?" Kester said with alarm.

Miss Wellbeloved tutted, glaring at her colleague. "Mike likes to come up with all sorts of preposterous inventions," she explained quickly, entwining her spindly fingers across her hollow stomach. "Don't listen to him."

"None of the rest of us do," Serena added.

"Preposterous?" Mike squawked. "Honestly, you ladies have

no appreciation of what I do. I'm the one who makes all of this possible, and you know it. I'm what keeps this company modern and cutting edge."

"I do not believe there is anything 'cutting edge' about this place," Miss Wellbeloved snipped. "But let's not get off the subject. Kester, will you please tell us more about why your mother sent you here?"

Kester shifted uncomfortably, crossing one leg over the other. "There's nothing much else I can tell you, really. On the night that she died, she told me to find Dr Ribero. Until that night, I'd never heard the name before." He gratefully accepted the mug of tea that Pamela gave him, though he now felt guilty about the three sugars. His mother had often told him to cut back, but he liked the taste too much. He swore it helped him to think better.

"I fully understand why she didn't mention it," Miss Wellbeloved muttered. Her expression darkened, and she turned away. Kester studied her intently, unable to interpret her reaction. *Did she have a problem with my mother?* he wondered. There was something going on here, but he wasn't sure quite what.

"What do you mean?" he asked, sitting straighter.

"Well," Pamela said, sipping from a chipped porcelain cup. "It's not really the sort of thing you can easily explain to people, dear." She winked at him, then looked at Miss Wellbeloved with concern.

Kester frowned. There was something strange going on, a mystery that united these four people, from which he was firmly excluded. He couldn't even begin to imagine what it was, and by now he was feeling too exhausted to ponder on it much. It had been an odd day—perhaps one of the oddest in his life—and now that he had sat down, he felt his mind unravelling at the seams with tiredness.

"So," he said suddenly, struggling to stir himself. "Is there a Dr Ribero here or not? I presume that there once was, given your reaction when I mentioned his name. Did he work here too, at the same time as my mum?"

Pamela and Serena looked at one another and laughed.

"It's his company," Pamela explained, pointing to one of the doors at the back of the room.

"Does he not work here then?" Kester asked.

"He certainly does," Miss Wellbeloved answered. "Just through that door is his office."

Kester frowned, confused. "Well, can I talk to him?"

All four colleagues looked upwards at the clock mounted above the window.

"No, not quite yet," Miss Wellbeloved said finally.

"Why not?"

"He's always asleep until three o'clock," Serena replied with a grin. "And there's one rule in this office. Never, ever disturb Dr Ribero when he's having his siesta."

Kester looked at the clock. "It's practically three o'clock now," he said.

"Yeah, practically. But not actually. And that's a big difference," Mike replied, slamming his mug on to the desk and spilling tea over the leather.

Kester paused. "So," he said, mulling it over, "does that mean he'll be awake soon?"

"In two minutes and thirty-two seconds precisely," Miss Wellbeloved confirmed.

What sort of a man is this? Kester thought with bewilderment. *Who has a daily siesta that runs until exactly 3:00 pm, and not a second less?* And, more importantly, why had his mother decided that it was so important for her son to meet him? None of the facts were adding up, and it was making his head ache to think about it. He drank the rest of his tea, watching the slow progression of the clock.

As the long hand clicked into place at the twelve, he heard a low buzzer from somewhere behind Dr Ribero's mysterious office door.

"That'll mean it's safe to knock on his door now," Pamela explained kindly, tapping her watch for good measure.

"Shouldn't I give him some time to come to, if he's just woken up?"

"Oh no," Pamela replied, "he's always up like a bullet as soon as his alarm goes off. Let's go and get you two better acquainted."

Miss Wellbeloved took his empty mug, giving him a strange look. "I hope you're prepared for this," she muttered, pursing her lips together.

"What should I be prepared for?" Kester asked. He looked over at the door with growing anxiety, expecting it to fly open on its hinges at any moment. There was an air of pregnant expectancy in the room, and it was making him instinctively wary. This wasn't helped by the secretive glances the others were giving one another.

The two older women exchanged another meaningful look, just to further ignite his anxiety. Pamela raised an eyebrow, and Miss Wellbeloved shrugged. She smiled tightly, gesturing to the door. "I'll knock for you," she said. "Get back to work, everyone. Tea break is over."

Kester shuffled reluctantly towards the door, following the older woman like a large ship being pulled into harbour by a fast-paced tug-boat. She paused, bony fist hovering in the air, then knocked smartly in a series of authoritative raps.

"Come in," a low voice rumbled from within.

"Dr Ribero," Miss Wellbeloved said, as she pushed open the door. "This is Gretchen Lanner's boy, here to see you. Kester, I'd like to introduce you to Dr Ribero. Your father."

CHAPTER 3: THE INFAMOUS DR RIBERO

Kester froze. *My father?* he thought dumbly. *But that's ridiculous. I don't have a father. It's always been just me and my mother, no one else.*

"There's been some mistake," he croaked, backing away. His head started to spin, and the walls seemed suddenly a lot closer than they had been a few seconds previously. It didn't help that the room was small, as tightly enclosed as a womb, and windowless. It felt bewilderingly oppressive in the heat of the summer's day.

"No, this is definitely your father," Miss Wellbeloved confirmed, oblivious to his distress. She nodded curtly, then retreated. "I'll leave you to have a private chat," she concluded. The door snapped into place with a loud click, leaving the room in stifling silence.

Kester wiped the sweat away from his brow, then reluctantly faced the man he'd been left alone with. They stared at one another for an indeterminable amount of time.

"Well, this is unusual, yes?" Dr Ribero announced finally. His accent was surprisingly rich, and the words flowed round the room like velvet, laden with Spanish undulations, like the tossing of a midnight ocean.

The owner of the magnificent voice sat in a leather armchair in the corner, fingers folded neatly as a judge, looking upon Kester as though he were a fascinating specimen in a laboratory. Kester stared back, gormless as a puppy, the word *father* still echoing in his ears. There was nothing fatherly about this figure. And certainly there was absolutely nothing about his appearance that seemed to connect Kester to him.

Dr Ribero was leonine. There was no other word for him. He exuded elegance, from his long, pointed shoes, right up to his aquiline nose. He was handsome, especially given his advanced age. His hair, though grey, was lustrous—smoothed back with wax, it formed a perfectly shiny wave over his scalp. A dashing moustache curled from under his nose like a pair of inquisitive grey worms. His eyes were dark, but twinkled with electricity. He reached slowly across to his side table, picking up a cigarette holder complete with half-smoked cigarette, then lit it with one deft flick of a silver lighter.

"Isn't it illegal to smoke in a public place?" Kester squeaked.

Dr Ribero shrugged. "My office, my rules," he replied, his voice rolling languorously over the vowels and consonants. "I take it you do not like to smoke. So, I will not offer you one." Kester stared, struck dumb by the shock of it all, unsure where to put himself. Dr Ribero surveyed him, before gesturing with a regal nod. "Please, sit."

He looked around. There was a cluttered desk at the other end of the room, complete with a studded leather swivel chair. Unceremoniously, he plumped himself onto its rigid seat, and tried to resist the natural momentum as the chair threatened to swing him in the wrong direction.

"So, I can see that you are Gretchen's boy," Dr Ribero said at last, after studying him for the best part of a minute.

"How can you see?" Kester asked.

Dr Ribero pointed two elongated fingers at Kester's eyes like a pair of tiny cannons. "It's all there," he replied, with a cryptic nod.

Kester said nothing. He fixed his gaze on the floor, focusing in on the bright rug below his feet, a sea of ruby-red geometric patterns that separated him from the doctor. *This is insane,* he thought. *What on earth am I doing here? And why did that woman say he was my father? That's just ridiculous. It's simply impossible.* Ruefully, he acknowledged that there was no way such a handsome chap could have produced him. His real father, whoever he may have been, must have been every bit as paunchy and pale as himself. It didn't make sense.

"So, what do you think?" the doctor continued, interrupting his thoughts. He exhaled, slowly pistoning out a stream of smoke. It curled languidly, masking his face briefly before billowing out towards the ceiling, which Kester could see was a mottled shade of beige from years of nicotine exposure.

"What do I think about what?"

"About all of this, of course. What do you think of my agency?"

Well, that's a peculiar question, given he's just been told that I'm his son, Kester thought. *What a strange man. Though of course, it can't be true. Mother would have told me if I had a father who was alive. She never would have kept it from me.*

Doctor Ribero studied him intently. "You are deep in thought, I can see," he said finally. "I think perhaps you are confused, yes?"

Kester nodded dumbly.

"Well," the doctor continued. "Why don't we start at the beginning? If you are my son, that means you are Gretchen's boy. It's a pleasure to finally meet you, Kester."

"Why aren't you surprised?" Kester spluttered. "You look

so . . . so unmoved by finding out that you have a son!"

Dr Ribero chuckled, an earthy rumble, like the precursor to an earthquake. "You presume that because it is a shock for you, it must also be a shock for me. However . . ." He paused, letting the word hang in the air. "I have known about you for a very long time, my boy."

Kester swallowed hard and ended up choking. Coughing, he fought to regain control of his lungs as his face grew redder, banging his fist against his chest. Dr Ribero gestured to a jug of water on his desk. His expression didn't alter, even while Kester's cheeks turned to a deeper shade of plum. Kester ignored him, feeling more ridiculous with every sputtering moment.

"Why didn't you ever come to visit me?" he eventually wheezed, loosening his collar. "If you knew I existed?"

The older man leaned back in his chair with a sigh. He gazed around the office, as though seeking inspiration, before taking another deep tug on his cigarette. "This is a very serious conversation to be having, so late on a Friday afternoon," he stated finally. "Allow me to ask some questions instead, yes? How is your dear mother?"

"Dead," Kester blurted out.

Dr Ribero paled. He remained motionless for a minute or so, as composed as an owl in a thunderstorm, before slowly placing his cigarette holder on the ash tray. Kester noticed then that his hand was shaking.

"I'm sorry, I didn't realise you'd be upset," he said.

"Gretchen is dead?" Ribero repeated weakly. Kester nodded.

The room rang with the weight of the words. They seemed to grow larger in the silence, filling the space with their brutal finality, puffing out with unbearable pressure. That one word. Dead. It was shocking how it could change the atmosphere so much. It made everything greyer, colder. Kester had noticed that a lot in the last fortnight. Death still wasn't a concept he'd wrapped his head around yet. *Death.* Even the word itself was like a final, icy breath.

"How did it happen?" Ribero whispered, all exuberance sucked from him like a vacuum cleaner. He looked haggard, as if he'd aged a decade in the space of only a few minutes.

"Cancer."

"But Gretchen was always so healthy," he mumbled. "None of this poison." Ribero jabbed an accusing finger at his smouldering cigarette, as if it was directly responsible. "Always so slim, so energetic, so sensible. How could she get cancer?" He muttered something in Spanish, looking down to the floor.

"I think it can happen to anyone," Kester said, as kindly as he could. He suddenly felt sorry for the man in front of him, this suave man, reduced to a morsel of his former self in a matter of moments; he felt guilty for having caused the change.

With a shake, Ribero composed himself, straightening against the back of the chair. He drew back, studying Kester hard, black eyes burrowing tunnels into Kester's own.

"And now you are on your own, and this is why you are here? Because you don't know where else to go?"

Kester shook his head, then nodded. "No. Well, yes, partly. I'm certainly on my own, but that's not the reason I'm here. My mother told me to come and find you. When she was . . . when she was dying. That's why I'm here. I'm fulfilling her final wishes. But to be honest, I'm not sure what good it has done."

Ribero gave a grim shake of the head, pressing his chin against his fingers. He appeared lost in thought, staring at the wall behind Kester's head as though waiting for the solution to the problem to magically appear. Kester waited, as the minutes stretched on. The mantelpiece clock ticked gently. Ribero's cigarette fizzled to a limp line of ash.

This is madness, Kester thought. He stood awkwardly, then offered a hand. Dr Ribero didn't take it, only narrowed his gaze, still staring at the wall. Eventually, Kester lowered his arm.

"I'll say goodbye then," he said. "Don't worry, you won't

hear from me again. I don't want anything from you. My mother obviously didn't expect you to provide for me, so I shan't either."

The doctor's head snapped up, like a puppet pulled to attention. He pointed a finger directly at his son's face. "My boy, you may leave, if that is what you want. However, I have to correct you on that last point. I have been providing for you since you were born. Perhaps not emotionally, but financially, very much so, yes."

Kester's eyes widened. The doctor nodded.

"I didn't know that," he stuttered, the wind taken out of him.

"How did you think your mother had that nice house?" Dr Ribero asked in disbelief. "She didn't work, surely you must have wondered."

Kester paused, blushing. "I . . . I don't believe I did, no." It pained him to admit it, and he felt suddenly incredibly stupid. *Have I really been that naïve?* he wondered. *Why have I never questioned it before?*

The truth was, he had never stopped to give it any thought. It was the way it had always been, he and his mother in their cosy semi-detached house in the quiet Cambridge suburbs, tucked away from the bustle of the city. He had always presumed it had been left to them by the dead father his mother sometimes alluded to, but never spoke directly of, and he'd never asked any questions about the matter.

Except that his father wasn't dead. He was alive, very much alive, and living in Exeter, only a matter of hours away. The weight of it all crashed upon him like a sack of wet sand, and his knees weakened with the horror of it all. He sank back into the chair, cradling his head in his hands.

"Gosh, I had no idea," he murmured. *What a fool he must think I am*, he thought. *To have lived this long, and never stopped to wonder how my mother could afford to keep me? How could I not have realised?* His mother had always said he was too accepting of things. Now he appreciated exactly how right she was.

Finally, he looked up. "Was it you who put me through university then?"

"Yes."

"And you own the house? Our house in Cambridge, I mean?"

The doctor shook his head. "No. I bought it for your mother. She needed somewhere to live. It was . . . how do you say it? The least that I could do."

Kester felt a little lightheaded. The combination of grief, tiredness, and unexpected revelations rendered him stupid, speechless, unable to determine the correct response. *After all,* he thought, running a hand through his hair, *how are you meant to speak to your father, when you meet him for the first time? It's not exactly the sort of thing we get taught at school.*

"Why didn't you ever come and visit me?" he asked. "I mean, weren't you curious? Or do you have other children, is that it? Do you have another family?" Looking at the doctor, he could well imagine a succession of women falling for his charms. Although old, the force of his masculinity was still strong, and Kester could only imagine how attractive he had been as a younger man. The thought made him rather jealous. If indeed this was his father, why had none of those handsome genes passed on to him?

"No, no, nothing like that," Dr Ribero snapped, reading Kester's expression correctly. He reached across for his cigarette, realised it had gone out, and relit it with a flick of his lighter; he tugged on it sombrely. "No, I have never married. I am not that kind of a man, Kester. Not like you think. I am not the Lothario or the Casanova, no."

"So why never come and see me then?"

It was a pleading, plaintive question, and it surprised him, even as the childish reprimand left his lips. *Why do I even care?* he thought, as he surveyed the old man, who had, before three o'clock this afternoon, been completely unknown to him. *Why should it bother me that he's never been to see me? Why am I even still here?*

Yet it did bother him. It nettled him, and the sting of rejection ached within him like a fist to the stomach. *What was wrong with me?* he wondered. *What could have possibly been so very unpleasant about me that my own father never wanted to see me?* The notion of it made him feel unnervingly anchorless, as though an unseen carpet had been whipped from under his feet.

To his surprise, instead of answering, the doctor stood, straightening his knees with an audible crack. He gestured sternly to the door. Kester gulped.

"You want me to go?" he mumbled, shocked. His feelings of rejection multiplied in the space of a second.

Dr Ribero pulled open the door with force, the gust fluttering his paperwork across his desk. "Miss Wellbeloved!" he bellowed. Kester winced.

The woman slid into the room as though on rails. Her swift arrival indicated that she must have been listening to their conversation, or at least standing very close to the room. Without a single glance at Kester, she quietly closed the door behind her.

"Tell him," Dr Ribero said, stalking back to his chair like an alpha lion returning to its rock.

Miss Wellbeloved frowned. "About which part?"

Ribero grunted. "About the agency, Jennifer. The rest can wait."

"It would be better coming from you," she replied. "It's hardly my place."

The doctor waved an impatient hand, batting her comment away like an imaginary wasp. "It's every bit as much your place as mine. And I do not know where to begin. Please, Jennifer. You explain it. I have only just woken; I am still tired. This is all too much for me."

She sighed, then walked across to the desk, resting herself on the edge.

"Kester," she said, glaring in Ribero's direction. "Your father wants me to tell you about this agency. After I've finished, his absence in your life will probably make a lot more sense."

So she was listening, Kester thought, with bewilderment and irritation. *She heard every word of what we were saying. She isn't even bothering to conceal the fact.* He'd always been raised to believe that eavesdropping was the height of bad manners, and it shocked him to see such an austere woman so comfortable with listening in on the conversation of others.

"What has this agency got to do with him not visiting me?" he asked, looking at Dr Ribero. The older man sank his chin on to his fingers, brows knitted. He didn't meet Kester's gaze.

"Oh goodness me, this really is rather difficult," Miss Wellbeloved said testily. "Julio, are you sure I can't convince you to step in?"

The doctor grunted.

"Hmm," Miss Wellbeloved concluded, after an uncomfortable silence. She raised a hand, studying her fingernails as though seeking strength from each well-manicured cuticle. "Well, I suppose I should just come out with it. Stop beating around the bush. It seems silly to string things out."

"String what out?" Kester said. He was getting exasperated. "I really don't have the foggiest what you're talking about."

"This agency . . ."

"Yes?"

"Well, it's an agency for supernatural investigations."

Kester choked, then chuckled. The others looked at him expectantly. Kester laughed again, waiting for a giggle or wry wink, anything to indicate that he was currently the butt of a rather peculiar joke.

"Excuse me?"

"I said, it's an agency for—"

"Yes, I heard you the first time. I just don't have the faintest idea what that means."

Dr Ribero grunted. "It is not so difficult a concept. We are an agency for the supernatural."

"So you keep saying," Kester replied. "But that still makes no sense at all!"

Miss Wellbeloved massaged her brow, wincing. She frowned at Ribero, who pursed his lips together, shaking his head like a disappointed headmaster.

"Do you know what the supernatural is?" she asked, adopting the slow tones normally reserved for small and dim-witted children.

"Of course I do," Kester replied. "Ghosts and all that stuff. But that's made up, it's not real. So you can't have an agency to investigate something that's made up. That's nonsensical."

"Why would you say it was nonsensical?" Dr Ribero interrupted, bushy eyebrows bobbing up and down in a rather alarming manner.

"Because ghosts don't exist. It's been proven," Kester replied, feeling rather hot and bothered. The questions were baffling him and he couldn't work out whether they were teasing him or were stark-raving mad. But why would they tease him? Paternal claim aside, they were complete strangers. Did they normally tease people they didn't know? If so, that was a little bit mad too, wasn't it?

I wonder how one is meant to act when surrounded by insane people? He looked around for something to defend himself with. The best he could find was an antique paperknife on the desk behind him, though its tarnished blade suggested it had seen better days. Was it improper to threaten lunatics with a paperknife? Or should he simply try to escape at the first opportunity?

"I hate to tell you this, Kester, but that's actually not true," Miss Wellbeloved said, interrupting his thoughts. "It's what the government would have you believe, but the reality of the situation is very different. The supernatural is very real indeed."

Kester straightened his collar. "I'm ever so sorry," he said in as polite a tone as he could muster. "But I'm afraid I don't believe you. Not one little bit."

"*Dios mio*! And you're meant to be my son?" Dr Ribero exclaimed, shaking a fist at the ceiling, as though berating the heavens themselves. "But that cannot be! I could never produce so narrow-minded a creature, no?"

"Dr Ribero, please remember, this is all very new to him," Miss Wellbeloved said warningly. She turned to Kester. "This is precisely why your mother asked him to stay away from you. We run a very unusual type of business here, and she didn't want you involved in it when you were a child."

"Hang on," Kester said heavily. "Just a moment please."

Miss Wellbeloved and Dr Ribero waited patiently, observing him with implacable severity. He felt like a beetle under a microscope, about to be squashed.

What on earth am I meant to do? he wondered. Nothing in his twenty-two years of life so far had prepared him for this kind of situation, and he felt utterly helpless. All that he had learnt about social etiquette seemed completely useless in this current situation. There had never been a time at Cambridge where he'd been educated on how to address people who were potentially mad.

He cast his mind to Alice in Wonderland, one of his favourite childhood books. How had Alice dealt with the Mad Hatter? *Humour him,* he thought, with sudden clarity. *Humour them both. That's the way out of this situation.*

However, there was something in their faces that deterred him from this approach. Neither looked at all mad, despite their outrageous claims. In fact, a more classic image of sanity would be hard to find. The austere ruler-straightness of Miss Wellbeloved and the charismatic elegance of Ribero didn't work at all with his preconceived notions of insanity.

"You said earlier my mum used to work here," he began, proceeding with the delicacy of a tiptoeing ballet dancer. "Are you seriously telling me that my mother used to investigate ghosts?"

"Aha, now he finally starts to grasp it!" Dr Ribero said, with a sarcastic slap of the thigh. Miss Wellbeloved shot him a look. She leaned over, grasping Kester by the arm.

"Come on," she said firmly. "Perhaps if the others tell you more about what they do, you'll understand things a bit better."

"Hey, you are not having this conversation without me," Dr Ribero said hastily, rising from the chair with an energy quite at odds with his age. "I will come with you."

"Hang on, I'm not sure I want to come with you myself yet!" Kester squawked, pulling his arm from her grip as politely as he could. He smoothed down his hair, shoved his glasses up his nose, and eyed them with deep suspicion.

"What are you going to do instead, cower in my office all afternoon?" Dr Ribero said.

"Well, no. No, of course not. But I rather thought I might leave. This is all a bit too silly."

"You still don't believe us?" Ribero barked.

"Of course I don't believe you!" Kester replied, finally losing his cool. "You're telling me you investigate ghosts for a living, which is just plain bloody mad!"

"Oh dear," muttered Miss Wellbeloved with a sigh.

"If you go now, do not expect to be welcomed back!" Dr Ribero said, raising his voice.

"That's probably fine with me," Kester flustered. "To be honest, I think you're quite insane, and I'm not sure you're my father either. So it's probably best I leave."

"Fine, if that is your choice!"

"I think it is my choice, yes."

"Oh for goodness' sake, will you both stop being so ridiculous!" Miss Wellbeloved flared, her icy tones heating up by a significant margin. "Julio, I said it was better for you to tell him. I've handled it badly, and you've been no help in the matter either."

She turned to Kester and her face softened a little, like a glacier starting to drip. "Look here," she said, tucking a stray grey curl behind her ear. "This is a shock to you, I know. But we're telling the absolute truth. We do run a supernatural agency." She stopped, narrowing her eyes at Ribero. "And this is very much your father. I can vouch for that. I was there when Gretchen announced she was pregnant with you."

At the mention of his mother's name, Kester slumped, the fight taken from him. *This woman knew me when I was in my mother's womb,* he realised. He also couldn't help but notice the look she was giving Dr Ribero. It was full of reproach, like a whipped dog. The doctor met her gaze, then looked away, rubbing his eyes.

"Will you come with me to talk to the others?" Miss Wellbeloved said finally, gesturing out the door.

Kester sighed. "Yes," he agreed, standing. "I suppose so." *After all,* he thought. *What choice do I have?*

"And will you behave yourself and stop working yourself into a temper?" Miss Wellbeloved snapped at Ribero.

Dr Ribero, contrite, shifted awkwardly from foot to foot. "Yes."

"Good. Well, let's go and discuss things with the others."

Sweeping the door open, she ushered Kester back into the airy office, like a hen flapping out an intrusive chick. It was a welcome change from the musty heat of Dr Ribero's inner sanctum and he felt his head clearing as the breeze from the window grazed his face. At their desks, Pamela, Serena, and Mike looked up in unison: three pets awaiting their master's command.

Miss Wellbeloved raised an imperious hand, calling for

attention. "I've told him about our agency," she said, pointing at Kester. "But, unsurprisingly, he doesn't believe a word of it. I rather thought you might all be able to help. Can you just clarify things by telling him what you do? Pamela, you start."

Pamela stood, smoothing down the ruffles on her blouse, which billowed over her large bosom like a waterfall. "Goodness me, I don't normally have to explain to people what I do for a job, I'm not sure where to start."

"Just a simple explanation will suffice."

"Very well." Pamela smiled. "I'm the agency's resident psychic. If you don't know what that is, it's a—"

"I know what one is," Kester replied. "They're people who predict the future, right?"

Pamela knotted her hands in a tumble of awkwardness. "Yes, sort of," she wavered, looking at Miss Wellbeloved for help.

"How come you didn't predict that I'd come here today then?" Kester asked.

"It doesn't really work like that, I'm afraid."

That's convenient, Kester thought, but kept his reservations to himself. In spite of his belief that they were all completely bonkers, it was difficult to dislike this strange group of people, and he didn't want to upset them, even if they were certified lunatics. It was wisest to continue to humour them, then make a run for it at the next available moment.

"A psychic picks up on spirit energy," Miss Wellbeloved clarified. "Pamela visits haunted locations, and tells us whether a spirit is present or not, and what state of mind it's in."

"Oh, I see," Kester said, with a polite cough. He looked at the exit with renewed longing, wondering whether or not to make a run for it.

Serena coughed deliberately, waving a hand in the air. "I work as the extinguisher," she declared, then added as a challenging afterthought, "I bet you don't know what that is."

"Strangely enough, no. I don't," Kester replied, fighting to keep any trace of sarcasm from his voice.

"You might have heard of exorcists," Miss Wellbeloved added. "It's along those lines."

"I ask the spirits to vacate the premises," Serena said. "I'm sort of like a bailiff. I send them packing."

"It's not quite like that," Miss Wellbeloved interrupted, shaking her head. "We like to be respectful of spirits, and we don't just 'send them packing', do we, Serena?"

Serena shrugged, tapping a stilettoed toe on the floor.

Kester screwed up his eyes, struggling to make sense of it all. The words that they were saying were said so seriously, so professionally, that it seemed almost believable. But he knew that it was all complete nonsense. His natural sense of propriety was wrestling with his sense of incredulity, not to mention his growing curiosity. Despite his desire to leave as swiftly as possible, he couldn't help but want to hear more. He'd never heard anything so preposterous, and yet so intriguing, in his entire life.

"So what do you do?" he asked Miss Wellbeloved finally.

"I'm a conversant," she said primly. "I inherited the skill from my father, and my father's father. I can talk to spirits. Believe me, it's a real asset in this line of work. I operate almost as a lawyer does, facilitating between the spirit and the human on the receiving end."

"Her skills are very useful indeed," Dr Ribero added, with a respectful nod. "One of our biggest assets. Many times, Jennifer has calmed down very bad situations, yes?"

"I'm glad you realise that," Miss Wellbeloved replied, a hint of colour touching her cheeks.

"So what does Mike do then, if he's not really the IT guy?" Kester asked, looking over at the burly man, who was currently concealed under an unruly mountain of gadgets, wires, and batteries.

"No, he really is our IT guy," Serena said. "He sorts out our computers, runs the website—"

"You've got a website?" Kester said weakly.

"Not one that the public can access. It's an Swww.co.uk address."

"What?"

She rolled her eyes. "An Swww.co.uk address. Don't you understand basic website addresses?"

"Not weird ones like that, funnily enough."

Mike snorted, poking his head out of the mess like a meerkat. "Hang on a minute," he interrupted. "I really don't like this label of 'IT guy', Serena. I know you call me that just to bug the crap out of me." The two glowered at one another, before he continued, "I also design all the equipment that we use. And believe me, some of it is pretty impressive. Larry Higgins would love to get his hands on some of this stuff."

"Who's Larry Higgins?" Kester asked.

"Larry Higgins runs the Larry Higgins Agency in Essex," Serena said. "We all think he's a fat idiot, but he's doing very well for himself indeed. Dr Ribero can't stand him."

"Do not get me started on the Higgins," Ribero growled, folding his arms and glaring in Kester's direction.

"You mean there's more than one of these supernatural agencies?" Kester blinked, polishing his glasses on his shirt. He was finding it almost impossible to get his head around it all.

Serena sniggered at his lack of knowledge. "There's a few, yes. Higgins's company is the only other one in the south, apart from bloody Infinite Enterprises in London."

"Oh, those bastards," Mike grumbled. "Don't even get *me* started on them. Larry Higgins might be a pompous prat but at least he's not like bloody Infinite Enterprises."

"Infinite Enterprises are quite the government darlings," Miss Wellbeloved explained. "Which is why we're all very disapproving of them. It's jealousy, pure and simple. They snap up all the best jobs."

Government? Kester thought, bewildered. *Are they trying to suggest that the government hires these supernatural agencies? This is all getting more ridiculous by the minute!*

Dr Ribero stepped forward with the fluid grace of a leopard, reached out, and grasped Kester by the elbows. He studied his son intently, his dark eyes flitting restlessly over his face as though tracking a fly. The room fell silent.

"You don't believe a word of what we are telling you, do you." It was a statement, not a question.

Kester shrugged, unsure how to answer without causing offence. *No,* he thought, *but it's certainly fascinating, even if you are all living in a make-believe world.*

The doctor grunted, still examining the young man's features. Suddenly, he smiled. His face broke into light, a thousand beams of Latin sunshine manifesting themselves in his wrinkles and cracks. "Aha," he proclaimed, drawing Kester back to view him in his entirety.

"What?" Kester asked weakly, intimidated by the scrutiny.

Dr Ribero met his gaze, then chuckled. "I have finally seen myself in you."

"What do you mean?"

"At first, it was all your mother. A weak, plump version of your mother. Now, I see a little glimmer of me, right there." He pointed directly into Kester's eyes, making him wince. "It is there, that little twinkle of defiance and disbelief. I see the spirit of Argentina in you. Just a little, but it is there. That is a relief, yes?"

Silence filled the room. Kester blinked. Dr Ribero's smile widened.

"He still doesn't believe us though," Serena chimed, after a minute or so.

Mike guffawed, slapping his desk. "Of course he doesn't!" he bellowed. "Come on guys, we wouldn't believe us either, if we were hearing it for the first time. That's how we like it, isn't it?

It's that disbelief that means we can do our jobs in peace."

"Well, I don't see what more I can say to convince him," said Miss Wellbeloved, scratching her head and looking flustered.

Serena sidled around her desk, languid as an alley-cat. "Perhaps you shouldn't *say* anything else," she said, pixie-eyes glittering. She examined Kester at length, starting at his polished shoes, past his crisply ironed slacks and right up to his face, which was looking more baffled by the moment. Then she nodded. Kester swallowed hard.

"You should *show* him instead," she said finally. Her tone was full of ill-disguised glee, to such a degree that he almost expected her to start rubbing her hands together like a Machiavellian pantomime villain.

"Show me what?" Kester asked weakly. Her cunning grin convinced him that he really didn't want to know.

"Now that's an idea," Pamela said, flapping her hands towards the second of the doors at the back of the room. "We caught a Bean Si the other week, why don't we show Kester that one?"

"What on earth is a 'bean see'?" Kester looked from face to face with growing alarm. Wherever this was going, he was pretty positive he wasn't going to like it.

"I'm not sure that's a wise idea," Miss Wellbeloved interrupted, looking thoroughly disapproving. "She's a particularly volatile one. We don't want to scare him."

"Oh come on, she wouldn't scare him, a harmless little thing like that," Serena replied.

"I don't know, she's pretty noisy when she gets going," Mike added merrily.

Miss Wellbeloved tutted. "I think that's a rather unprofessional suggestion," she muttered. "Not to mention disrespectful to the Bean Si in question."

"Oh come on, she won't mind being let out for a bit. She could probably do with a stretch before she gets deported anyway."

"Excuse me, I am still here you know," Kester said, as assertively as possible. He placed his hands on his hips, and tried to stand a little straighter. Then felt marginally ridiculous and slumped back into his usual posture. Authority wasn't really his thing. "I don't know what this bean thing is," he said loudly, "and I'm not sure I want to see it."

"A Bean Si, a Bean Si!" said Dr Ribero, punching Kester's arm a little too enthusiastically. "You must have heard this name, yes?"

"No."

"Banshee is the more common term," Serena said, winking at the others.

"A banshee?" Kester echoed.

"Yes, a banshee," Miss Wellbeloved confirmed. "Have you heard of such a creature?"

Kester considered. "Well," he pondered, "My mother used to say to me, when I was a boy, that I cried like a banshee."

"How old were you when she said that?" Serena asked.

"About thirteen or fourteen?"

Serena snorted.

"Oh dear," murmured Pamela faintly.

"A banshee, or Bean Si as they're known in their native land," continued Miss Wellbeloved, delivering Serena a withering look, "is a female spirit that wails loudly before a person is about to die. However, that's not entirely based on truth. Although they do enjoy howling whenever death is in the air, they actually wail whatever the occasion."

"However, as you can imagine, it's very unsettling for the person who ends up with her in their home," Pamela added.

"Christ, yes, they make a right bloody din," Mike added. "We all have to wear earmuffs when we deal with a Bean Si, the noise goes right through you."

"Is that what happened with this Bean Si then? Was she in

someone's home?" Kester asked. Then he suddenly realised what he was asking. *Why am I humouring them?* he asked himself. *Don't encourage them! It'll only make it worse!* Yet he couldn't seem to stop himself. In spite of the oddness of the situation, not to mention his own disbelief, he was curious to learn more. There was a strange logic to their words that wormed its way into his head, making him almost believe them.

"Yeah, down near Torquay," Mike replied, leaning casually against his desk and knocking off a bundle of wires in the process. "She was a pretty easy case actually, a quick two-hour job. Those are the sort we like. None of these protracted haunting projects. They're a right pain in the—"

"Yes, thank you, Mike," Miss Wellbeloved interrupted firmly. She looked helplessly at Dr Ribero, who shrugged.

"I'll go and get her then," said Pamela. Delving into the deep pockets of her voluminous skirts, she pulled out a key, then puffed over to the door like a sponge bobbing in bathwater.

"I still don't think this is very wise," Miss Wellbeloved muttered. "I do wish you'd say something, Julio."

Dr Ribero smiled wryly. "Serena is probably right," he said slowly. "Only way to convince this boy is to show him. Look at him, Jennifer. You see? He is not believing us yet."

Miss Wellbeloved sighed, pressing her arms across her flat, buttoned-up chest, but said nothing more.

After a minute or so, Pamela emerged from the darkened room clutching what appeared to be a plastic bottle of mineral water. However, as she came closer, Kester could see something shifting inside, something with a faintly greyish tinge, smoky and fiery in the centre. As Pamela held it up, he thought, for one ludicrous moment, that he could detect a small hand, no larger than a daisy-head, pressing against the grooves of the plastic. Then it disappeared, retreating back into the strange, billowing mist.

"Is that a plastic bottle?" he asked stupidly. He'd never seen anything like it in his life.

"It's as good a way of storing spirits as any," Mike said, with a hint of defensiveness. "Of course, Infinite Enterprises have got state-of-the-art storage devices, but we don't have the money for those. So water bottles do the job nicely. We just have to make sure none go out with the recycling by mistake."

Kester blanched. "I see." He couldn't take his eyes off the bottle. There was definitely something in there, but he couldn't work out what it was. It pulsed, as though aware it was being watched. Kester shivered.

"Are you ready to let her out?" Serena said wickedly. Her face was full of merriment.

"Hang on, hang on!" Miss Wellbeloved snapped. "Get the earmuffs please! If you're going to let her out, I don't want us all to be deafened. And Serena, only a minute please, then put her right back inside. Is that agreed?"

Serena nodded, whilst Mike walked back to his desk, fishing out some earmuffs from one of his drawers. He threw Kester a pair, who looked at them in disbelief. *What am I doing?* he thought incredulously, even as he pulled them down over his ears. He eyed the bottle nervously, unsure what to expect. The entire day was starting to feel rather like a bad dream. *Maybe it doesn't matter what I do,* he thought, looking at the others. *Maybe I'll just wake up in a moment.* There was comfort in the prospect of waking up in his single bed back home and forgetting that any of this nonsense ever happened.

Before he had a chance to review the situation more sensibly, Pamela held the bottle at arm's length and unscrewed the lid in one deft movement. Kester opened his mouth to protest, but was stunned into silence by an overwhelming hiss—a deep, throaty noise that rampaged into the room—bringing with it a huge cloud of black smoke.

It reminded him of a storybook he had owned as a child. The front cover had depicted a genie, curling enigmatically out of a lamp. What was happening in front of him now was very much like that, only a lot less charming and a lot more terrifying. In fact, he'd never seen anything more revoltingly, stomach-churningly horrible in all his life. It was like all his worst childhood nightmares, bundled together and repackaged for him to enjoy in adulthood.

Kester stumbled instinctively backwards. He tripped over his feet, nearly falling to the ground, as the cloud rolled and twisted above them, wrenching at itself like a mass of wrestling snakes. Then the screaming started. For one mad moment, he thought it was his own scream. Indeed, he did feel like screaming, and couldn't be completely sure that he wasn't making some sort of noise of terror. However, whatever sound was coming from his mouth was completely drowned by the deafening screech of the smoke in front of him. It tore at his eardrums, in spite of the ear muffs, and he fell to his knees, more terrified than he ever had been before.

What the hell is that thing? he thought crazily, unable to take it in. The sight, the sound, even the clinging wet-leaf smell of it was too much for his brain to process. It was by far and away the most awful thing he had ever witnessed in his entire life. He felt his head start to fuzz, as though someone was slowly squirting expanding foam into his ears.

He was dimly aware of an arm, draped over his shoulder, plus some other far away, confusing noises, all virtually drowned out by the tinnitus-inducing wail of the thing in front of him. Out of his wits with fear, he looked up, then wished he hadn't. The cloud had a face. An ugly face. A repulsive, gnarled, cruel face, looming toothily over him. Not to mention a pair of twisted hands, with winter-twig fingers, reaching out, coming straight towards him.

And, perhaps most confusing of all, a doorway behind her. More maw than door—a ragged tear in the air, like the entrance to a cave. Shimmering, hanging impossibly above the ground. A doorway to another place, another place he didn't even want to think about imagining.

His vision began to fluff at the edges and he keeled over, unconscious, onto the office floor.

CHAPTER 4: MORE DOORS

Kester awoke to the sight of a high, white ceiling, almost ecclesiastical in style. *Am I in a church?* he wondered, with the hint of a smile. He'd always liked churches. Their peacefulness appealed to him, not to mention their stoic conservatism. It was tempting to drift back to unconsciousness again. There was something in his head, a little urgent voice, insisting it would be better to go back to sleep. A whole lot better.

Why are my ears hurting? A shrill ringing needled at his eardrums, making his head feel like it was being assaulted by an army of angry, vocal rodents. He felt sick. Even more alarmingly, there were people next to him, which he wasn't expecting. With great reluctance, he turned his head. Five faces floated into focus, studying him with varying degrees of concern. *I'm definitely not in a church,* he realised, blinking. Then he remembered.

"Oh dear lord, no," he said. The awfulness of the memory hurled itself back into his head and he groaned. "Dear god, that was awful."

"Ah, you are back with us!" Dr Ribero boomed, clapping his hands. Kester peered up at them, all huddled together like a group of vultures surveying a helpless antelope, from his horizontal position on the sofa. He felt bile rising to his throat, and fought hard to swallow it down.

"I—what was—? What just happened?" he finally burbled, shaking his head. He sat up, then wished he hadn't. Blood rushed to his cheeks, making him feel faint again.

"Well, I knew you'd be scared, but I didn't think you'd pass out," Serena said scathingly, kicking a patent heel against the floor.

"I know, he was like the big sissy, was he not?" Dr Ribero chuckled, nudging her in a conspiratorial manner.

Miss Wellbeloved scowled. "Julio!" she chastised. "Remember who you're talking about!"

Dr Ribero had the decency to look abashed, but not for long. Adjusting his trouser legs, he deposited himself next to Kester with the grace of a landing eagle.

"My boy, you have seen your first spirit," he declared, beaming. "And how did it feel?"

"Horrendous," Kester said, rubbing his forehead. "What the hell was that thing?" The memory of it was coming back fast, the evil screeching, the swirling black smoke, the terrible face, leering out at him. He shuddered. There was no way he was going to be able to sleep tonight. Or perhaps ever again.

"Just a very low-grade Bean Si," Serena sneered. "Gosh, if you can't cope with one of those, then I don't know what you'll be able to cope with."

"Serena, remember he didn't even believe in spirits before today," Pamela chastised, flapping her arms at the younger woman like a disapproving hen. "Be kind. He's very young still. And he is Gretchen's boy, after all."

Kester looked warily around the office, expecting to see the creature still hovering in the air, waiting for him to notice it. Thankfully, the room had returned to normal, and not a wisp of the evil thing remained.

"Where is it now?" he asked hesitantly.

"Back in the bottle," Pamela said, in a soothing voice. "Don't worry, we've put her right back in, and she's now locked up again in that room. She can't get out, love; I promise you."

"She's a loud one, isn't she?" Mike shook his head, as though trying to dislodge water from his ears. "Dunno about you, but my ears are still going. It's the only thing I really dislike about them actually, that awful noise they make. Always gives me a headache after."

"Why was she leaning towards me?" Kester asked. He didn't want to ask the question, but he felt that he needed to. During the event, he had had the horrible sensation that the Bean Si had been reaching out for him in some way, reaching out for him, and him alone. He very much hoped that he had been mistaken.

"Yes, I noticed that." Miss Wellbeloved perched on the armrest of the sofa. "That was most strange. I did wonder if it was due to the fact that you'd recently had a family member die."

"It's normally before the death that they latch on to people though, isn't it?" Mike interjected. "I've not heard of a Bean Si reaching for a human after the death's happened. They might hang around, scream a bit, unsettle everyone; but they don't target just one person, do they?"

"Great, that makes me feel much better," Kester muttered, massaging his temples. He knew what Mike meant about the headache.

"Maybe she thought you were handsome and fell in love with you," Serena said sarcastically. Both Miss Wellbeloved and Pamela shot her a severe look.

"What was the doorway?" Kester asked, suddenly remembering.

"What doorway?" Dr Ribero asked.

"The doorway, behind that creature."

"You mean the doorway at the back of the room?"

Kester shook his head. "No. Not that one. The weird cave-like door. It was like the air had ripped open behind her. It was the oddest thing I've ever seen. Even odder than that horrible creature."

"Hang on, hang on. Just one minute, please. What do you mean, door?" Dr Ribero asked, suddenly serious.

Kester straightened himself, addressing the problem of his shirt, which had untucked, revealing his pale belly, which bulged most unflatteringly over his belt. "When that—that thing came out of the bottle, there was a weird door right behind it. It wasn't like a normal door; it was like—"

"Yes?" Dr Ribero said, leaning closer. His eyes were gleaming.

Kester shrank back. "It was probably nothing," he concluded. "I was so terrified; I would have imagined anything. Tell me, was that creature real? It wasn't just some horrible joke you were all playing on me, was it?"

"God, that would be one elaborate practical joke, wouldn't it?" Serena said sarcastically. "Do you imagine we have a holographic projector system and state-of-the-art, top-volume hi-fi system, rigged up and waiting to trick unsuspecting visitors?"

"Well, Mike is an IT guy," Kester replied crossly.

"Electronics expert," Mike snapped. "And you're right. If I wanted to create a machine that produced a realistic Bean Si, I'd certainly have the expertise to do it. But for the record, you were looking at the real thing. No trickery at all, I'm afraid."

"That is strange, that you would see a door," Dr Ribero muttered. He looked up at Miss Wellbeloved, who shrugged.

"I'd say the whole experience was rather strange," said Kester, shuddering. The memory was still grotesquely fresh. He didn't think he'd ever forget that craggy, misty face hanging over him, like a ghastly haunted tree. It was all his worst nightmares, all compressed into one dreadful minute of his life, and he wished fervently that there was a way that he could empty his mind of it, or at least reverse time and never experience any of it.

He rose to his feet, wobbled, and steadied himself against the nearest desk. "I think I'll be heading off now," he announced, fighting to keep his voice from shaking. His head was beginning to throb, and he wanted nothing more than to retreat to the pink-frilled Victorian safety of his B&B. The idea of burying his head into the worn eiderdown and trying his hardest to ignore the events of the day was very appealing indeed.

"Really, you're going so soon?" Pamela said, surprised. They all looked instinctively at the clock.

"I don't feel very well," Kester replied. "I think I need to lie down somewhere, take some time to think things through. It's been quite an afternoon."

"I'll say," Mike said jovially. "Not every day you meet the father you never knew you had, and come face to face with a banshee."

"Indeed," Kester agreed faintly.

"Why not join us for a pint after work?" Mike continued, oblivious to Kester's obvious state of distress. "We're popping down to the Fat Pig for a drink or two, did you want to come?"

"That's very kind of you, but I really think I need to be alone. My head is pounding."

"Bloody banshees," Mike acknowledged. "You'd think someone would ask them to come equipped with painkillers."

"Just a moment!" Ribero barked, as Kester scooped up his bag. "How long are you staying in Exeter, hey? When are you returning to Cambridge?"

"I've only booked the one night," Kester replied. "I'm catching the train back tomorrow." *Tomorrow can't come soon enough,* he thought wistfully, thinking of his own familiar bedroom, his cosy living room, reading in the sunlight in the garden. *Except he's actually the one who paid for that house, not mother,* he realised, eyeing Dr Ribero warily. *I wonder if he'll want it back, now she's dead?*

"Hmm," Ribero grunted. He scratched his chin, then stood. "Perhaps you would like to stay a little longer, yes? Maybe a few days?"

"Why?" Kester asked. He knew it wasn't the politest way of responding, but at present, his desire for social etiquette had rather been overwhelmed by his need to snuggle under the nearest duvet.

"Ah, well," the doctor said, coughing. "You know, we have only just met, and it seems a shame for the visit to be so brief, does it not?"

"I think what Julio is trying to say is that he'd like to get to know you better," said Miss Wellbeloved with a wry grin.

Kester studied the floorboards, dismayed and overwhelmed by it all. His head felt as though it was going to explode, not just because of his headache, but because of the confusion of the day. It was simply too much to cope with. He wished that he had never come, that he'd resisted booking the train ticket down, that he'd ignored his mother's dying wish entirely. So far, it had brought him nothing but rotten luck, and everything he'd discovered since being here had shaken his world to the core.

"I've only booked one night in the bed and breakfast," he mumbled, hoping the excuse would be adequate. "I don't think I can extend it any further, I think she was fairly fully booked, what with it being the summer and everything."

"Ah, that is not a big problem," the doctor persisted, patting Kester on the shoulder like a groom calming a skittish horse. "We can find you somewhere. You should stay a little while, see what we do here. What do you think, eh?"

"I really think I should be getting back," Kester persisted, edging subtly towards the door. "Though perhaps we can arrange another time, in the future, to meet up again?"

Dr Ribero shook his head earnestly. "No, Kester, my boy, no. That will not do. You are here now, right? So we must make the most of it. After all, we have only just met."

"Julio, perhaps don't force him," Miss Wellbeloved murmured, narrowing her eyes. Kester shot her a grateful look.

Ribero shrugged her comment off with a dismissive wave. "Ah, he is not being forced. He just wants the formal invite, don't you, Kester? It is because he is polite, you see. Raised by his mother to be a good boy. That is all."

"Kester, you're more than welcome to stay at mine for a while, if you'd like," Pamela offered, bustling up to him like a bobbing balloon. "I've only got a small back room, but it's quite cosy. As long as you don't mind the dog jumping on you first thing in the morning."

"And the fact that her house stinks of mince and mashed potatoes," Serena added, wrinkling up her nose.

"Serena, it was just that one time, and that was because I actually had been cooking mince and potatoes," Pamela chastised. She leaned towards Kester earnestly and added, "it doesn't smell of that all the time, I promise you."

"Well, it still smells of damp dog hairs," Serena said with a snort. "Your dog moults for England. It's amazing it's not completely bald yet. I thought your lounge had a carpet until I realised it was just dog hair I was treading on."

"Please don't exaggerate."

"Every time you inhale in your house, you get a nose full of dog hairs."

"Serena, will you just give it a rest, please?"

"Well, I'm just pointing out that—"

"Please!" Kester shouted. It was a little louder than he had anticipated, and he felt his face redden. The others fell silent, looking at him with mild amazement.

"Please," he continued, a little more quietly. "I feel like I'm going a little mad. I've not even been here an hour, and in that time I've found out I have a father, who I didn't even know existed, and I've also discovered that there are horrible ghosts lurking around the place. I just need some time to myself. I can't . . . I can't hear myself think in here."

"Oh, you poor thing," Pamela said, placing a soft hand on his shoulder. "Of course. This is just all too much for you, isn't it? Especially given what you've gone through recently."

"It is a bit," Kester said, fighting the urge to sniff. He was feeling oddly emotional, and worryingly close to tears. It was most unlike him, but then, this day had been quite unlike any other he'd ever known. He supposed an unusual reaction was only to be expected.

"Why don't you just stay one more night and come out with us tomorrow?" Dr Ribero suggested. There was a strident ring to his tone, a stony obstinacy, that suggested he wasn't going to take no for an answer.

"Come out with you tomorrow?" Kester said, blinking in confusion. "What's happening tomorrow?"

"Oh, it's the woodland job tomorrow, isn't it? I completely forgot about that one," Mike said, before he chortled. "Well, it's certainly an interesting job to bring Kester along on."

"Wait a minute, is this another supernatural thing?" Kester said, stuttering slightly. *No way,* he thought. *I can't believe they'd even think there was a remote possibility that I'd want to join them.*

"Well, of course it's a supernatural thing!" Serena said, confirming his fears. "What else would it be?" She shook her head, folding her thin arms in a neat concertina across her relatively flat chest.

"No," Kester said firmly. "Not a chance. Thank you anyway." He moved with greater urgency towards the door.

"This one isn't a frightening job," Dr Ribero continued, stepping nimbly around him and blocking his path. "It's unusual, but not at all scary. I promise you. You will love it."

"I doubt that very much."

"It's just a small, little, lost ghost. Nothing at all to be bothered by."

Kester shook his head with disbelief. "You said that the Bean Si was nothing to be bothered by, and that was the most awful thing I've ever had the misfortune to see. Why would I want to see anything else?"

Pamela coughed. "Well, this one might make you feel a bit less negative about spirits. It's honestly not scary at all. Just a tiny little spirit that's lost its way. It's quite sad really. We've found where it's hiding, now we just need to help him home."

Kester paused. There was something about the image of a lost little ghost that moved him slightly. But only slightly. After all, it was still a ghost at the end of the day. And he didn't much relish the idea of hanging around in a wood, actively seeking one out. However, judging by the faces surrounding him, they weren't going to let the subject drop. And in spite of everything, there was a tiny part of him that was just a little bit curious.

"If I do come," he began, "can I go home after that?"

Dr Ribero tweaked his moustache between his thumb and finger, pulling it into a point with a flourish. "If you still want to," he said slowly. "Yes, yes, absolutely. We are not trying to make you stay against your wishes, no. Of course not."

"No, that's definitely not what we're trying to do," Mike added. His amused expression suggested the exact opposite.

"I'm sure you can easily change your train times," Pamela said. "And if you do want to stay longer, the offer to sleep at my place is still there."

"Well, that's very kind of you," Kester said quietly, giving up all hope of getting out of it. "Do you want me to come here tomorrow then?" *If I really must,* he added silently.

"No, we'll pick you up in the van," Mike said. "What B&B are you at?"

Kester gave him the address, then laughed. "Is it like the Scooby Doo van?"

Dr Ribero glared at him. "It is nothing like the Scooby Doo van. That is a cartoon, yes? No, it is not like that. We are a serious company, not a joke. Thank you."

Kester cleared his throat. "Okay." He resisted the urge to laugh again, aware that there was a slight note of hysteria to it. "So, shall I wait outside?"

"Yep, wait out on the street at around six o'clock," Mike said.

"Six in the morning?" Kester squeaked. He never normally got out of bed until at least gone nine.

"Yeah, think you can manage to wake up at that time?" Serena said with the vaguest hint of a sneer.

"I'm sure that won't be a problem," he snapped, though privately thought exactly the opposite. His only consolation was that, as he wouldn't be able to sleep, thanks to the banshee, he would probably be awake anyway. Whether or not he'd be functioning properly as a human being would be another matter entirely.

"And maybe you'll see that door again," Dr Ribero added, finally moving out of the way to allow him to pass.

"Door?" Kester repeated with a blank look, his attention focused on the office exit, which was now unblocked and presenting a tempting passage out into the normal world.

"The door, the spirit door," the doctor repeated impatiently.

"The one you saw behind the Bean Si," Pamela added.

"Oh, was that what it was?" he asked, without much real enthusiasm. He had reached the point of being beyond caring. Now, all that filled his mind was thoughts of getting out of here, out into the afternoon sunshine, where things were normal, and ghosts simply didn't exist.

"Yes, very interesting you should see it, very interesting indeed," Dr Ribero muttered thoughtfully. Shaking himself like a dog coming in from the rain, he gestured grandly towards the exit. "But we can discuss it more tomorrow. I can see that you are tired and overwrought. You go now. Get some sleep. Recover. Big day tomorrow."

Kester smiled weakly, already regretting his decision to agree to join them. *What was I thinking?* he wondered as he scuffled from the office, closing the door with great relief behind him. *What on earth was I thinking?*

In the pitch blackness of the upper hallway, he shuddered suddenly. Visions of the Bean Si, its plumes of evil-smelling smoke, suddenly came to mind with horrible clarity. *Who knows what other creatures are lurking in the darkness with me?* he thought, then wished he hadn't. He staggered in the direction of the staircase, cursing when his knee made sharp contact with the bannister. Images of monsters, ready to pounce, propelled him into the dim light of the downstairs corridor.

As he emerged on to the dusty, aged alleyway, he didn't think he'd ever been so relieved to see the daylight.

CHAPTER 5: THE MISPLACED GHOST

True to Mike's word, the van rolled up outside Kester's B&B at exactly six o'clock. Apart from a solitary pigeon, roosting on the lamppost opposite, the street was entirely deserted. If he hadn't been so tired, Kester might have enjoyed the serenity of the summer's morning; the sun was easing up over the distant hills and bathing the fields with soft amber light. As it was, he hardly noticed any of it, and focused instead on how cross he was at having to be out at this ridiculous hour.

"You look bloody awful," Mike said jovially, as Kester clambered into the passenger seat next to Miss Wellbeloved. The suspension groaned under the additional weight, like an asthmatic pensioner, and Kester shifted in the seat, worrying that it would collapse under him. "Rough night's sleep?"

"Just a bit." Kester grimaced. He wished he'd had time to get some breakfast. Preferably something sweet, like a *pain au chocolat* and a mug of steaming hot cocoa, like his mother used to make. The prospect of coping with the day ahead, without even the tiniest bit of granulated sugar to push him through, was not an attractive one.

"I hope you weren't scared last night," said Pamela, leaning over from the backseat. She patted his shoulder, finishing with a grasp of his elbow. "Any nightmares?" She looked sickeningly fresh and alert, given the early hour.

"I didn't get much sleep," Kester replied wearily. His eyes felt as though someone had stuffed them with grit, then sanded them down for good measure.

"Ah, but tonight, you will sleep like a baby," Dr Ribero announced grandly from the backseat. "You will be so worn out by today, you will not be able to stop yourself. You will see."

Oh great, thought Kester resentfully. *So whatever we're doing today not only involves the supernatural, but it's going to involve physical exertion too.* It felt like the world's worst combination—his two most hated things. The unexpected and sport.

Pamela squawked as the van bounced over a speedbump with a protesting creak. "I wish you'd book this thing in for a service," she complained. "Every time it goes over a bump, it feels like the bottom's about to fall out."

"Well, it does have to cope with rather a heavy load, doesn't it," drawled Serena, who was curled up in the other corner.

"Was that a jibe about my weight?"

"Of course not," Serena said, in a voice that implied exactly the opposite.

"Well, not all of us can be blessed with the figures of stick insects," Pamela replied, poking her in the ribs. "And at least I've got breasts."

"No question of that," Serena agreed, with a wry look at Pamela's voluminous bosom.

"Ladies, ladies, it's too early in the morning for that sort of talk," Mike said, changing up a gear. "I'm a red-blooded man, after all." The van crunched under his abrasive handling.

"Oh Mike, you are funny," Pamela tittered. Serena snorted,

shutting her eyes.

"Would you like a quinoa and hemp bar?" Miss Wellbeloved offered, rummaging around in her handbag. "They're exceptionally good at providing you with slow-release energy."

Kester didn't have the foggiest idea what she was talking about, but nodded anyway. The mention of the word "bar" implied some sort of snack product, which hopefully might have a chocolate coating, or at the very least, a peanut or two. He was disappointed to be delivered a thin slab of something distinctly homemade, which looked about the same colour as wallpaper paste. Upon nibbling it, he realised it tasted like wallpaper paste too, but he nibbled through it nonetheless. At least it was food, albeit not terribly edible.

"So, did you manage to get any sleep last night?" Mike asked, roaring the van up into another gear and narrowly missing the kerb. "Or were thoughts of banshees keeping you awake?"

Kester pulled a face. He thought he might have dozed off for an hour or so at one point, but mostly, he'd been plagued by images of the horrible creature he'd seen the day before. It went without saying that he had left the light on all night. "I might have had a bit of sleep," he replied curtly. "Not much though."

"Everyone is frightened the first time they see something supernatural," Pamela consoled. "It's a very normal reaction, don't worry."

"Yeah, I absolutely wet myself when I first saw a spirit," Mike interrupted.

"He means that literally," Serena added. "I'd like to clarify that when I first saw a spirit, I was only a child, and I wasn't frightened at all."

"That's because you frightened it instead." Mike swung round the bend, throwing them around like ragdolls. "It probably took one look at you and fled back to the spirit world at top speed."

"Shut up, Mike."

Pamela tapped Kester on the back. "You do get used to it, after a while."

"What, spirits or Serena's constant snide comments?" Mike asked. Serena delivered a glare of pure fury, before rolling over and feigning sleep.

"I'm not sure I want to get used to it," Kester replied. "I think I was quite happy not knowing any of it existed, actually."

"Ah well, mate, too late for that now. Might as well adjust to the idea," Mike said, with a cheerful nod. "Some spirits are alright actually. I got challenged to a drinking contest by one in Ireland once. That was a night and a half, I can tell you."

"How on earth do you have a drinking contest with a ghost?" Kester said, eyes widening.

Mike laughed. "Well, let's just say he drank me under the table. Unfair advantage really, given he could float above the table instead. But there we go."

"You'll swiftly realise," Serena added, opening her eyes again, "that Mike seizes any opportunity to be drunk under the table. We might as well set up a permanent residence for him underneath a pub table, actually."

"Whereas Serena will sip one little thimble-full of vodka, go a bit cross-eyed, start spouting ancient Greek philosophy, and pass out in the nearest corner," Mike replied merrily.

"Oh yes, I'd forgotten about that night," Pamela laughed. "That was funny. Especially when she threw up all over that poor man's shoes."

"Yes, well I think it's been much exaggerated over the years," Serena snarled.

"Oh of course, of course," Pamela replied. "No truth in it at all, eh?" She winked at the other girl, who glowered in response.

"Where are we actually driving to?" Kester asked, scanning outside for clues. In the mellow grey gloom of the morning, he could see that they were leaving the city, and heading out on to a quieter road, flanked by the occasional thatched cottage. The vast Devonshire countryside rolled ahead of them, like a giant green carpet that someone had flung across the landscape as a casual afterthought.

"We're off to an estate, just a few miles from here," Miss Wellbeloved said. "Thorngrove Manor. Well, the woodlands next to Thorngrove Manor, to be precise."

"Why did we need to leave so early then?" Kester asked.

"All spirits have their own natural rhythms," Miss Wellbeloved replied. "Times at which they are active. This one is in completely the wrong time zone, so is most active early in the morning, until about nine."

"What on earth do you mean, 'wrong time zone'?" Kester asked.

"Didn't we say?" Miss Wellbeloved peered into the windscreen mirror, smoothing her hair. "It's a Japanese spirit. Completely dislocated, poor thing. Hasn't got a clue where it is, and it's wandering round causing all sorts of problems on the estate."

"A Japanese spirit?" Kester repeated. "What? I didn't even realise ghosts could have a nationality."

"Of course they can!" Dr Ribero declared loudly. "Just like you and me, yes? It is the same for them."

"Well, that's simplifying things a bit," Miss Wellbeloved interrupted firmly. "Spirits live in the spirit world, but have links here, as you've already experienced. They link with specific places in our world, but this one had managed to get itself completely muddled, and has ended up in the wrong country. Now it can't get back, and as you can imagine, that's making him rather miserable."

"I suppose that's a little bit sad," Kester said thoughtfully. "How do you know it's miserable?"

"Because it won't stop bloody crying," Mike retorted. "It's putting the toffs right off their shooting parties. Every time they head out to bag some pheasants, they find the birds have flown off, because they're scared by this ghost. Quite funny really, when you think about it."

"Anyway," Miss Wellbeloved continued, ignoring Mike. "The owner of the property is an MP, so as you can imagine, he's not too pleased. Hence we've been called in to sort things out."

"Yeah, he's a right fat prat," Mike laughed. "Looks a bit like a blow-up dingy with an angry little red face at the top."

Miss Wellbeloved sighed. "Anyway," she continued. "We're the nearest agency, so we got the job. It caused us a bit of a headache at first, because we couldn't find the spirit, but once we'd worked out where it was and when it appeared, it made things a lot easier."

"So, will you just be sending it back to its, er, what do you call it? Its spirit home?"

"No, we can't just send it back right away," Serena cut in scathingly, as though staggered by his stupidity at suggesting such a thing. "You need to be able to access the spirit world, which very few people can do."

"Okay," Kester said, "what do you do with them then?"

"We gather the spirit into a storage receptacle," Miss Wellbeloved explained.

"A water bottle," Mike added helpfully.

"And then," Miss Wellbeloved continued, forging ahead in spite of the interruption, "we take it back to our premises for safe storage."

"So we stuff 'em in a cupboard, basically."

"Yes, Mike, thank you very much," she snapped. "We put them in our secure, locked cupboard. Then we take them to the spirit depot once a month, in London."

"The what?" Kester said, more confused by the minute. Images of a busy sorting depot, stuffed to the brim with loud, terrifying ghosts, filled his head, and he didn't know whether to laugh or feel utterly depressed that such a thing might actually exist.

"It's just a drop off point, run by Infinite Enterprises, where all ghosts are taken and delivered safely back into their own world," Mike said. "It's me who normally gets saddled with the spirit run. Bit of a boring job really."

"Infinite Enterprises are quite important then, are they?" Kester asked. Mike snorted and refused to reply.

"They're the only people with the facilities to open spirit doors manually," Serena clarified. "It's cutting-edge technology. Costs a fortune. Which is precisely why we don't have it."

"Which is why people who can open spirit doors are so valuable," Ribero muttered. "They're a lot cheaper." Miss Wellbeloved looked over her shoulder, shooting him a look.

They sat in silence for a while. The sun gradually filtered colour through the landscape, and the pastel blue hue of the sky hinted at another bright, cloudless day. In spite of his tiredness, Kester enjoyed the sight of the rolling hills in the distance, turning from milk-grey to green under the caress of the sun. Back in Cambridge, there wasn't much in the way of hills. Here, there was a wildness that made him think of ancient times, before mankind had trampled all over the planet and urbanised it into an endless succession of cities and towns.

"Would anyone like another quinoa and hemp bar?" Miss Wellbeloved offered, pulling the Tupperware pot out of her bag.

"No." The response was unanimous.

"We're here now, anyway," Mike said, swinging through an imposing wrought iron gate. "Not bad timing, either. That's the perks of driving early."

They started to jiggle around like pebbles as the van rattled up the extensive driveway. Kester quickly grabbed on to the side of the door for support, mainly to save himself the embarrassment of rolling into Miss Wellbeloved's lap.

"Rather impressive house," he said.

"I'll say. Landed bloody gentry," Mike grumbled. "All the

privileges a title can bring."

The estate loomed ahead—a giant stone behemoth squatting in the midst of some exceptionally neatly landscaped gardens. It spoke volumes about its owner: important, imposing, and rather self-satisfied.

"I'm not really dressed for meeting anyone important," Kester said nervously.

"Oh, these lot aren't important," Mike said with a growl. "Just because they got born with a silver spoon stuck firmly up their—"

"Yes, thank you, Mike," Miss Wellbeloved interrupted. She turned to Kester, observing his faded t-shirt with an appraising eye. "You'll do fine," she concluded. "They'll just presume you're here to tidy up afterwards or something."

"Oh great," Kester mumbled. He knew he should have worn his shirt.

He stumbled out onto the driveway, scratching his head in dismay. *What am I about to let myself in for?* he wondered, looking over at the woodland in the distance, a silhouette of treetops huddled behind an expanse of immaculate lawn. *Is there really another ghost, lurking somewhere in those trees?* Even if it was only a small, sobbing spirit, he wasn't really sure he was in the mood to meet it.

A door slammed, startling him out of his thoughts. He looked over to see a portly figure marching down the stone stairs to greet them. His stomach was only just contained by his dressing gown, which threatened to come loose with every forceful step.

"Oh, here we go," Serena muttered. "Here comes Lord Flab-gut now,"

"Flanburgh, not Flab-gut, and don't be so rude," Miss Wellbeloved hissed. Pamela giggled.

"Aha, so you're here," the man declared, as he pulled slowly to a stop, like a steam train creaking into a station. His strident tones startled a gull roosting on the roof above, sending it flapping into the sky. "Well, I'm glad you've come. The whole situation is becoming quite unmanageable."

"What has happened?" Dr Ribero said, striding over to take charge of the situation. "No threatening behaviour, I hope?"

"Oh no, no, nothing of that sort," Lord Flanburgh said, tightening his dressing gown. "It's just the crying. It's such a god-awful nuisance. I shall be glad to be rid of it. It's quite ruined my shooting season; I can tell you. Not to mention all the mud it's produced. Loud, messy little bugger, it really is."

Mike snorted, and quickly turned it into a cough.

Lord Flanburgh eyed him suspiciously before continuing. "No, that ruddy thing has been exceptional trouble, and obviously having to keep everything hush hush has been rather tricky. I was worried that a few of the lads on the shoot might run off to the press, and we couldn't have that now, could we?" He gave a meaningful nod, a gesture ruined by the fact that he could only tilt his head slightly, due to the size of his double chin.

"Well, we are here now, and we will have this spirit gone within an hour or so, okay?" Dr Ribero said, rubbing his hands together. "This is not a difficult case, now we know where the little chap is hiding."

Lord Flanburgh chortled. "I'd hardly call it a little chap. Little monster more like. Ruddy odd creature. Glad to be shot of it, sir, glad to be shot of it. Still, as the wife said, at least it wasn't in the house. That never would have done. Ruining all our Queen Anne furniture. Doesn't even bear thinking about."

"Shall we get started then?" Miss Wellbeloved said, looking at her watch. "We don't want to lose our opportunity."

"Quite so, yes. Do carry on. Do what needs to be done to get the little blighter gone, won't you?"

Ribero nodded graciously. "Ah yes. The little 'blighter' will be out of your wood in no time at all, yes? Now, if you will excuse us, your Lordship."

Lord Flanburgh gave his stomach a reflective pat. Kester suspected he might be contemplating his breakfast, which would be a lot better than a quinoa and hemp bar. "Yes, good luck to you," he concluded, then spun on his heel and headed back towards the house.

"He is a strange man," Dr Ribero whispered, as they watched the elephantine figure wobble back into the house.

"A fat bastard more like," Mike muttered. This time, no one disagreed with him.

"Right, shall we get going?" Serena said. "Mike, why don't you go and get the kit?"

"Why do I have to go and get the kit?" Mike grumbled. "You've got hands, haven't you?"

"Yes, but you're always going on about your rippling muscles," Serena retorted. "Time to put them to work." She stalked off in the direction of the woods without a backward glance. Pamela scuttled after her eagerly. Miss Wellbeloved looked at Dr Ribero, sighed, and followed suit. Kester saw no other option but to scurry after them, heart pounding. He was anxious about what he was about to see, but oddly excited too. In fact, in spite of his tiredness, he felt more awake than he had done in weeks, months perhaps. It was all rather exhilarating, despite his deep-seated fear of what lay ahead.

The trees were much larger than they'd looked from a distance. Great oaks hulked above them, weighed down with bumpy leaves, and tall birches towered like elderly men, reaching haphazardly to the sky. Walking through their trunks, he suddenly felt rather small and awed, much like he often felt when entering a cathedral. The air was still. Strangely still, in fact. He couldn't detect a single bird chirruping, in spite of the fact that it was early morning. It was as though someone had pressed the mute button, draining the wood of all noise.

"Quiet, isn't it?" Mike chimed, out of breath from running

to catch up.

"Why is it so silent?" Kester asked, looking nervously over his shoulder. He half-expected to see ghosts leaping out from behind every tree.

"Animals generally don't like spirits," Miss Wellbeloved explained. "If a spirit takes up residence, you can be sure that most of the animals will have moved out within a day or so. There's something about the supernatural that sets their teeth on edge."

Much like me, Kester thought. *I really can't say I blame them.*

"How much further do we have to go?" he asked.

"It's quite a way in," Pamela explained. She was already beginning to pant a bit. "Probably another twenty minutes' walk?"

As it turned out, twenty minutes was more like three-quarters of an hour. The wood was far larger than he had realised, and part of the journey was a steep uphill climb. Soon, despite the coolness of the morning air, Kester had worked up a sweat, and was struggling to catch his breath. He was heartily relieved he hadn't worn his smart shirt after all.

"So, when did you first get into all of this?" he asked Pamela, as much to break the eerie silence as anything else.

"What, you mean when did I join the agency?"

He nodded.

"Well, I always knew I wasn't normal," she said, patting the perspiration off her cheeks. Her frizzy hair was pasted down against her forehead, forming a round helmet of sweat. "I used to pick up on spirits all the time when I was little. My parents were terrified. Luckily, I eventually met the right people, who guided me in the direction of Ribero's agency."

"Then you realised there were other people like you?"

She grinned. "That's right. It's comforting to know you're not alone."

"And what was my mum like?"

Pamela paused, glancing over at Miss Wellbeloved. She looked uncomfortable. "Your mum was a very gentle, sweet-natured person," she said, choosing her words carefully. "And of course, celebrated across the country, because of her unique talents."

"I was also highlighted as a great talent when I joined the agency," Serena interrupted, sidling up behind them. She was still wearing stilettos, but seemed unfazed about trampling through the woods in them. *Maybe she even wears them to bed,* Kester thought, irritated by her presence. He'd wanted to hear more about his mother.

"Were you?" he asked, without much enthusiasm.

"Yes. I'm young, but I've already got a reputation as one of the best extinguishers in the country." She looked upwards, her green eyes twinkling in the mottled sunlight. "Put it like this. I take no prisoners. I'm not down with this woolly, softly-softly approach. I get rid of spirits and I don't mess around."

"You know Jennifer doesn't like you talking like that," Pamela reminded her.

"No, I don't." Miss Wellbeloved looked over her shoulder, giving Serena a warning look. "Spirits have every much right to be respected as you do."

"Aha, we are very nearly there," Dr Ribero announced, as they started to clamber downhill along a narrow path.

"How can you tell?" puffed Kester, marginally peeved to see that Dr Ribero didn't appear remotely tired after the brisk walk. *For an older man, he really is in good shape,* he thought enviously, noting his father's flat stomach underneath the white shirt. He looked down at his own quivering paunch and frowned.

"Can you not hear it?" Dr Ribero whispered, halting him with a gentle press of the hand. "Listen."

Kester paused. Sure enough, as his ears adjusted once more to the silence, he could detect a faint noise floating on the still air. A whispery, but undeniably clear sob. The hairs on his neck promptly stood on end.

"My goodness," he breathed, astonished. "It sounds like a human crying."

"Not so much when you get up close," Dr Ribero said. "Then you can hear the difference. You will see."

I'm not sure I want to see, Kester thought, feeling suddenly cold. The madness of the situation hit him with sudden, brutal force. This time yesterday, he hadn't even believed in ghosts. Now, here he was, out searching for one in the middle of nowhere, with a group of people that he scarcely even knew. *What on earth has happened to my life?* he thought with bewilderment. *And how do I get back to being normal again?*

"Come on, let's get on with it," Serena grumbled. "I'm hungry."

"Yeah, I could do with a full English breakfast right now," Mike said, yawning. "Sausages, bacon, couple loaves of toast, that'd do me nicely."

They pressed forward, wrestling with the increasingly tangled undergrowth. The crying increased in volume. As they got closer, Kester could detect a distinct difference to the sobbing. It sounded hollow, like an echo through a tunnel, with a wispy after-note that hung in the air, vibrating to nothing. The nearer they got, the more Kester wished he could retreat again. Pamela noticed his discomfort and gave his arm a squeeze.

"Honestly, it's fine, love," she whispered. "Nothing to be scared of."

"Okay," he squeaked, wishing he could believe her. He felt utterly terrified.

Kester pressed after them, through a thicket of particularly dense foliage, trying not to sting his arms on the nettles. All the while, the crying became louder and more insistent, combined with another sound that he couldn't quite identify. A grainy, rhythmic noise, like gravel being thrown against a wall. What was it? It sounded so familiar, yet he couldn't quite place it.

Then, as he stepped into the clearing and saw the cause of the sound, he realised instantly what it was.

"Oh my goodness, it's raining on him," he breathed. He tried to speak further, but the sight struck him speechless, his mouth gaping open and shut like a surprised haddock.

Standing alone in the clearing stood a tiny creature, as perfectly formed as a china doll, though he stood no taller than an average sized dog. He, if indeed it was male, was dressed in an impossibly white gown, which glowed with the intensity of a celestial body. Initially, Kester was confused by what appeared to be a huge disc, hovering above the spirit's head. Then he realised. It was a delicate little parasol. *This ghost is carrying an umbrella!* he thought incredulously, unsure whether to start laughing or tear out of the woods in horror.

The sound that he had heard was the noise of heavy raindrops falling on the ghost, and the ghost alone. All around the creature's bare little feet, the ground had turned to thick mud. In fact, the whole clearing was virtually a bog. It was a stark contrast to the parched ground they'd walked on to get here.

"*Amefurikozo*," Miss Wellbeloved said, stepping forward. "*Koko ni kunasai.*"

"What does that mean?" Kester whispered to Serena.

"I haven't got the foggiest," Serena replied. "Jennifer's probably just learnt a few phrases of Japanese to put the spirit at ease."

"*Amefurikozo* is its name," Dr Ribero corrected. "He is a Japanese *yokai*. A little child spirit. You see?"

Whatever Miss Wellbeloved had said to the ghost, it appeared to have worked. The creature looked up, umbrella tilted like a halo. Two huge, black eyes, empty and knowing as a field mouse, surveyed each of them in turn. Kester couldn't tell whether it was the result of the crying or the rain, but moisture had started to corrode the spirit's white cheeks, melting them like candle wax.

"*Koko ni kunasai*," Miss Wellbeloved repeated, gesturing to the ghost. "*Koko ni kunasai.*"

"What are you saying to him now?" Ribero whispered.

"I think I'm asking him to come here, in Japanese," she replied.

"Hang on, where did you learn the phrase?" Mike asked.

Miss Wellbeloved rolled her eyes. "On the internet, like anyone else would," she hissed. "Why?"

"Was it a proper website?"

"What do you mean?"

"Well, you could be saying anything to him, like 'do you need the toilet' or 'your burger's about to fall out of its bun' or something like that, couldn't you? If it's not a reputable site."

"Oh do shut up, Mike."

Serena laughed out loud, and the spirit wailed at the noise, a mournful yowl that swept through the clearing like a bitter breeze. It held its porcelain-pale hands out to ward them off, and glided backwards over the turbulent mud.

"Oh for goodness' sake," Miss Wellbeloved said, glaring at them all. "Will you all please be quiet?" She edged towards the trembling ghost, who was sobbing with renewed vigour.

"What a sad creature," Kester said, touched in spite of himself. He'd never seen such a morose, frightened sight. Although its face, with its billiard ball eyes and colourless features, was horribly unnatural, its inner turmoil was so raw that it was impossible not to be moved.

"Kester," Dr Ribero whispered, sidling up beside him, quiet as a serpent. "Tell me, do you see this door again?"

"What door?"

"You know, you know," Ribero spluttered back, poking him in the ribs. "The one you saw with the Bean Si, yes? You remember. It was only yesterday, right? Can you see it now?"

"You mean the weird opening I saw behind the banshee?"

"Yes, of course that is what I mean! Do you see it?"

Kester looked back at the little spirit, who had stopped retreating and was now watching Miss Wellbeloved fearfully, clasping its bird-like hands together in a ball of anxiety. Kester squinted hard, scanning the area for signs of the strange ragged opening he had seen behind the banshee, but he couldn't see anything. Only trees, a little raincloud, and a lot of mud.

"No, sorry," he said finally. "Why do you ask?" It was a curious question. *Why does this door thing matter so much to the old man?* he wondered. *It's about the fifth time he's mentioned it, it's obviously of some importance. I hardly like to tell him I think I imagined it all.*

"Hmm, that is strange," Dr Ribero muttered, clearly disappointed. "Very strange indeed. I would have thought you would have been able to see it again."

"Could everyone please stop gossiping and help instead?" Miss Wellbeloved whispered, throwing them a filthy look. "I rather feel as though I'm doing all the work here."

Serena yanked the bag off Mike's shoulder, nearly pulling him over with it.

"Oi, watch out!" Mike barked, rubbing his arm. Serena rolled her eyes and knelt down, pulling various contraptions out of the bag, until she found what she was looking for. She held the water bottle in the air.

"Are you ready for me to start then?" she asked, tiptoeing closer.

"Not quite," the older woman replied. "I'm trying telepathic calming, it seems to be having some effect, but we need him a lot more settled than this before we get him into storage. That's why it really would help if everyone would stop talking. It's difficult enough to communicate with a foreign spirit as it is."

"Just let me stuff him in the bottle!" Serena snapped. "Otherwise we'll be here all day."

"No, we'll treat him with the respect he deserves," Miss Wellbeloved snapped back. "We don't need another frightened spirit, Serena. Remember the last time."

Serena groaned theatrically, stuffing her hands into her tight black jeans.

"*Watashitachi wa tasukemasu,*" Miss Wellbeloved continued, holding her hands out. "Come on, little thing. We're trying to help you."

The spirit sniffed in a manner that was uncommonly like a human, wiping its tiny doll nose on its sleeve. *It's actually quite sweet,* Kester thought, entranced by its delicate features. He smiled. *Perhaps this isn't so bad after all.*

Almost as if to prove him wrong, the spirit suddenly poured out a whirlwind of gibberish, a string of foreign words that caught the air, gusting it into a frenzy. Kester felt moisture on his arms, first a light mist, then a steady drizzle. The creature started to wail, flinging its spidery arms into the air.

"Oh dear," Pamela said, looking upwards. "He's made it rain on us. Jennifer, are you sure you got that Japanese translation right?"

"You probably just insulted his mother without meaning to, or told him he had a face like a bison's backside," Mike added. "You should never rely on the internet. It's a minefield of misinformation."

"What is he doing?" Kester asked with growing alarm. The wind collecting in the clearing was blowing harder, flying round and round like a mini whirlwind, dragging leaves off the nearby bushes and trees and flinging them into their faces. Above their heads, clouds were forming, miniature storms, throwing down rain upon them. The little spirit stood in the middle of it all, now howling at the sky, its mouth distended into a maw of distress and anger.

"Hmm," Miss Wellbeloved tutted, putting her hands on her hips and surveying the situation. "This is unfortunate."

"Time for me to get him in the bottle?" Serena suggested, with more than a trace of sarcasm.

"Yes, I think it is definitely the time for you to get him into the bottle!" Dr Ribero said, his voice hardly audible over the shrieking wind, not to mention the shrill screech of the spirit. "Let's waste no more time here, I am getting very wet and this is an expensive shirt."

Serena nodded, flicking her soaking fringe from her eyes, then unscrewed the lid of the bottle.

"Stop!" Kester suddenly shouted, wiping the wetness from his glasses. They looked at him expectantly. He pointed to the creature. "Look! Can't you see it?"

"Can't we see what?" Dr Ribero asked, peering through the sheets of rain at the spirit, who was now starting to spin around like a miniature dervish.

"That door thing!" Kester said, half-scared, half-excited. "It just appeared again, as he started doing all this scary stuff. It's there, right behind him!"

The opening in the air was much thinner this time. The narrow slit was like a fissure in a cliff, only just big enough for a child to clamber through. Beyond the door was only darkness, though the edges glittered, like moisture shining in the moon-light.

"Can't you guys see it?" he asked again, looking round in bewilderment. However, surveying the rest of them, it was amazing anybody could see anything. The rain was now falling as solidly as a power-shower, causing mist and spray to fly round them like a waterfall.

"You see the door again?" Dr Ribero squawked. "Are you serious?" He clapped his hands together with undisguised glee. "Where is it, where is it?"

"It's right there, behind that spirit," Kester said, pointing again. Then he started to laugh. The whole situation was so ridiculous that he simply couldn't be scared anymore. He'd entered a world of madness, a world where the old rules no longer applied. It was like stepping directly into Oz, walking straight through the rabbit hole and into insanity. *Perhaps I have gone completely crazy,* he thought, and started to laugh harder. *Oh well, if I have, I'm clearly in good company.*

"Get the spirit through the door!" Dr Ribero shouted, giving him a ferocious poke. Kester stumbled, slipping in the mud.

"What do you mean, get it through the door?" he said, wiping the water from his face.

"Push it! Just push it through!"

Kester blinked stupidly. "Push it through?"

"Yes!"

"I'm not going to do that, that's a bit . . . it's a bit rude, isn't it?"

"This is not a social occasion! Forget the manners! Go on, push the spirit through, do it quickly!"

Kester turned back, then saw that the door had gone. Completely disappeared. It was as though it had never been there in the first place.

"It's gone," he announced dumbly. "The door, it's vanished. I don't know where it's gone to."

"Oh, for goodness' sake," Serena snarled. "While you're having fun and games, I'm getting completely drenched!" She stepped forward towards the creature, who was now spinning at an eye-wateringly frightening speed, his umbrella forming a perfect moon-like disc above its head.

"This has all gone a bit tits-up, hasn't it?" Mike commented, wiping the water from his face.

Serena ignored him. Instead, she haughtily raised the bottle into the air, tilting it in the direction of the whirling ghost. Kester watched her with fascination as she frowned, closing her eyes and muttering under her breath.

The spirit, aware of her presence, started to glow, throwing out sparks. Kester backed away, frightened again. He was not only scared for himself, but for Serena, who was now being showered by bright-white embers. However, they bounced harmlessly off her, falling into the mud with a hiss. Indeed, she hardly seemed to notice them. Her lips were now moving at a greater speed, and she started to thrust the bottle at the spirit, pushing it outwards in its direction, then pulling it back again.

"What's she doing?" Kester whispered.

"Shh," Pamela said. "You mustn't disturb her. It's a serious business."

The spirit started to screech. It was a dreadful noise, a raw scream of fear, childlike and terrifying in equal measures. It started to spin more haphazardly, tracing widening circles in the mud like a spinning top running out of momentum. Serena started to chant aloud, eerie words that Kester had never heard before, deep and guttural and filled with resonance. The spirit stumbled, skittering across the clearing. It flung itself into the air, then appeared to be pulled down by invisible ropes.

The rain began to cease. Within a few seconds, it had stopped completely. Kester watched with amazement as the creature, with one final yowl, vanished completely.

Serena swiftly screwed the lid on the bottle and nodded. "Job done," she announced. "Next time, don't all mess around so much, eh?"

"Where did it go?" Kester asked, shaking the water off his hair.

Serena jiggled the bottle in his direction. "Where do you think it went?"

"But I didn't see it go in there."

"That's why what I do is called extinguishing," Serena snapped. "I literally extinguish them out of the air, and put them anywhere I please. Which in this case, is this storage unit." She caught Mike's eye and added, "The water bottle."

"Well, that was all very badly handled," Miss Wellbeloved scolded, wiping down her blouse. "Serena, you must stop treating spirits with such disrespect. It's exceptionally bad for spirit-human relations."

"What else would you have had us do?" Serena spluttered indignantly. "You'd completely lost control of the situation. What other option did we have?"

"Yes, but incidences like this only increase hostile hauntings, which you're very well aware of," Miss Wellbeloved barked back. "It angers them, Serena, and I cannot say I blame them."

"Perhaps I could have tried to reach into its mind," Pamela said, looking troubled.

"No, it wouldn't have worked," Miss Wellbeloved said. "You know as well as I do that if they don't understand your language, it's as good as pointless."

"Look, the spirit is captured, and that is all that matters, is it not?" Dr Ribero said, patting the ladies on the back. "Come on, this is not worth having squabbles over. We have done our job, we will get paid, and now we can have our breakfast, yes?"

"Would it have helped if I'd have been able to push it through that door?" Kester asked suddenly. They all looked at him, as though only just noticing his presence.

"Yes, it would have done," Dr Ribero said, after a pause. "I believe you are seeing a door directly through to the spirit world. If that is the case, then it is a marvellous gift indeed."

"I don't think I have any gifts like that," Kester said, tittering, then straightening his expression when he realised his father was being serious. "I mean," he clarified, "I'm not like all of you. I'm normal. There's nothing special about me."

"But you do not deny that it is twice you have now seen this doorway?" Dr Ribero said, folding his arms across his dripping wet chest.

Kester pondered for a moment. "I think so," he said slowly. "But I'm not sure what it was, to be honest. And as I said, I'm the least likely person to have any sort of supernatural gift. That's just not me."

"You can say that again," Serena drawled. "You're about as in tune with the spirit world as a boulder."

"It would not surprise me at all if you could see the doorway to the spirits," Dr Ribero said, glaring at Serena. He draped an arm around Kester's shoulders, grinning. "After all, that's what your mother could do."

Kester jumped, dislodging Dr Ribero's arm. "What? You're saying my mother could see doors to the spirit world? But that's ridiculous! She would have told me!"

"Just like she told you about me, and about my agency?" Ribero said, with a dry chuckle. "I think, Kester, you must understand that your mother had more secrets than you realise."

"Yes, you can certainly say that again," Miss Wellbeloved muttered. She coughed, straightening herself. "But it is true. Gretchen had a remarkable gift. That's part of the reason we were England's finest supernatural agency in those days. Every other agency was desperate to hire her. It's a very rare thing to be able to do."

"Look, can we start walking back?" Mike interrupted, shivering. "Not being funny, but I feel like someone's chucked a bucket of icy water over me. Oh, wait a minute, that's pretty much what happened."

"Yes, let's get back, I'm freezing," Pamela agreed. Her thin blouse had gone alarmingly see-through in the rain, revealing an enormous bra with straps like an industrial crane. However, she seemed completely unfazed by her exposure, and kept drawing attention to it by flapping her wet top outwards and letting it flop back on to her skin with a squelchy thump.

They started to trudge back along the path they'd come in by. Kester felt strangely elated. Energy coursed through him like electricity. *Is there really something special about me?* he wondered. *Have I really got a gift?* He'd become so accustomed to people finding him dull that he rather liked the idea of having a special power. Even if it was a supernatural one.

Still, he wondered why his mother had never told him about her own gift. Why had she kept so many things from him? Wouldn't they all have been happier if they had lived with Dr Ribero instead? Why hadn't the doctor asked his mother to marry him? And what was Miss Wellbeloved's problem with his mum? There were so many unanswered questions, that it made him feel light-headed. Watching the Argentinian doctor stride ahead, he felt even more confused. *What other secrets is he hiding?* he wondered. *What else does he know, that he's not telling me?*

Pamela nudged him, interrupting his thoughts. "So," she said in a confidential tone. "Are you going to stay a bit longer then? You're not still planning on going back to Cambridge today, are you?"

Kester considered. "I don't really know," he confessed. Part of him still wanted to go back to the peace and quiet of his home. But he couldn't deny the fact that his curiosity had been aroused. It was all too interesting. Unnerving. Occasionally terrifying. But fascinating, nonetheless.

"You know that you're welcome to stay at mine for a few nights, if that helps. The offer is still there."

"That's very kind of you," he replied, reluctant to commit just yet. He wanted to think things over first, and properly weigh up his options.

The walk back seemed a lot shorter than the walk there, mainly because they were walking downhill, not up. As they emerged onto the sunny lawn, it seemed as though they'd passed through a time warp into the present day. The difference between the quiet forest and the perfectly mowed grass was extreme.

"Oh look, old flab-gut has spotted us already," Serena grumbled as they paced towards the driveway. Sure enough, the familiar spherical form of Lord Flanburgh could be seen, marching down the stone stairs to greet them. Thankfully, he was fully clothed this time.

"How did you get on?" he bellowed, startling yet more birds from the gutters above him. "All sorted, is it?"

"Ah yes, it most certainly is," Dr Ribero announced, stepping forward with a flourish. "No more spirit. We have him captured."

"Well, that's ruddy good news. Glad to hear it," Flanburgh replied. He paused, staring incredulously at them all. Although the worst of the water had dripped off, they were still soaked, not to mention steaming slightly in the mid-morning heat.

"Dear god, what happened to you all?" he asked, stuffing his hands into his mustard-coloured jacket. "Did you fall in the stream or something?"

"Ah, no. It is a long story," Dr Ribero answered, rubbing his shirt down.

Lord Flanburgh chortled. "Ah, the little sod gave you a soaking, did he? That's a bit unfortunate. Ah well, at least it's warm. You'll dry out in no time." He leant over, smacking the doctor on the back. "The main thing is, you've solved my problem. I'll see to it that Millicent pays the money over straight away."

"Wonderful, thank you," Dr Ribero said.

"I must say," Lord Flanburgh continued, as he led them to the van, "I had my doubts about your team. The government weren't exactly singing your praises, if you know what I mean. Infinite Enterprises tend to be the chaps that are called out these days, aren't they? But you've done a good job, well done you."

Dr Ribero grimaced at the mention of Infinite Enterprises, not to mention the distinctly patronising tone of the other man. Mike chuckled, helping the doctor into the van by giving him a hearty shove on the backside.

"Plus you're a good sight cheaper!" Flanburgh continued, calling over Mike's broad shoulder. "I shall make sure to mention it when I'm next in the Houses of Parliament."

"Very kind of you," Dr Ribero said wearily from the back seat. "Just let us know if you need our help again, okay?"

"Yes, of course, of course. Quite so. Why hire a team of

London professionals when you've got a perfectly good little local company who can just about handle the job instead, eh?"

Dr Ribero growled in response, which was thankfully muffled by the slamming of the van door.

"What a prat," Mike said, spinning the van round in a haphazard arc around Flanburgh. No one contradicted him.

"Oh, by the way everyone," Pamela announced, as they bounced along the driveway. "Good news."

"What is that?" Ribero asked, folding his arms and looking very much as though he was about to take a nap.

"Kester said he was going to stay at mine for a few days," she said. "So Julio, you've got your son around for a little bit longer."

"Er, well, I didn't definitely say I was going to stay," Kester began, but his protests were drowned out by Ribero's exclamations. It seemed that the announcement had suddenly galvanised him into action, propelling him forward to give Kester a hearty slap on the back.

"That is wonderful news!" he said, with a toothy smile that seemed to extend across his entire face. In spite of himself, Kester grinned in response. It had been a strange twenty-four hours. Undoubtedly the strangest he'd ever experienced. But for the first time in a long while, he felt excited.

"Well then, I suppose he could come along for the Green Lady job, couldn't he?" Serena stated. There was a distinct air of challenge in her voice.

"Oh goodness, I'm not sure about that," Miss Wellbeloved said quickly. "He's vastly inexperienced, regardless of whatever special gifts he might possess."

"Well, his 'special gifts' might be rather useful with this job, don't you think?" Serena answered, sneering in his direction. Kester couldn't ignore the drip of sarcasm lacing the comment. *Why is she so hostile all the time?* he wondered. *It's like she gets a kick out of being mean to me.*

"I think that would be a wonderful idea," Dr Ribero said,

still beaming. "Kester, would you like to join us on this job tomorrow?"

"Well, I don't know anything about it," he replied, feeling a little overwhelmed. He grabbed hold of the door handle as Mike hurtled the van round a particularly tight bend.

"Why don't you give him the diary to read?" Pamela suggested. "After all, you always say it's good to brush up on the case before starting, don't you?"

"That is a good idea," Dr Ribero said. "We will give it to you to read this afternoon, and then you will be prepared for tomorrow, yes?"

"Erm, if you say so," Kester stuttered. Once again, he felt as though events were racing ahead of him, leaving him no time to think about things. It was unnervingly like sitting on the world's fastest rollercoaster, without knowing whether or not it had been safety tested first.

"I'm still not sure this is a wise idea," Miss Wellbeloved scolded. "I rather think you're becoming too obsessed with his ability to see the spirit door, and less interested in his welfare, Julio."

Dr Ribero swatted her comment away with an elegant flick of the wrist. "Ah, he will be fine. He is not some little boy, Jennifer. He is a man, look at him!"

Miss Wellbeloved glanced over at Kester and sighed.

"Don't say I didn't warn you," she muttered.

Kester wasn't quite sure who she was warning—Dr Ribero or himself. Neither prospect made him feel entirely comfortable.

"I will give you the diary when we return to the office," Dr Ribero said earnestly, before curling up cat-like in the back and shutting his eyes.

CHAPTER 6: THE HAUNTING OF COLETON CRESCENT — EMMELINE'S DIARY

4th December, 1891

I do not like our new house on Coleton Crescent. I do not like it at all. I hardly like to admit it to Algie, who is so taken with it. I feel that my lack of enthusiasm will somehow dampen his, and I do not want to put an end to his pleasure. After all, as he keeps reminding me, it is a sign that we have "reached high," that we can afford a property on the crescent, overlooking the river, in the most prominent place in the city.

Even when we viewed it for the first time, I felt uncomfortable here. There is an unnatural stillness to the property, a watchfulness, perhaps; I detected it even then. I attempted to address the issue with Algie, but he waved aside my protestations, insisting they were simply "womanish hysteria." He told me he could sense nothing of the sort, and that the house had a most welcoming demeanour. I cannot imagine how he could feel such a thing. The house is nothing if not sombre and forbidding, at best.

Now that we have moved in, the uncomfortable sensation has become more pronounced. It has only been two days, and already I feel I am an unwanted guest here, that the house itself wishes to expel me from the premises, to forcibly throw me out of the door, never to return.

Margery has been a staunch support, as always. She tells me that it is normal for a new house to feel strange, and that I shouldn't "feel amiss." I am so glad we kept her. Algie wanted a new maid, but Margery has been with the family for such a long time, I should be desperately sad to see her go. She is right, I suppose. All houses must feel a little odd to begin with. After all, one becomes accustomed to familiar surroundings, and when placed somewhere new, it's only natural to become a little unsettled.

Perhaps Algie is right, perhaps we should throw a party to celebrate our arrival. Some entertainment may lighten the mood and bring some life into this old house. Certainly it needs it. No matter how many windows I throw open, it always seems so dark.

16th December, 1891

I met with Mary today for afternoon tea at Molls. It was so very pleasant to see her, and so kind of her to travel this distance to see me. She told me all the news of Totnes, and I will confess, it made me miss it dearly. Ah, Totnes with its simpler, smaller-scale pleasures! I am still not convinced that city life agrees with me, though I understand of course that

Algie needs to be here for his work.

Mary told me that Constance is to be married this coming spring. I was most pleased for her, although it pained me that I could only hear the news second-hand. After all, were we not all thick as thieves when we were younger? It made me feel so distanced from it all, as though I no longer existed in that world.

Her husband-to-be is a well-to-do farmer. It means she will stay near Totnes, close to her family. I confess, I do envy her a little. Although my family are not a long distance away, it is too far for my liking. I wish Mama lived closer. I do not like the thought of her living alone, even if Millicent regularly visits to check on her.

After our tea, I took Mary back to the house. She was eager to see it, especially after what I had told her. She admitted that it seemed "too quiet" as we sat in the parlour, and that it had a still quality to it, as though it was waiting for something to happen. I believe that was an apt way of describing it. Trust Mary to capture the mood so perfectly; she has always been so gifted with words.

However, she said that our furniture looked "capital" and that we had selected it well. Algie had allowed me to choose from the latest fabrics, and I had selected a William Morris wallpaper for the living room. It looks beautiful, like a garden brought indoors. Our dining table is especially magnificent and is made of polished cherry wood. Mary declared it the handsomest thing she had ever seen, and I am inclined to agree with her. The candelabra looks almost lost in the midst of it, like a tree stranded in a polished field!

It made me most happy to see Mary again and show her around our new home, though after she had left, I will admit, I felt all the lonelier without her. Margery was at market and the new cook is a dour old thing, I do not feel I can simply enter the kitchen for a conversation. She has the typically broad accent of someone from the north, and indeed, I struggle to understand her meaning behind all those spherical vowels and rumbling consonants.

The sun is setting now. Algie will be home soon. Or at least, I do hope that he will be home soon. It is most dismal to be alone in this house, with only the views of the River Exe to keep me company. The ticking of the mantelpiece clock is almost insufferable when I am alone, and the house most dreadfully cold in spite of the fire.

26th December, 1891

How I wish I had never ventured into the attic. He has brought it down. Algie, I mean. He has brought that horrible painting down, into the living room, and now I shall never be away from it. It is monstrous. He cannot see it, but I can. My Christmas has been ruined.

3rd January, 1892

Goodness, my last entry was short, and rather muddled. I do confess, Margery had provided me with some laudanum for my nerves, which have become worse of late. I feel I should explain my sentiments regarding the painting, or otherwise, dear reader, you shall remain quite perplexed forever.

A few days before Christmas, I was alone in the house. I often am, you see. It is not as it was in Totnes. Here, I am not surrounded by friendly faces, family, and acquain-

tances. Here, I am isolated, horribly so. Left alone in this dreadful house, which I am sad to say, I loathe more than ever.

I was alone, and sewing in the parlour, when I detected a noise above my head. I could not tell you what the noise was. Only that it was low, thrumming, and full of menace. It was as though a cacophony of whispers were filling my head: a terrible chorus of murmured threats and incantations. I know this must sound strange. Indeed, as I write it down I realise that anyone reading this may wonder if I am not a little mad. However, all I can say is that I do not feel mad. I feel quite sane. Sometimes I wonder if madness would be easier.

I sat in fright in the parlour, my sewing forgotten. The noise did not cease. It increased in volume until it seemed to shake the very walls of the house itself. Then, came the knocking. A loud, authoritative knock pounding through the floorboards. I discerned then that the noise was coming from the attic. I called out, but no one answered. Then I remembered it was Mrs Trevalley's afternoon off, and Margery was purchasing cloth from the fabric shop. Fraser may have been pottering around in the garden, but if so, he was too far away to hear my cries.

The knock came again, and I knew I must answer it. I felt compelled to do so, as though drawn to the sound on a piece of string. Every fibre of my body was pulling me towards the source of the noise, though I desperately did not want to investigate. Against my will, I reluctantly climbed the stairs, then the narrow stairs leading to the attic door.

As I turned the handle, the noise stopped as abruptly as it had started. Silence surrounded me. And I felt the unbearable sensation of being watched. Eyes were burning into me;

I could swear it. Fierce, malevolent eyes full of hatred and rage, all of it directed at my person.

I stepped into the attic, all the time suspecting that something dreadful would leap out upon me, seize me, and torment me. However, the attic was empty. Only packing cases, some pieces of furniture left by the previous owner, and in the corner, what looked to be a large painting, covered by a dusty cloth.

I do not know what compelled me to do it. And how I wish that I never had! Some dread spirit possessed me that day, something I had no control of. I marched towards the painting and tugged the cloth off in a cloud of thick dust.

And there it was. There she was. A portrait of a lady, dressed entirely in green. She would have been beautiful, I believe. Were it not for those eyes.

Oh, those eyes. I have not slept properly since I first saw them. Full of such venom, such malignant power. All of it fixed resolutely upon my trembling person. I believe I may have fainted. Certainly I found myself somehow on the floor, cowering, covering my own eyes to avoid meeting her gaze.

I pray, dear reader, you never see such a thing. They are eyes sent straight from the bowels of hell itself.

"That's bloody horrible!" Kester exclaimed, quite forgetting himself. Beside him, Pamela looked up from her own book, peering over her reading glasses.

"Quite a read, isn't it!" she said cheerfully, pointing at the diary.

Kester closed the book with a resolute thud and leant back in the deckchair. Although Pamela's courtyard garden was small, it was a pleasant place to rest, especially on a sunny afternoon. The sunlight filtered through the branches of the apple tree, and bees were making themselves busy among the wildflowers. It felt quite at odds with the horrible book he was reading. *What a dreadful tale,* he thought anxiously. *And all presumably true, given that it's a diary. Unless of course, she was mad. Poor Emmeline, whoever she may have been.*

"What happens next?" he asked, basking in the sunlight. Hemingway, Pamela's shaggy sheepdog, snuffled over to sit beside them, and Kester gave him an absentminded pat, trying not to mind as the dog deposited several hairs all over his trousers.

"What, you mean in Emmeline's diary?" Pamela asked.

"Yes."

"Well, all sorts of terrible things happen with the painting, as you've probably already guessed."

"What happened in the end? Did she manage to destroy it?"

Pamela nodded. "Yes, but that's the problem."

"What do you mean?"

"Well, Emmeline destroyed it, but some idiot decided to send it to be restored, a few months ago. As you can imagine, it's caused a bit of a stir."

Kester pondered for a moment. "I see. It's a bit odd, isn't it? A possessed painting?"

Pamela put down her book and reached for her iced tea. "No, not at all actually," she said. "It's relatively common for spirits to attach themselves to inanimate objects." She sipped noisily. "Makes it that much harder to get rid of them though, especially if they've woven themselves into the fabric of the item."

"But I've never heard of a ghost possessing an object before. A person, yes, but not an object."

Pamela chuckled. "I think you'd be surprised. Djinn are very fond of living in inanimate objects."

"What? Sorry, I didn't catch that."

"Djinn. Genies. You've heard of Aladdin's lamp, I presume? That type of thing. We don't get many djinn in Europe though. They can't stand the cold."

Kester sighed. He wasn't sure he'd ever adjust to this talk of ghosts; the supernatural being discussed as frankly as though chatting about the weather. In spite of having seen two spirits in as many days, he still found the whole concept challenging to swallow. Beside him, Hemingway started to lick at his iced tea, which rather put him off drinking it again.

"What about poltergeists?" he said suddenly. "Do they like to live in objects?"

Pamela shook her head. "No, they just like to smash them around a lot. They're incredibly annoying, to be honest. We've had some poltergeist cases that have been real hard work. We had one that was in a stationery cupboard recently."

"I beg your pardon?"

"In an office, in Bristol. It wasn't particularly harmful, it just liked throwing the pencils around. It was a nuisance to get rid of though, particularly as I kept getting paperclips thrown at my hair. I was picking them out for hours afterwards."

Kester considered the notion of a haunted painting. It wasn't a concept he liked the thought of at all, and the diary's description of a malevolent portrait, complete with demonic eyes, made him feel distinctly uncomfortable.

"Where's the painting now?" he asked, swatting at a hoverfly, which was threatening to land on his nose. "Is it in the same house?"

"Remarkably, yes it is," Pamela replied, finishing off her drink. "The woman must have destroyed it then stuffed it in the attic again, only to be discovered a hundred or so years later. Although you'd be amazed how often that happens."

"It's rather creepy," Kester said. "I'm not sure I like the idea of a ghostly painting. Especially one with evil eyes."

Pamela giggled. "I'm sure this painting's most malicious glare is nothing compared to our Serena. Maybe they should have a staring match. My money's on Serena, every time."

"Should I carry on reading?" he said, looking at the diary reluctantly. It was such a beautiful day, that he didn't relish the thought of burrowing his head in a book, when he could fall asleep in the sun instead.

Pamela nodded. "Yep, Julio said you should try to get through as much as possible. Tell you what, I'll leave you in peace while I go and make dinner."

Kester smiled as she stood. It was incredibly kind of the older woman to let him stay at her house, even though it was rather filled with dog hairs, as Serena had correctly claimed. Hemingway followed his owner with a cheerful bark, wagging his tail so hard that a few neighbouring flowers lost their petals.

"Well, here goes," he muttered, picking up the diary again. The very next entry he read made him wish that he hadn't.

20th April, 1892

I have lost the baby. I know it for a fact. I saw what issued from me; there can be no doubt. Such pain I've never experienced before. Margery kept me as comfortable as possible until the doctor was able to come, but by then it was too late. I feel empty, hollow, as though the last essence of life within me has been extinguished. It is agony. Algie has taken it badly too. He paled when he saw the bloodied bedsheets, and couldn't move from the spot, not even when Margery told him it "wasn't a man's business."

I tried to tell him that it was the fault of the painting. But Algie would not listen. I have begged him several times to listen to me, but now, I am convinced that the portrait holds some power over him, a dreadful spell that he finds impossible to resist. Indeed, many times now I have seen him, standing motionless in front of it in the living room, staring open-mouthed at the lady in green, as though admiring a lover from afar. He is transfixed, and once, I even heard him murmur the word "beautiful" as he gazed at her.

Oh, but she is monstrous! I cannot understand why Algie loves her so! I have become too terrified to enter that room now. The simple act of walking past the door is a trial. Even if the door is closed, I can still feel those eyes, burning into me, hurting me from the inside. It is a wicked, dreadful thing. Whomever the lady may once have been, she was a terrible person, of this I am certain.

Even Margery agrees with me. She told me that the Green Lady has started to haunt her dreams; she now sleeps with the candle burning. She said that she had nightmares of the lady reaching out of the very canvas itself, grasping out with skeletal hands, trying to pull her in. She says she can no longer look at mirrors, for she sees the Green Lady staring back at her, instead of her own reflection.

I know exactly what she means, I have had similar visions myself. The Green Lady wishes to remove us from our world and trap us in hers. She is evil.

Why cannot Algie see it?

10th May, 1892

The doctor came today. I was subjected to the most intrusive of examinations. He refused to speak to me throughout, even though I questioned him greatly. I confess, I took an instant dislike to him, with his thick spectacles and prying hands. He looked rather as though he enjoyed his task a little too much, if I may say so.

Afterwards, I overheard him discussing me with Algie in the study. I heard the word "hysteria," on more than one occasion. I know exactly what they think of me. Algie even called me mad to my face last night. He told me that I "must desist with this nonsense" then informed me darkly that "there would be consequences" if I remained unable to control myself.

I know that I must try harder to be the wife he expects me to be. But it is so very difficult when that painting has taken over everything. Algie is very much changed since that terrible day it was brought down from the attic. I remember with great sadness the small acts of kindness he used to deliver to me—the gentle words, the little gifts. Ever since the painting was brought down, he has been a different person. Colder. Harder. And so horribly unkind. He even struck me once. It was not hard, but nonetheless, I wept. I wept more for what we had become, rather than from pain of the blow. I believed that we had a most happy marriage. Now I fear that this is no longer the case.

1ˢᵗ June, 1892

My own bad dreams have started. I see the Lady. Always I see the Lady. And always it is the same. I am transfixed, held to the painting by unseen hands, unable to move, nor even to turn my head away by the merest fraction. And she moves, fixing her eyes upon me. Those eyes! Even the thought of them turns my skin to ice. They pierce, they wound, they rip my very heart in two! They are the evillest things that I have ever seen.

In the dream, she is not content to merely glare. She reaches out of the canvas, as though stepping through a doorway. She leans towards me, full of malicious intent. And she seizes me. Those cold, skeleton fingers pierce through my skin, and my blood drips upon the floorboards.

It is then that I usually wake up, drenched in sweat, often screaming. I dare not sleep, but I am so weary. Why will Algie not destroy that painting? Why will he not listen to his wife and take a knife to it, tearing it into pieces? Does he not love me anymore? I begin to suspect that he loves her instead, the Green Lady. He has fallen under her evil spell; he is not the Algie I married.

Margery said we should return to Totnes. The thought is very tempting. Return home, escape this horrible, silent house, with its torture and its cruelty. It is a house under a curse; I believe that most strongly. It is haunted. I have smashed the mirror in my room. At least that will stop her watching me while I am asleep.

4ᵗʰ June, 1892

He has locked me in my bedroom! I can scarce believe that he would subject me to such indignity! He told me that "it was for my own good" and that I would have to remain here until the doctor could come.

The reason for my incarceration is that Margery and I tried to make our escape. Early this morning, long before the sun had risen, we gathered some belongings with the intention of hiring a hansom cab to take us to Totnes. I will admit that I stole some money from my husband, a fact which, upon discovery, he was most enraged by. However, it was in desperate circumstances! Never would I normally commit such a crime! I begged my innocence, but he refused to listen. He grasped me by the arm, so firmly that I cried out, and dragged me upstairs, throwing me down upon the bed.

Never had I seen him so angry. His face was lit as though by fire, and he pointed at me with a most devilish, venomous rage. He told me that I had "brought shame" on his house, and that I was "quite insane" and "an intolerable burden." I believe I may have laughed at this point. In truth, I did feel most unhinged and quite unable to control myself. I told him that he had fallen in love with a painting, and he sneered at me most cruelly. He said that "at least the lady in the painting had probably been perfectly sane in real life," and that she had "probably been able to produce children too."

Oh, how that last comment wounded me, like a dagger to my heart. It is not my fault that the baby was lost. Can he not see my pain over it? I think of my child every day, what might have been, had it lived. He does not, cannot, understand how dreadful that day was. And it was the Green Lady's fault, of that I swear. She has not ceased in her haunting of me, not since that terrible day I first discovered her in the attic. She wants to kill me. I can feel it. She will not rest until I am no longer alive.

8ᵗʰ June, 1892

I am frightened. So terribly, terribly frightened. I fear I may not be able to write for much longer. Last night, while I was in bed, Algie came to me. But his eyes were hers. The Green Lady's, I mean. They glowed with the ferocity of a devil unleashed upon the world. I thought at first that he planned to embrace me. He leaned closer, a silhouette over my bed, and I thought he would try to kiss me, all the time impaling me with that horrible hot glare.

Instead, he tried to throttle me. Good Lord, it pains me to write it down! He placed his hands around my neck and began to squeeze, and all the while, his eyes glowed in the darkness.

She was in him. The Lady in Green was inside him, possessing him, making him perform this unspeakable act against me. I could see her within him, triumphant, delighting in my misery and distress. I kicked out at him, and he fell to the ground, groaning. Then I screamed. I screamed as loudly as I could. Margery came running. I told her what he had done. Algie said I was mad and that I had fabricated it all, but I could see that she believed me. She nodded, ever so slightly, to let me know she did not doubt my tale. Only Margery knows how dark things have become in this house.

How long can I bear this? He threatens me with the lunatic asylum. It would be preferable to the madness I endure each day that I am here. I cannot remain locked in this room much longer. I must break free. I must escape from her.

CHAPTER 7: MEETING THE GREEN LADY

"Nice house," Mike said, taking in the pillars, the sash windows, and the neoclassical brickwork. "Bit of class, that is." Across the road from the house, the River Exe shimmered in the morning sunlight, the people on the iron footbridge just about visible from their elevated viewpoint.

"Dream on," Serena said, surveying her red nails. "Out of your league."

"Certainly on what he's paying me," Mike grumbled, scooping up the kit bag. "If I'd have gone to Infinite Enterprises, who knows what I'd bloody be on now."

"Nothing stopping you."

Mike snorted, glowering from underneath his Legoland cap.

"So, is this really the same house that was written about in Emmeline's diary?" Kester asked. By the look of the sombre granite stones, the imposing black door, and the broken pediments flanking each window like frowning eyes, he could well believe it. It was an expensive-looking property, but it definitely had a touch of hostility about it.

"Yes, the exact same house, right?" Dr Ribero said, striding up to the door. He seized the brass knocker and issued a succession of deafening raps. "I have been told that the painting is in the lounge, so we will go straight there and assess the situation."

"I'm a bit nervous," Kester admitted, looking around at the rest of the group.

"Oh, a haunted painting isn't going to do you any harm," Serena tutted. She tapped the pavement impatiently with one pointy, high-heeled toe, eyeing the house with irritation. "You've read Emmeline's diary. What's the worst that can happen? Some old bag in a green dress is going to look at you a bit funny?"

"Well, it sounded a lot worse than that," Kester said defensively. "I didn't like what she wrote at all. It sounded very unpleasant." He glanced at the dark window, half-expecting to see a furious spirit leering out at them at that very moment.

"Remember that people often get very scared by the supernatural," Miss Wellbeloved explained. "For normal folk, it's common to overreact to these sorts of things."

"Or pass out, like you did the other day with the banshee," Serena added. "That was about as big an overreaction as I've ever seen, actually. Apart from soiling yourself. Which you might well have done, for all I know."

"I didn't soil myself," Kester clarified.

"That's what you say."

"They're taking a long time to answer the door, aren't they?" Pamela said, peering into the nearest window. "Do you think they've forgotten we're coming today?"

"I very much hope not," Dr Ribero said, twirling his moustache between his fingers. "They were insistent that we must address the situation as fast as possible, yes? I have cleared time in our diary especially. I will not be happy if they have messed us around, I will not."

"Ah, come on boss," Mike said, leaning against the railing.

"It's not like we're swamped with work at the moment."

As though responding to his comment, the front door swung inward with a shrill creak. A pale face peered out, round and flaccid as an orangutan.

"Are you the ghost crew?" she croaked. Each line in her aged face was so caked in powder that it looked as though a forensics team had dusted her down for fingerprints.

"Er, well, we are the supernatural agency," Dr Ribero said, looking at the others.

"Yeah, ghosts and all that, right?" the old woman said. "Things that go bump in the night?"

"Indeed," Dr Ribero confirmed, pursing his lips together. "May we come in?"

"Hang on, let me get my daughter," the woman mumbled. Without warning, she swung round with the momentum of a wrecking ball and bellowed at the top of her voice. "Isabelle? Izzie? Them people are here! The ones who want to look at your painting!" She turned back round to them, grinning. "Why don't you come inside, and I'll make you all a nice cup of tea."

"So, you are Mrs Diderot's mother?" Dr Ribero asked politely, stepping into the hallway.

"Yep. Izzie's not been having too good a time of it recently, as you know. So I've come down to keep her company. Didn't have much else on, it weren't a problem really."

Kester hovered by the coat stand, unsure where to put himself. A mottled mirror hanging by the door revealed how at odds he looked with the rest of the group, his paunch hanging over his belt like a toad's burlap. *I really must do something about that,* he thought, noticing Dr Ribero's wiry torso and Mike's solidly built stomach, and comparing himself unfavourably to both.

A sound diverted his attention. He looked up to see a woman standing at the top of the stairs. By the look of her, he guessed that she was around forty, though her haggard expression aged her considerably. Her mouse-brown hair was scraped into a hasty bun, pulled back from her face, which, with its high cheekbones and delicate jaw, would have been attractive in different circumstances. She floated down the stairs like a wraith, clutching the bannister for support.

"I am so relieved you're here," she said, without preamble. Up close, the hollows of her eyes indicated that she hadn't slept in days, weeks perhaps.

"Ah, Mrs Diderot," Dr Ribero said, offering his hand. "It is a pleasure to finally meet you."

"Isabelle, please," she said, extending her own thin hand to meet his. "And this is my mother, Jane." She had a hint of her mother's east-London drawl to her voice, but clearly marriage or education had refined it, polishing it to a more neutral accent.

"Is your husband here?" Dr Ribero asked.

"No, François is away," she answered. "I think that's what's made it all so difficult to cope with. He's away so often, and I'm left here alone, you see."

"Don't you have any children?" Pamela asked, looking around for signs of younger inhabitants.

Isabelle shook her head. "No," she stated, without further explanation. "No, I don't."

"Well, we've read through the diary carefully," Miss Wellbeloved said, taking charge of the situation. "Thank you for sending it to us in the post, it's been most informative. A fascinating case."

"I'm not sure fascinating is the word I would use," Isabelle said, looking down at the floor. "It's been horrendous. When I read that diary, I realised that I was experiencing exactly what that poor woman had gone through. Ever since we found that painting, it's been a nightmare."

"Ah, try not to worry too much about it," Mike said, with a grin. "It sounds like a pretty basic haunting to me. Only thing is, this one's managed to get itself well and truly welded into an object, which can make them a little tricky to package off to the spirit world. However," he added, shaking his shoulder bag in her direction, "I've been working on a piece of equipment that I believe might do the trick. It's not been road-tested thoroughly yet, but—"

"Yes, thank you Mike," Dr Ribero interrupted. He leant towards Isabelle, giving her the full extent of his Argentinian charm. "Don't worry, we will get this sorted for you. You have my many words."

"Just one word. *You have my word*," Miss Wellbeloved corrected quietly. Ribero's jaw tightened.

"That's good to know," Isabelle murmured. She looked over at her mother. "Are you going to make the tea, mum?"

"Yes, yes, I'll go and do that now," her mother said reluctantly. She was obviously fascinated by them all, and wanted to make sure she didn't miss a thing.

Pamela suddenly looked upwards, as though she had just detected a bad smell emanating from the ceiling. She opened her mouth, about to say something, then shut it again, shaking her head.

"Picking up anything?" Dr Ribero asked.

Pamela nodded. "Oh yes," she said. "Yes. It's a particularly bad energy actually. Most unpleasant. I think we've got a rotter on our hands here."

"Oh no, really?" Mike groaned, dropping the bag unceremoniously to the floor. Whatever was inside made a dull metallic clang as it hit the Victorian tiles, echoing through the long hallway. "I'm really not in the mood for a tricky one today. I had a bit of a late one last night."

"Well, we suspected this wouldn't be an easy case," Miss Wellbeloved said. She turned to Mrs Diderot, whose eyes were widening with every word. "It might be best if you went elsewhere while we take a look at it. Where do you find the most comfortable place to be in the house? Your bedroom? The kitchen?"

"The kitchen isn't so bad," Isabelle replied, scanning the ceiling to see what Pamela had been looking at. She rolled her hands into a fretful ball. "I'll go and help mother with the tea. Would anyone like some biscuits?"

"Yes please, I wouldn't say no," Mike said enthusiastically. "Have you got any chocolate ones?"

"Mike, do you ever stop thinking about your stomach?" Serena asked.

"Never. It's my very favourite organ," Mike replied.

"Could have fooled me," Serena muttered.

"I've got some digestives?" Isabella offered, moving backwards down the hallway.

"Chocolate covered ones?"

"No, just the normal ones I'm afraid. I could make you a hot chocolate to dip them into if you like?"

Mike beamed. "That'd be smashing. Ta very much."

"Right, now we have addressed the important issue of Mike's stomach, shall we continue work?" Ribero barked. Isabelle gave a weak smile and scuttled off to the kitchen, her satin slippers hissing on the polished floor.

"I have to say, the energy in this house is horrendous," Pamela said in a low voice, checking that Mrs Diderot was no longer in earshot. "It's really dense, heavy stuff. Far worse than I expected."

"Well, we knew we were dealing with a hostile spirit, just from talking to Mrs Diderot on the phone. Not to mention the contents of the diary," Mrs Wellbeloved replied, craning her neck to peer inside the lounge. "Let's go and see what we're up against, shall we?"

They trooped into the lounge, then stopped, silent.

The room was impressive in a classically Georgian way. It had high ceilings, a magnificent marble fireplace, and huge leather sofas. However, it wasn't the room that had rendered them speechless. It was the painting that hung directly above the fireplace, taking up a good deal of the available wall space.

"Wow," Pamela breathed quietly.

"It's a lot bigger than I expected," Serena whispered, momentarily stunned out of sarcasm.

Kester stared at the painting. He'd been anticipating something more awful than could be imagined, complete with rabid red eyes and terrifying expression. Instead, all he saw was an elegant oil painting of a young woman, dressed in a rich emerald-green dress. A smart little hat rested upon her bright red hair, and she gazed out of the canvas with a face that was neither frightening nor hostile. It wasn't what he had been expecting at all, and it took him by surprise.

"Is that it?" he said, staring at the others. "That's not scary at all!"

Pamela grimaced. "Can't you feel it?" she asked.

"I certainly can," Serena said, frowning. "She's got a face on her, that one, hasn't she?"

"Whatever do you mean?" Kester exclaimed. "I think she's got a very nice face."

Miss Wellbeloved pitched a perfectly raised eyebrow in his direction. "That's interesting," she said. "Julio, Mike, what do you think?"

"I think that she is very pretty," Dr Ribero drawled, studying the painting with a little bit too much enthusiasm.

"I'll say. I think she's a bit of a scorcher myself, very nice looking," Mike added.

"As I thought," Miss Wellbeloved concluded, placing her hands on her narrow hips. "We've got ourselves a woman-hater."

"A woman-hater?" Kester echoed. "Why do you say that? She doesn't look as though she's doing anything particularly hateful to me."

"Pamela, myself, and Serena can all clearly see her hostility," Miss Wellbeloved explained. "Yet you men can only see her beauty. For some reason, this Green Lady doesn't like women. That's most interesting. However, it will only make our job harder."

"Yes, if she's got issues with half our team, it's going to throw a real spanner in the works," Pamela said, studying the painting with dislike. "She'll try extra hard to work against us."

"But I don't understand how you can think she's hostile!" Kester exclaimed. He examined the portrait more closely, taking in the fine brushwork and the rich details. Whoever had painted her was clearly a skilled artist. Her dress seemed to glow with an inner light, making her seem like an angel, and her delicate face was quite the most beautiful thing he'd ever seen. *I wish I owned this painting,* he thought, following the undulating brushstrokes and splashes of colour. *I wonder if they'd consider giving it to me? After all, the owners of the house obviously don't want it.* He could imagine it now, sitting in his lounge above the dining table. It would look perfect there. And then, he could look at it while he was eating.

"Hey," Serena snapped, clicking her fingers in front of Kester's eyes. She did the same to Mike. "Wakey wakey you two. You both look like you've gone into a trance."

"I'm not sure having Kester or Mike here is such a good idea," Pamela said, biting her lip.

"Why do you think that?" Dr Ribero asked, eyes still fixed upon the painting.

Pamela rolled her eyes. "Because you're all becoming infatuated with her after only being in the room five minutes! Look at you! Your tongue is practically hanging out to the floor."

"Ah," Dr Ribero grunted, pulling himself up to his full height. "You think because I am looking long and hard at this painting that I am falling under her spell, yes?"

Pamela, Miss Wellbeloved, and Serena nodded in unison.

"No," he continued, thrusting a finger into the air. "Remember, I see the things that the spirits do not want me to see. And I can see this spirit, hiding in the brushstrokes. I think she is old. Very old. An old, malicious thing, concealed behind a very pretty painting."

"What do you mean, you see things that the spirits don't want you to see?" Kester asked. He was still staring upwards, reluctant to take his eyes off the Green Lady. It was as though the rest of the room had dimmed, leaving just himself and her, all alone. Plus, he could have sworn her mouth had turned up a little at the corners, as though pleased to see him. *I never want to leave this room,* he thought euphorically. *If that is a spirit, it's the kindest, sweetest spirit I've ever seen. Now that's the sort of ghost I like.*

"Kester? Kester, I will tell you, if you look at me," Dr Ribero said. His voice was little more than a distant buzz in his ear, as minor a distraction as a passing bluebottle. He moved away, straining to see the painting over Ribero's shoulder. Suddenly, he felt hands grasp his shoulders and shake him. Ribero spun him round with the ease of a ballet dancer, so he was facing the opposite direction.

"Hey!" Kester shouted, startled. "What did you do that for?" His head felt fuzzy, like someone had jammed a bag of cotton wool into his ears.

"At least you are looking at me now and not her," Ribero said. He grabbed Kester's chin, preventing him from turning back again.

"Take your hands off me!" Kester said, squirming, trying to see the painting again. "I wasn't doing anything wrong!"

"No, but she was," Serena glowered, nodding over to the Green Lady. "Get him out of the room. I should have known he'd be a liability. Mind you, Mike isn't much better. Look at him. He's like a randy dog who's fallen for a chair leg."

"I'm alright, thank you very much," Mike retorted. Reluctantly, he tore his eyes away from the painting. "Though I will admit, she's got a lot of power, that one."

"What do you think we should do?" Pamela said, looking concerned. "If she isn't going to respond to me or Jennifer or Serena, we've got a bit of a problem."

"Hey, I can still stuff her into a bottle, regardless of whether she likes me or not," Serena said. "However, it's getting her out of the painting in the first place that's going to be difficult."

"Could we remove the painting from this room and put it into storage?" Pamela suggested.

"Our broom cupboard isn't really the most effective place to bang up a problem ghost," Mike said. "Now, if we were Infinite Enterprises, we'd have a state-of-the-art, ultra-secure storage facility. I suppose we could ask them if we could take it there?"

"No." Ribero rolled up his shirt sleeves. "We will not be doing that. It only makes us look as though we cannot cope with our own problems. Plus, no amount of storage will get that spirit out of the painting, no? We cannot just leave her in there."

"You sure?" Mike said. "I could take her up to London with me on the next spirit run, leave her round the back or something, then run off."

"No, we will not be doing that," Dr Ribero barked. "That is a silly idea, Mike."

"Plus, Infinite Enterprises have got security cameras and they'll see you doing it," Pamela added.

"Then they'll think you're an even bigger moron than they did before," Serena added.

"Yes, but we were not considering it anyway, okay?" Dr Ribero snapped. "Now, can we please focus on the task at hand? Let us go out of the room. This painting is making my head hurt, and Kester is getting very peculiar over it."

"I am not," Kester protested, aware that his voice had risen to a mulish whine. Wrenching away from Ribero's grip, he stole one last longing look at the painting, before being hauled away like a naughty toddler in a sweetshop.

"I was just about to let you know that tea's ready," Isabelle's mum said, as she saw them emerge into the hallway. "Do you want me to bring it in there?"

"No, we'll come and join you in the kitchen." Ribero shoved Kester forward, blocking the path back into the lounge. "Come on," he ordered, giving him an extra push in the small of his back. "No time to get soppy over a painting, you silly boy. Especially not a possessed one, no?"

"Suppose not." Kester allowed himself to be pushed down the hallway. Already, he could feel his head beginning to clear. The brightness of the kitchen certainly helped. Daylight washed through the paned windows, bleaching the oak units and ceramic tiles.

"How did you get on?" Isabelle asked. She was slumped at one end of an enormous farmhouse-style table, nursing a mug of tea in her hands. A vase of sunflowers wilted on the dresser beside her. "You weren't in there very long."

Ribero pulled out a chair next to her. "No, but in that short time, I think we managed to see the extent of the problem very clearly, Mrs Diderot."

"Call me Isabelle, please."

"Very well, Isabelle," Dr Ribero crooned, edging a little nearer. He gestured at the others to sit, in a regal manner that suggested he owned the house, not Mrs Diderot. "To begin with, do you mind me asking where you found the painting?"

"It wasn't me who found it." Isabelle sighed, stroking the rim of the mug. "My husband found it when he was clearing out the attic. As I told you on the phone, it was in shreds, as though someone had ripped right through it with their fingers."

"That's interesting," Ribero replied. He nodded at the others.

"I understand now why someone might have wanted to do that," Isabelle said with a sniff. "These last six weeks have been torturous. I just want that painting gone. But every time I try to deal with the situation, something stops me. It's as though I simply cannot bring myself to do it."

"Do what?" Pamela asked.

"Tear the damned thing to shreds!" Isabelle exclaimed, then started to cry. Dr Ribero gracefully pulled a handkerchief from his pocket and offered it to her, which she seized, patting her eyes. "I do apologise," she sniffed. "It has been such a terrible time. I didn't believe in ghosts until I moved here."

You and me both, Kester thought, staring back at the hallway. Now he was out of the room, the Green Lady's effect had worn off a little, though he still found himself unable to stop thinking about her attractive features; not to mention her sweet, yet rather sexy expression.

"Izzie was always such a practical little thing," Mrs Diderot's mother interjected from her position by the sink. She seemed wholly unperturbed by it all, as pragmatic as a vast ocean liner in a minor sea storm. "But since you moved here, oh the problems you've had, eh dear? It's played havoc on her marriage, I can tell you."

"Ah, that is another question I wanted to ask you," Dr Ribero continued, wagging a finger in her direction. "How has your husband acted towards this painting?"

"When he found it, he was very excited," Isabelle said. "Looking back on it now, his excitement was quite unnatural, I suppose. He insisted we take it to a restorer. At the time I didn't mind. I hadn't linked the strangeness of the house with the painting, so it seemed like a harmless enough idea."

"Were things strange even before you fixed the painting then?" Miss Wellbeloved asked.

"Oh, yes," Isabelle replied, nodding. She cupped her tea as though desperate to hold on to something solid. Kester noticed that her hands were trembling.

"In what way?"

"The first time we viewed the house, I thought it was strange. It was too quiet. I don't know, I suppose it was like someone had sucked all the air out. I didn't like it at all. But it was on the market at a ridiculously low price. The estate agent told us that it had been for sale for over a year, but nobody wanted it. I can now see why that was."

"Yes, that does make sense," Ribero said, stroking his chin. "What made you buy the house then?"

"I didn't want to," Isabelle said. "But François can get very enthusiastic about things. He quite convinced me that it was the perfect house for us, and I suppose I got swept up in it all. But from the first day we moved in, I regretted it."

"Yes, you phoned me that very evening, didn't you love?" Isabelle's mother chimed in. "Said that she thought the house was strange and that eyes were watching her. I'll admit, I told her not to be so silly. I thought she was just tired after all the effort of moving in."

"So your husband, he has been very enthusiastic about this painting?" Ribero asked, casting a meaningful look in Miss Well-beloved's direction.

"Oh yes," Isabelle said. "It's awful. It's like he's in love with it or something. I know, that must sound strange."

"Not at all," said Serena with a snide glance at Kester. "Men are a bit like that. Powerless at the sight of an attractive woman."

"Well, that's what was so strange," Isabelle replied. "François was an amazing man. I met him in Paris. We've always had a wonderful marriage, in spite of . . . well, in spite of various things. But ever since he laid eyes on that painting, he's been different. It was far worse after the painting was restored. It's as though he's besotted with it. I catch him in there all the time, talking to it." Without warning, she burst into fresh tears. "I feel like I've lost him! I feel like he's having an affair or something, and that whatever it is in that painting wants me dead!"

Kester gasped. It was so similar to the story he had read in the diary that it sent a shiver right through his body. "Just like Emmeline," he said quietly, more to himself than to anyone else.

"Yes, just like Emmeline, poor woman," Pamela agreed.

Isabelle blew her nose into Ribero's handkerchief, sounding a little like a trumpeting elephant.

"Well, we've got ourselves a right sod here, haven't we?" Serena said, folding her arms across the table. "A ghost with a bit of a taste for tormenting women. I'll enjoy giving this one the heave-ho back into the spirit world." She stuck her chin out, as though daring anyone else around the table to contradict her.

"Well, we'll try resolving this amicably first," Miss Wellbeloved corrected.

"So when are you going to get started?" Isabelle asked. She wiped down her face, handing back the sodden, mascara-smeared handkerchief to Dr Ribero. "When can you get rid of it? When can I start leading a normal life again?"

Dr Ribero eased back into his chair, puffing out his cheeks. "My dear lady," he said, choosing his words carefully. "There are a few things which stand in our path here, and I will lay them out for you thoroughly, so you understand exactly what is going on, yes?"

She nodded, biting her lip.

"Firstly," he continued. "We suspect we cannot get this spirit out of the painting by conventional means. Normally, my colleagues here would coax out the spirit, then trap it within a special storage unit, ready for disposal."

Mike coughed, in a way which sounded distinctly like "water bottle". Dr Ribero ignored him.

"However," Ribero paused for dramatic effect, sweeping the room with a dark stare, "in this instance, I suspect the spirit will not come. She does not like women, that is clear. Also, she is an old spirit. She has entrenched herself deep into that painting. She will not come out without a fight. So we cannot do this the simple way, sadly."

"I see," said Isabelle. "But you can get rid of it, can't you?"

"I need to think this through," Ribero answered. "We do not want to cause this spirit distress or make it angry. Older spirits are more powerful. If this one is upset, we do not know how she will react. Plus, if she decides to flee from the painting, we are not sure where she will next attach herself. In the worst case scenario, she could choose to attach herself to a person. And that would be very bad, yes?"

"You mean like a possession?" Isabelle said, open-mouthed.

"Gawd, like that famous horror film," her mother exclaimed, slapping the sink in excitement. "I didn't know that could happen in real life. Blimey, now there's a thing."

"Plus, there are the legal logistics of it all," Ribero continued.

"Legal logistics?" Isabelle echoed. "What legal logistics?"

"The painting, it is an object, an asset that you and your husband own," Ribero explained. "Without your permission, we cannot destroy it, otherwise you could legally accuse us of criminal damages."

"Yeah, and an expensive lawsuit is the last thing we need," Mike interrupted, swigging the last of his hot chocolate.

"But I own it, and I give you permission!" said Isabelle. A note of hysteria edged into her voice as she slammed the mug down on the table. "I don't see that it should be a problem."

"Ah," said Dr Ribero, rubbing his thumbs together. "But would your husband give us permission? We always have to be most careful in these situations, yes?"

"I suppose the house is in his name, so the painting must be in his name as well," Isabelle said, closing her eyes as though in pain. "So it's not as though you can simply throw it on a bonfire and have done with it. Damn it."

"Neither can we take it from the house," Ribero explained. "As this could be seen as theft."

"Not that we think either of those things will be able to get rid of the spirit for good," Serena said.

Ribero nodded. "I presume your husband does not know we are here?"

She shook her head, pursing her lips. He sighed, smoothing

down his moustache like a troubled animal in need of soothing. "As I thought. His lack of cooperation may cause us some problems; you see? To act without his knowledge, it would be, how do you say it? Unethical. We must keep to the law at all times, I am afraid."

"I understand," Isabelle sighed. "So, in the meantime, while you think of the best way to resolve the situation, what am I to do? I can't stay here with it much longer. It's unbearable."

"Why don't we find ourselves a nice room in a hotel for a while," her mother suggested helpfully. "Somewhere in Exeter, then we can just pop over and let these lot into the house whenever they need to come?"

"That's not a bad idea," Isabelle said, massaging her temples. She looked at Dr Ribero. "How long do you think it will take?"

He shrugged. "It's difficult to tell. But rest assured madam, we want this thing out of your house as much as you do. We charge a fixed price, remember, not by the hour. So it does not benefit us to take a long time on it. You understand?"

She nodded, then fell back against the chair, exhausted.

"Let's do that then," she said finally. "Lord knows I can't cope with this anymore."

"I'd be happy to take the painting from you," Kester piped up. All eyes swung round to look at him, and he felt his cheeks redden. "I mean, if you wanted to sell it to me or anything?"

Isabelle frowned, confused. Dr Ribero gave Kester a ferocious look.

"Ah, he is just joking," he explained, tweaking his shirt collar. "Aren't you, Kester?"

"Well . . ." Kester said, suddenly feeling foolish. What was it about that painting that had had such a profound effect on him? He'd made the offer to buy it almost without thinking. *Perhaps it is monstrous after all,* he thought. *It's certainly made me behave oddly.*

"He's not joking, he's just been a pillock and fallen in love with the painting too," Serena said with disgust. "Ignore him. He's new. He's just here to learn the ropes. He doesn't have a clue."

Dr Ribero went red in the face and directed his venomous stare from Kester on to Serena.

"That is quite enough," he muttered. "You will excuse my team," he said, addressing Isabelle. "This boy here is new, and this lady here has too big a mouth. But rest assured, they are both very good at their jobs." He shot them both another furious glare, eyebrows bobbing in a threatening manner, like tangoing toilet-brushes. Kester blushed. Serena looked mutinous, and threw Kester a particularly hostile glare.

The rest of the meeting passed without incident, though Kester found himself feeling increasingly angry towards Serena. *What is her problem?* he wondered, watching her pick at her nails as Dr Ribero concluded the conversation with Mrs Diderot. *Why does she have to attack me at every available opportunity?* Serena met his eyes and scowled. He looked away.

Outside, as the front door shut quietly behind them, Dr Ribero exploded into action. "What is the matter with you?" he hissed, poking a finger in Serena's direction like an attacking cobra. "What a way to behave in front of a client!"

"Hang on a minute," Serena snarled, folding her arms. "It was him that made the stupid comment, not me." She pointed at Kester, looking at him as though he was something a farmhand had cleared out of a particularly smelly stable.

"Ah, but he is silly and new and does not know better!" Dr Ribero exclaimed, stalking towards the van. "You, on the other hand, have worked with me for many years now—"

"Five, to be precise."

"Five, yes. Five. And you should know how to behave yourself! It is outrageous! Who do you think you are?"

"I know, she's got a bloody mouth on her, hasn't she," Mike added, grinning merrily at Serena's discomfort. "Can't take her anywhere."

"Oh, shut up, Mike," she snapped. "At least when I open my mouth, intelligent things come out."

"Could've fooled me."

"No, on this occasion, that was not an intelligent thing that popped out of your mouth, no!" Dr Ribero continued. He threw open the door of the van as though it had personally insulted him. It screamed on its hinges.

"Hang on, I'm not silly," Kester said, suddenly realising what his father had said. In truth, he'd been thinking about the painting again and hadn't really been paying much attention to the conversation.

"Oh yes, you bloody are," Serena said. "What made you offer to take the painting? Of all the idiotic things to say! You made us all look like morons."

"Well, I don't really know why I said that," Kester bumbled, moving out of the way to let her climb into the back seat. "I really don't. It was rather foolish."

"Damn right, it was foolish!" Serena squawked.

"I'm sorry," Kester said, clambering in and shutting the door. "I really am. The painting did something strange to me, and I apologise."

The frankness of his apology took the fire out of the argument, dampening the atmosphere to a morose preponderance. Kester shuffled in the seat as the van took off down the road, feeling like a schoolboy after a particularly harsh telling-off from the headmaster.

"Look, I'm going to be going back home anyway," he said awkwardly. "So I'll be out of your hair. You're right, Serena, I'm not suitable for this sort of thing at all. I'm an academic, not a ghost-hunter. I tell you what, if you'll just let me pick up my things from Pamela's, I'll then go to the train station, and you can all properly get on with your job."

Serena grunted and stared out of the window, her expression

unreadable.

"Oh, but we don't want you to go!" Pamela wailed. "There's still so much we haven't talked about, like your lovely mother!"

"Not to mention your ability to see the spirit door," Dr Ribero added. "You should not go yet. I ask you to reconsider, and I take back what I said about you being silly, okay?"

"Yeah mate," Mike said. "You should stick around a little while longer. Don't worry about making the odd mistake, we've all done it."

"But to be honest, I'm not sure I ever said anything about working long term with you all anyway!" Kester said. "It just all sort of happened, really. I haven't had a chance to think things through. Plus, I can't just leave my house deserted. Who knows what would happen to it?"

"Look," Serena piped up. "I didn't mean to have a go at you. Though I still stand by what I said. It was a stupid thing to say, and you should think before you open your mouth."

"Okay," Kester acknowledged.

"But," she continued, scrutinising the others, "why are you all so desperate for him to stay? It's just because you think he can open the spirit door, isn't it? That's why you think he's so special."

"Hey, I never said I was special," Kester protested.

"Isn't it enough to have a really good extinguisher on the team?" Serena's jaw tightened. "I mean, we manage alright, don't we?"

"No-one's saying you're not a good extinguisher, love," Pamela said, giving her a comforting squeeze.

"Well anyway, I'm going to be leaving, so you needn't worry about me causing any more disturbances," Kester said as firmly as possible.

"Tell you what," Mike said, swinging the steering wheel to the right and veering up the pavement. "I've got to do the monthly spirit run tomorrow, why don't I drop you in London?

Then you can just get the train from there."

"I don't want to cause you any trouble," Kester said.

"Nah, no trouble at all, I'd like the company," Mike said. "The tape deck's knackered in this van, so I can't even listen to music these days."

"I don't want to impose."

"You're more than welcome to stay another night," Pamela offered, leaning over the seat and patting him affectionately on the shoulder. "It's not a problem at all, the bed's still made up and ready. I'll tell Hemingway not to sleep in it tonight, I know you were a bit put off by him climbing in with you last night."

"Okay, thank you," Kester said, once again feeling rather swayed along by events.

"But you will come back down, won't you?" Dr Ribero said, nibbling on his fingernail and looking at him anxiously. "After all, we have a lot to talk about, you and I." He paused, before adding, "you are my son, after all."

Kester said nothing. He couldn't make the old man out. *Why is he so keen to keep me here, when he never once came to visit me before?* he wondered. *Is it that he genuinely wants a relationship? Or is it just because he's convinced I've got some special power, which he wants to make use of?*

With that unsettling thought, he slumped into his seat and tried to forget about the day. It wasn't so hard to do. He was blessed with a natural ability to put unpleasant things out of his mind.

However, forgetting about the Green Lady was going to be considerably trickier.

CHAPTER 8: HOME AGAIN

The drive up to London with Mike had been interesting, to put it mildly.

After a series of roars, rasps, and splutters, the van had eventually broken down entirely, leaving them stranded halfway round the M25. This wasn't exactly how Kester had planned to spend his morning—perched on a grubby grass verge and watching cars hurtle by at breakneck speed. To make matters worse, they had five spirits bouncing around in water bottles in the back of the van who released the occasional moan or howl, just to keep them on their toes.

For two hours, they'd entertained themselves by playing "guess that song," but it wasn't a great way to pass the time, given that they liked completely different music. Even after the emergency recovery man had managed to get them going again, the van had continued to splutter and jackrabbit with alarming frequency, leaving Kester quite fearing for his life as they drove into London and along the manic city streets.

However, it had been fascinating to see the headquarters of the famous Infinite Enterprises. Kester could see why Dr Ribero was so jealous of the company. The building was a soaring behemoth of glass and iron, glinting like a futuristic fortress in the heart of London's business district. It couldn't have been more different to Ribero's crumbling offices in Exeter if it had tried. It was a beacon of power, announcing its success in every sharp corner and polished window pane. Kester was suitably impressed. He was even more awed by the black-suited guards that opened the door round the back, taking Mike's battered water bottles without so much as a greeting.

Walking away, Mike had proceeded to remind him, in no uncertain terms, of the number of times he'd been approached directly by the company, but how he'd chosen to remain loyal to Ribero instead. Looking back at the building, then surveying Mike's scruffy shirt and jeans, Kester wasn't quite convinced.

After hopping on the train from London Liverpool Street to Cambridge, Kester finally arrived at the suburban avenue he'd grown up in, and was soon back in his own safe, quiet little house. Although he'd only been away a few days, it felt like far longer, and his home already had a rather sad, unloved feel. Dust lined the dado rail, the fluff was gathering momentum on the Persian rugs, and the undisturbed scatter cushions suggested, most emphatically, that nobody had sat on them for a while.

The brief absence made him realise how he'd neglected his home. Admittedly, he wasn't used to cleaning. When mother had been ill, Kester had given it his best shot, but after she had died, he simply hadn't bothered. The accumulation of dirt hadn't been so obvious then, but now it stood out, loud and offensive as a football hooligan, defying him to ignore it.

With an unexpected burst of energy, he threw on his mother's apron and seized the feather duster. After about twenty minutes of desperate cleaning, the saggy sofa by the window proved too tempting to resist. Kester collapsed, surveying the room. It didn't look at all different. *Why do people bother cleaning anyway?* he wondered cynically, wiping the sweat from his forehead. *It really is an awful waste of time.*

He sighed. The house felt somehow *wrong*, the weight of his mother's absence still hanging in the air. The grandfather clock plodded morosely in the corner like a death march. A fly buzzed against the window pane. But other than that, there was unnerving silence. He didn't remember it being like this. Was it because he'd become accustomed to the incessant chatter of Ribero and his crew over the last few days?

A rather unpleasant thought struck him. *I wonder if my mother's ghost is in here somewhere?* He glanced around the room, wondering if unseen eyes were watching him, right at this moment. He quickly stopped picking his nose. *She'd be really cross if she saw me doing that.* Prior to visiting Exeter, believing that his mother was a ghost would never have even occurred to him. But now, he found himself wondering whether it might be possible.

"Hello Mother?" he called out, feeling rather foolish. "Are you still here?"

He waited, cocking his head up to the ceiling, half expecting to see his mother's ghost bobbing around by the marbled ceiling light. To his disappointment and relief, the only response was the continued tick of the clock. The late afternoon sun blazed through the windows, the strong glow reassuring him that there was nothing supernatural in his vicinity.

Just because you happen to have seen a couple of ghosts in the last few days, doesn't necessarily mean there are spirits around every corner, he reminded himself, getting up to make some dinner. It was late, and he remembered that he hadn't eaten anything since Liverpool Street station, which seemed a very long time ago. Plus, it had only been a dried up Cornish pasty, so it really didn't count as proper food. And of course, neither did the salt and vinegar crisps or the bar of Dairy Milk.

Kester sloped out to the kitchen and put some water on to boil. The cheery sound of the kettle whistling on the hob raised his spirits. The sight of pasta, bubbling and bouncing in the saucepan, cheered him further. By the time he had sat down at the little Formica table to eat, he was positively happy. Happy to be home. Happy to have some food. Happy to have some time to think properly at last. It had been a mad few days, and he desperately needed time to review the situation and think about how to proceed.

However, by the end of the meal, he was none the wiser. A part of him wanted to stay at home, to hide away and ignore the rest of the world. The other half of him remained too curious to want to leave things as they were. There were so many unanswered questions lingering in Exeter, so many matters that felt unfinished. Not to mention the fact that he'd lost one parent, only to promptly inherit another. Despite spending some time with Dr Ribero, he still felt no closer to understanding the man, or his relationship with his mother.

Kester stumbled upstairs as the sun set, exhaustion finally getting the better of him. The last few days had been long, not mention bizarre. The house still felt strangely unfamiliar to him, as though it had been changed in a hundred imperceptible ways during his absence. The door at the top of the stairs looked vaguely menacing, hulking over him as he ascended. The cracked paint on the bannisters disturbed him in a way it never had done before. Even the sight of his own single bed, pushed against the wall of his tiny bedroom, seemed horribly empty. The sheets were too tightly tucked, and the quilt too faded and too ancient.

I think my mind's starting to run away with me, he thought, with a mixture of alarm and awe. He'd never been blessed with much of an imagination. He wasn't sure he liked it much.

His mother's bedroom door stood in front of him, implacable and strangely unforgiving. Kester could almost imagine being a child again—tapping on the door in the middle of the night, terrified from yet another bad dream. *I wonder, if I tap now, will anyone answer?* He shivered and pushed open the door.

There was her bed, just as he had left it—pink duvet tugged up to the pillows, like an old maid protecting her modesty. Her fitted wardrobes, with creamy, shiny paintwork. The little sink in the dresser. It was all the same, and yet it had changed. Or rather, he had changed, and now he was seeing it all with different eyes.

He moved to the wardrobe, pulling the doors open. The musty-sweet smell of his mother's clothes flew out, reminding him of her. *What am I doing?* he asked himself, bewildered by his own actions. Kester crouched and pulled a box from underneath her collection of plastic-wrapped coats.

"I wonder," he muttered, lifting the box up to the bed. He'd been deliberately avoiding sorting through her belongings. It had felt horribly invasive, rummaging through her things, even though she was no longer around to complain. They had always had an unwritten code of respect between them, acknowledging the other's right to privacy, and the fact that one of them was now dead did not make it feel any more appropriate.

Of all the things that he felt wrong about snooping through, this box was the worst. It was only a simple black cardboard box, a little worn at the edges. But he knew it was where she stored her private letters, bills, and diaries. He had never once wondered what was in there. Until a few moments ago, that was.

He lifted the lid. What lay inside was every bit as unremarkable as anticipated. Various documents, letters from the bank, correspondence to other people who he had never heard of before. An A5 folder, complete with bills from the last few years, all meticulously filed away. However, as he rummaged further, spreading the papers on the bed, he at last found something that caught his interest.

"Bingo." Kester pulled the yellowing bundle of letters on to his lap. The name at the bottom of the first letter confirmed his suspicions. *Julio.* These were letters from Dr Ribero. His heart began to pound. Again, he felt the pain of exclusion, of discovering that his mother had a whole life that she'd never told him about. The force of his father's absence and his mother's death walloped him in the stomach like a freight train. *Am I really sure I want to read these?* he wondered, stroking the pen marks on the page.

There were few letters, only a small handful in total. However, they might be enough to give him some more clues about the past. Kester prised away the ancient elastic band, which fell to pieces in his hand, and started to read.

My dear Gretchen,

You must come back. I know what I said, and I was wrong. I did not realise how wrong until now. What can I say to make it better? How can we make this situation work? I have no idea. But I do know I need to say sorry.

I did not mean to suggest that you get rid of our baby. I was desperate, you understand? The baby, it changes everything. You know that. But we can sort something out. We will manage. You need to come back. Our agency will fall apart without you. How else can we get rid of the spirits?

Do not think I care only about the business and nothing else. That is not true. I care about you also. And so does Jennifer. In spite of everything, she still loves you, as do I. It is me who has done the wrong thing here, not you. Do not run away.

Please, can we arrange a time to meet?

I await your reply,
Julio

Kester exhaled, blinking hard. *This is a Dr Ribero I hadn't expected,* he thought. *What did he do that was so wrong? And why did he want mother to get rid of her baby?* He also wondered why the letter mentioned Miss Wellbeloved, albeit by her first name. *Maybe it's another Jennifer,* he thought. But still, it seemed too much of a coincidence.

He picked up the next one, which was dated two weeks later.

My dear Gretchen,

Thank you for replying to me. I was so relieved to hear from you. It has been weighing on my conscience so much, and I am so glad that you are feeling well and that the pregnancy is progressing.

It seems so strange to think that it is already five months along and that you are showing. My baby. I did not ever think I would be a father. It is an odd feeling. I only wish it had been in different circumstances.

As to your request—oh Gretchen, you know that it is not possible. I have always been honest with you about my feelings for you. What happened between us—it was special, very special, and I treasure every moment I ever spent in your arms. Believe me when I say that, it is the truth.

But I cannot leave Jennifer. You know what her family has done for me. Gretchen, you know that they took me in when I arrived here, I cannot hurt their only daughter. It would be the worst insult. Plus, I love her too. I love her in a different way. With you, it is all fire, all life and soul. With Jennifer it is quieter, more peaceful. Calmer. Neither one is better, they are just different. I do not expect you to understand.

I do not know whether Jennifer and I will be married now. She is being so strong about it all, but she has doubts about the future. She is a remarkable woman. So are you. I know it sounds like a strange thing to say, but I feel blessed having you both in my life. I just wish I had handled it all better. I have been an idiot and I have hurt you both. I am sorry. I am lucky that you both don't hate me.

We do need to talk. But I cannot meet you behind Jennifer's back. We need to discuss your future. Where will you live? You cannot remain forever at your mother's, I know how much she drives you mad. We need also to discuss the baby. We need to talk very much, Gretchen. Please, call me.

Yours,
Julio

Kester placed the rest of the letters on the bed, shocked. *Miss Wellbeloved and Dr Ribero?* he thought with amazement. He couldn't imagine the two of them together. Miss Wellbeloved was so austere, and Ribero so fiery and excitable. There was definitely a familiarity between them, but he'd presumed that was a result of working together for so long. *Obviously there's a whole lot more to it than I realised,* he grimaced. The image of the pencil-thin woman and the doctor as lovers wasn't especially pleasant. *Mind you,* he rationalised, *it's a lot better than imagining Ribero with my own mother.*

"So, my mother was the 'other woman'?" he mused aloud, leaning back on his elbows. It didn't make sense. His mother had always been so morally upstanding! She'd always instilled in him a strong sense of right and wrong, from a very early age. How was it possible that she had been someone's mistress?

Stroking the ageing letters thoughtfully under his thumb, he noticed there was one at the bottom that was a different colour than the rest. Removing it from the pile, he saw that it was a hastily written note, in his mother's familiar handwriting. It was addressed to him.

My darling Kester,

I wonder how long it will take you to discover this? If you are reading it now, then I think that must mean I am no longer with you, otherwise you would not be looking through my things. I hope you are well, my dear boy, and that you are coping without me.

I have chosen to write this letter on the day they told me I have incurable cancer—so I know I do not have long to live. You were so brave when you heard the news, so stoic.

There is much I need to tell you, and even now, I cannot find the right words. I am writing this with the presumption that I will not have told you before my death—and I hope you can forgive me for my cowardice. I should have been more open with you.

I take it you have now read the letters attached to this one, and now know the truth about your father. I am so sorry I did not tell you sooner. There was too much to reveal, too much that was strange and unbelievable, and the longer I left it, the harder it became. Soon, it was easier not to tell you anything at all. But perhaps I was wrong to leave you in the dark.

I hope that you will visit your father, Julio Ribero. I have discovered that he is still running his business from the same location—99 Mirabel Street, Exeter. There, you will find him, and you will also find Jennifer Wellbeloved—a dear lady that I once did a terrible wrong to. I only pray that she can forgive me for what I did. I am sure they will be kind to you once they know who you are, even Jennifer. They will tell you everything you need to know.

All I will say is have an open mind. Julio runs a strange business. I was once a part of it. And the gift I have, I believe you have inherited. When you were a boy, you used to see openings to the spirit world all the time. It frightened you. I told you it was your imagination, but I was not being truthful, my darling. I told you to block the spirit doors, and I should not have done so. It is your gift to control, not mine. I apologise, my love.

I read this letter back now, and know that it sounds confusing. The cancer is making me feel so old, and it is so difficult to concentrate. There is nothing worse than feeling your mind start to unravel. I hope it will never happen to you.

Go to Dr Ribero. Sell the house if you need money. The southwest is far lovelier than here anyway. The sea air will do you good. Julio will help you. Despite what you may think from reading the letters, he is not a bad man. Indeed, he has a wonderful heart. It is just his brain that isn't always very reliable. He will help you to understand your gift, but do not let him pressurise you into doing anything you feel uncomfortable with. Julio gets carried away and forgets himself sometimes. Be firm with him. And remember, he is your father, and he owes you much.

Know that I am always with you, in your heart. I think exciting things are ahead, my darling—if you seize the opportunity. I love you and I am so proud of you.

With love,
Mother x

Kester paused, placing the letter very carefully back on the bed. He smoothed it, touching the places where the pen had dented the paper. Then, with animal ferocity, he started to sob. It was as though she had been speaking to him out loud, as though the separation between them was as thin as the paper the letter had been written on. But the separation was there. It was total, undeniable and irresolute, and nothing could ever unite them again. The weight of the knowledge crushed him, squeezing the breath from him, and he howled, the pain of missing her raging out for the first time since she'd died.

After a while, he composed himself. He wasn't the type to allow emotions to take control for too long. It was his mother's Germanic practicality. *Perhaps those tears were a little bit of Argentinian emotion bursting out of me,* he thought, wiping his face. *Maybe I am more like Ribero than I realise.* The room had gone dark; the sun had set, casting long shadows across the thick carpet and past the door. He felt suddenly, uncomfortably alone.

Kester tiptoed to bed, turning on every available light-switch in the process. Then, quite surprising himself, he pulled out his mobile phone and located Pamela's number. He didn't want to call her, especially given the late hour. Instead, he sent her a quick text message, informing her that he would be coming back to Exeter within a few days.

Putting down his phone, he nodded, knowing it was the right decision. There was nothing for him here. Whereas in Exeter, there was a father, some pretty interesting people, and a highly attractive green-dressed ghost awaiting him.

CHAPTER 9: BACK TO EXETER

Kester's first job the following morning had been to call the estate agent to put the house on the market. His second job was cancelling the newspaper delivery. The third, letting his neighbour, Miss Winterbottom, know he was leaving, which caused her to sniff and offer him the largest slice of her freshly baked apple cake.

After he had done these jobs, and eaten the cake, he booked a train ticket and turned his attention to packing. He soon realised that most of his books would have to stay put for now, unless he wanted to break his back carrying the case on the London Underground. The same went for his collection of rare coins, which he supposed he'd have to either sell or put into storage for a while, or at least until he was set up in Exeter.

However, in spite of the burden of responsibility, he felt excited, though he still questioned the sanity of his decision. He couldn't quite believe how bold and decisive he was being. It was as though someone else had stepped into his skin, making him unusually proactive; he felt worried that the sensation might leave him as swiftly as it had arrived.

Although the thought of leaving the house was upsetting, he knew it was time to go. Walking around, taking in the floral wallpaper, the gilt picture frames, the little oval mirrors hanging over every gas heater, he realised that his time here had come to an end. It was his mother's home really, and like her, it had become ghost-like—a faded memory of itself. If he remained here, he suspected he would start to disappear too, and absorb into the fabric of the house like lingering smoke.

After the estate agent's visit, he accepted the terms, happily signed the documents, left them the keys, and made towards the station, ready to start afresh. He felt surprisingly cheerful, in spite of everything, and the feeling didn't diminish, even after several hours on the train. The sun poured relentlessly through the windows as he whizzed from cityscapes to verdant fields and hills, as though spurring him on in his journey.

To his surprise, he found Pamela outside Exeter's St David's station, waiting for him next to her rustic Ford Fiesta. She waved, and he waved back, grinning. It felt good to be back again. It wasn't just the city; it was the whole experience—the excitement of the new.

"We thought you might be back, but hadn't realised it would be quite so soon," she said, crushing him against her ample bosoms as she drew him in for a hug. "You just couldn't stay away, could you?"

Kester smiled, piling the suitcase into the boot, which groaned under the weight. "I don't know what it was," he replied. "I got home, and it didn't feel much like home anymore. So I thought I'd better come back and see if I could make my home here instead."

Pamela clapped her hands, clearly delighted. "Well, as I said," she beamed, "you're welcome to stay at mine as long as you need to. It's comfier than a bed and breakfast anyway."

"Well, if you don't mind," Kester said. "I don't want to impose on you."

"Oh, you silly boy," Pamela said, squeezing herself into the driver's seat. "It would be a pleasure. I get lonely by myself, even though Hemingway is excellent company. But you can't have much of a conversation with a dog, can you?"

Kester agreed that the statement was true, as he climbed into the car to join her. The overwhelming smell of the air freshener caused his eyes to water, but still didn't manage to conceal the distinct odour of wet dog coming from the back.

"The others are all at the office," Pamela continued, reversing at an alarming rate and nearly knocking over a pensioner, who proceeded to shake his walking stick at them angrily. "Did you want to come back with me and chat things through with everyone? Or did you want to go back to mine and freshen up?"

"I presume Dr Ribero is having his afternoon nap, isn't he?" Kester said, raising an apologetic hand to the old man, who was still mouthing obscenities at them, his whiskery face red with anger.

Pamela chuckled, completely oblivious. "He'll be up in ten minutes though. You know what he's like, very punctual with his sleeping."

"Mind out for that bollard."

"Yes, I saw it, thank you anyway," she cheerily replied, sailing the car out of the car park and bouncing over the kerb instead. "Let's get back and have a nice cup of tea at the office then."

Instead of parking near the front of the offices, Pamela squeezed her car down a minute alleyway, which led to an equally tiny carpark. Kester looked around with mild confusion, trying to get his bearings, then realised they were at the back of the building. Peering up, he could see that the back wasn't in any better state than the front, with peeling whitewash paint, crumbling brickwork and an iron escape ladder that looked as though it had definitely seen better days.

However, inside, Kester was surprised. "It's much nicer than your front entrance," he commented, as they climbed the stairs.

"Oh, nobody ever goes in the front entrance," Pamela said, grasping the stair rail to haul her considerable bulk upwards. "Mind you, no one ever comes this way either, apart from us. We don't get many visitors."

"Why was the front door open when I first came here then?" Kester asked.

She looked over her shoulder. "I don't know. It shouldn't have been. Maybe the lock's broken. We should probably look into that."

"Probably," Kester agreed. Out of breath at the top of the stairs, he once again vowed that he really should try to get in shape. However, this was a vow he made at least once a day, and so far he'd done nothing to make it happen.

Pamela threw open the door at the top of the stairs, leading them into the familiar darkness of the upper landing. Kester stumbled after her as she danced her way to the office, like a newborn lamb following its mother.

"Look who I've got here!" Pamela exclaimed, gesturing to Kester as though he were a prize display at an exhibition.

Serena glanced up, rolling her eyes. "We know you've got him, Pamela. You told us you were going to collect him, remember?"

Mike jumped out of his seat, covering the office floor in two huge strides, and pumped Kester's hand. "Hello again!" he exclaimed. "Didn't expect to see you back so soon! What made you change your mind?"

"Ah, well, you know. The house just didn't feel the same when I went back," Kester bumbled, feeling rather overwhelmed.

Miss Wellbeloved rose slowly from her desk, the ghost of a smile tightening her lips. "Glad you decided to come back," she said. "I think Julio was quite morose at the prospect of you going."

Kester swallowed, remembering the letters he'd found in his mother's room. *Why is she being nice to me, when my mother had an affair with her ex-fiancé?* he fretted. *If I was her, I wouldn't want anything to do with me.*

"It's nice to be back," he stuttered. It was true. Although he'd never visited Exeter prior to this week, it already felt strangely like home. "Is Dr Ribero awake yet?"

"You know, you'll have to start calling him dad, won't you?" Mike said amiably. Miss Wellbeloved winced, then straightened her features.

"His alarm went off a few minutes ago, so we can safely presume he's in there having his usual mid-afternoon smoke," Serena declared, hammering away at her keyboard as though it had personally insulted her.

With a dramatic crash, Ribero's office door swung open, revealing the doctor himself, arms outstretched and a grin wrapped round his smouldering cigarette holder.

"Aha!" he cried out, plucking the cigarette from his mouth and waving it in the air, smoke billowing like the trail of a spectral snail. "I knew you would come back! Hello there, my boy!"

"Hello," Kester said uncertainly, giving a little wave, then feeling a bit silly and putting his hand down again. However, in spite of his awkwardness, he liked their obvious pleasure at his return. It certainly made him feel a good deal more wanted than he had felt when he'd first come to the office a few days ago.

"And now you are coming to Exeter to stay, yes?" Ribero continued, fixing him with the full force of his dark, South American gaze, as though daring him to disagree. Kester shrugged, then hastily changed the gesture to a nod.

"I think so," he said. "I've arranged for the house to be sold." Then he remembered who had bought the house, and added, "If that's alright with you, of course."

"Ah yes, but of course. It was your mother's house, now it

is yours. That is how it should be," Ribero declared, waltzing across the room with all the loose-limbed elegance of an ageing leopard. He stood in front of Kester, then grasped him by the shoulders, planting a whiskery kiss on each cheek.

"I am glad you are here," he said, suddenly looking serious. "Plus, I think we may need your help with this difficult case, no?"

"You mean the Green Lady painting?" Kester asked.

"Yeah, it's proving a lot more bloody tricky than originally thought," Mike said with a grimace. "It's a real case of all hands on deck with this one."

"As long as you think you can stop yourself from going all soppy over her again," Serena interrupted, with a frosty grin. "You were practically dry humping the canvas last time."

"Oh Serena, really," Pamela chastised. "That's unkind. It's not Kester's fault that the spirit was having a peculiar effect on him."

"I certainly wasn't doing any dry humping, thank you very much," Kester said, with as much dignity as he could muster.

"Well, something was clearly going on in your pants, that's all I'm saying. Honestly, you couldn't have looked more excited had you—"

"Serena!" Miss Wellbeloved and Pamela exclaimed in unison.

Mike laughed loudly. "Serena's just jealous. She doesn't like ladies that are more attractive than she is."

"If you're attracted to half-crazed murderous spirits, then that's fine with me," she spat back.

"As opposed to half-crazed, murderous humans like yourself, you mean?"

"Ah, let us stop this nonsense," Dr Ribero barked, flapping a hand at them all, as though putting out a fire. "All this silliness with dried out humping and murder. We need to discuss the case, not this."

"Down the pub then?" Mike suggested.

"Ooh, that sounds like a good idea," Pamela agreed. "Fat Pig?"

"You certainly are," Serena said.

Pamela pummelled Serena's arm, smiling. "You just can't stop yourself, can you love?" she replied. "I suppose if we named a pub after you, we'd have to call it the Long-Faced, Mardy-Arsed Cow. Which doesn't have quite the same ring to it."

Mike roared with laughter, much to Serena's irritation. However, after a few seconds she joined in, albeit rather stiffly.

After gathering all their belongings, they headed out of the office, down the alleyway, and onto the high street, past rows of overstuffed vintage shops and tiny cafes. The mid-afternoon sun blazed overhead, baking the worn pavements and glinting off shop windows. Kester trotted dutifully behind them, feeling like the runt of the litter, struggling to keep up. Suddenly, the team turned into an alleyway, moving pack-like from the busy street to the quiet of the narrow path beyond. At the end, Kester could quite clearly make out the antique pub sign, hanging still on the breezeless day, complete with brightly coloured pig painted upon it.

Mike punched open the door, striding inside like a lord returning to his manor. "Afternoon, Bill," he announced without preamble, saluting the barman. "I see you're a bit quiet today."

The man behind the bar looked up and grinned. He was a generously proportioned chap, with the general physique of a woolly mammoth, not to mention a verdant ginger beard that jutted proudly in front of him like the prow of a ship.

"Hello there, my good man!" he said jovially, leaning across the bar. "We're only quiet because it's early in the day, and only people like you start drinking at this hour. I see you've brought your *compadres* with you?"

"Yes, it's a team-building exercise," Mike replied. Kester looked curiously around the room. He didn't visit pubs very often. His experiences with pubs in the past had been almost entirely unpleasant. On one occasion, he had been slapped around the face by a pensioner who'd been irritated by his lack of desire to enter into a drinking contest. On the other, he'd managed to get his foot caught up on a table leg, causing the entire table, not to mention its contents, to crash to the floor. He'd been slapped that time too, by two very large, very angry young men. Or rather, punched quite hard in the belly. Whichever way you looked at it, it hadn't made for a great experience.

Thankfully, this pub was unthreateningly small. Indeed, it looked almost like someone's lounge, complete with iron fireplace, squidgy window seat, and smart floorboards. It had been crammed to capacity with a variety of wooden tables and chairs, all practically knocking into one another. Kester could imagine the atmosphere being quite intimate when full. However, at present, they were the only ones there, so instead, the room looked a little forlorn.

"What can I get you to drink?" the barman continued, scooping up a beer glass in readiness. Mike frowned diligently over the selection, before pointing to one directly in front of him.

"Make mine a large, dry white," Pamela bustled. She pointed at Serena. "I suspect this miserable young lass will make do with a fat-free gin and slimline tonic."

"No, I'll just have a diet coke, thank you," Serena snipped. "It's a bit early in the day to be drinking."

"Never too early for drinking," Mike declared, taking a reverent sip of his drink. He exhaled enthusiastically, smacking his lips. "That's a good one, that is."

"Yeah, it's a nice little local ale," Bill agreed, smoothing down his sideburns. He hooked his thumbs into the pockets of his waistcoat. "I suspect as it's a nice day, you'll be wanting to sit outside, ladies and gentlemen?"

"That would be very nice, I think," Dr Ribero said. "Make the most of this lovely weather, yes?"

After pouring the rest of their drinks, Bill diligently strode over to unlock the stained-glass door, waving them outside.

"Yes, make the most of it," he said. "I've heard a storm's on its way. By all accounts, it's something of a doozy."

Pamela groaned, squashing herself into the narrow space between table and bench. "Oh typical. You never can rely on the English weather, can you?"

"That you certainly cannot, madam," the barman agreed solemnly. He saluted them, turning on his heel. "Let me know if you want anything else," he called over his shoulder. "I'll leave you chaps to it."

Kester settled onto a narrow stool, enjoying the natural sun trap of the enclosed courtyard. Sparrows fluttered and chirruped within the ivy clinging to the red-brick walls, and somewhere in the distance, he could hear the melodic chiming of church bells. It was a pleasant spot, and he was tempted to shut his eyes for a while and enjoy the momentary peace.

"Right, shall we get started then?" Miss Wellbeloved suggested, sipping at her glass of water. "I don't want to take too long, I need to get home to bake a cake for my Art Appreciation Club."

"Perhaps it is best if we bring Kester up to speed first?" Dr Ribero said, winking at his son, who was presently fighting the urge to nod off. Kester quickly prodded his glasses up his nose and sat up straight.

"There's not that much to tell, is there?" Serena said. "It's only the last visit he missed."

"I'll fill him in," Mike said, slamming his ale down on the blistered table top. "Right Kester, the main problems we're facing are as follows. Are you ready?"

"Oh yes, I'm ready," Kester blustered, trying to look as professional as possible. "Do carry on."

"Problem one. The machine I've been working on to drag this Green Lady spirit out of the painting doesn't work."

"Which comes as no surprise to anyone," Serena added.

"I'll have you know," Mike continued, raising a finger with totem-like authority, "that it's nothing to do with my designs. My designs, as ever, are faultless. The problem lies with this bloody spirit. She's somehow spread out across the canvas, so she's not situated in one specific location."

Kester paused. "So," he started slowly, trying to get his mind around the concept, "she's all over the painting, rather than in one spot? How does that work?"

Dr Ribero rapped his fingers on the table. "It is irregular. Normally, spirits need to remain in one piece, regardless of what object they're living in. This one has unusual powers. It makes it virtually impossible to extract her in the usual way."

"Secondly," Mike continued, after releasing a loud belch, "we've been asking Isabelle Diderot a few more questions, and it appears this spirit is rather indestructible. Not that we'd want to destroy it anyway, because we respect spirits," he added, catching the steely glint in Miss Wellbeloved's eye.

"Why do you think the spirit is indestructible? Because that diary suggested that Emmeline managed to rip it to pieces and the spirit survived?" Kester guessed.

"More than that," Mike continued. "Quite frankly, from what we've learnt, it's amazing Emmeline was able to destroy it, if indeed it was her and not someone else. Isabelle was telling us that every time she's tried to damage the canvas, she's been repelled."

"Repelled?"

"Spirit repulsion is a common enough skill," Serena added. "Certain types of spirit can exude an antiforce that can quite literally knock a human off their feet, if they're powerful enough."

Kester scratched his head, fighting off a yawn. "Hang on a moment, an anti what?" His brain was struggling to cope after a long day travelling and a leisurely sit in the glorious sunshine.

Heat and tiredness were not the best combination when concentration was required.

"An antiforce," Mike repeated. "If you understand magnetic forces, you'll have a fair old idea of how spirit forces work. Humans naturally produce a certain kind of energy, and spirits can use negative energy to buffer them back—a bit like identical poles of two magnets, repelling each other."

"I see," Kester said sagely, though he didn't really.

"So, in short," Miss Wellbeloved concluded, "we have a spirit that we can't get out of the painting, and who can actively repel us when we get too close. It's a bit of a conundrum."

"So what are you going to do?" Kester asked.

Dr Ribero slapped his thigh. "That is precisely where you come in, my boy!" He grinned, revealing a mouthful of white teeth. "We think you might be able to help us with your unique and special gift."

Serena tutted. Kester felt a little like tutting too. *Not this again,* he thought anxiously. *I don't even know how to make the door appear!*

"I think you're pinning a bit too much hope on my limited ability," he replied nervously.

"I'll say," Serena muttered.

Dr Ribero shrugged. "If you cannot do it, you cannot do it. We will understand. But at the moment, it is the only solution we can think of, yes? Otherwise, we have to hand the case over to another company."

"Like Larry Higgins," Mike grumbled. "Or even worse, the big You-Know-Who."

"Oh dear," Kester said. "Well, that wouldn't be good, would it?"

"No, it would not!" Dr Ribero said with sudden animation, rising from his seat in his excitement. "My boy, it would be a terrible thing, yes? Our reputation would be damaged!"

"More than it is already," Miss Wellbeloved added.

"Christ, can you imagine," Pamela said. "People thinking even less of us than they do now."

Dr Ribero glowered at the ladies, with all the imposing self-righteousness of a wronged man. "Exactly," he continued. "This agency was going down the toilet, yes? But then Kester turns up. And suddenly, we have hope again. If he can open spirit doors, then this is something that even Infinite Enterprises cannot compete with, right?"

"Right," the rest of the group echoed.

"But I'm not sure I can!" Kester protested. "Besides," he added, "if you can't even get the spirit out of the painting, how can you expect to get her through a spirit door?"

Dr Ribero smacked the table, jiggling the glasses. "That is the beauty of it," he said, pausing for dramatic effect. "Spirits cannot resist the lure of the spirit door. It calls to them, because it leads to their true home. It is a call they must obey, sooner or later, no matter how much they don't want to. If you can hold the door open for a while, she will come out. She will have to."

Kester gulped. "But so far, I've only been able to see it for a few seconds at a time," he said. "How can I make it stay there?"

"Well, you just have to focus on not wetting yourself with fear or getting all aroused by a silly oil painting, that would be a good start," Serena snapped, smoothing out her bob. She crossed her legs, pointing a pillar-box red stiletto directly at him, like an accusation. He tried to ignore the rather lovely shape of her exposed calf, settling his eyes on the wall instead.

"Anyway," Dr Ribero continued, "we are doing an observation tonight, so you will join us and then we will see what more we can learn. Is everyone still coming?"

"As long as I get enough time to bake my cake," Miss Well-beloved said. "I promised the ladies I would. They'll be most put out if they don't get one."

"Yes, yes, enough with the cake," Dr Ribero said. "I under-stand; cake is important to ladies. As long as everyone else is still okay with the time? Nine o'clock this evening, yes?"

"Excuse me, what's this observation?" Kester asked, stomach sinking. He suspected he knew already. It sounded uncannily as though they would be performing some sort of night vigil on the painting, which wasn't exactly a prospect that filled him with delight. He was tired from his day, and wasn't in the right frame of mind to cope with a haunted house, let alone a hostile spirit.

"Haven't we talked through observations with you yet?" Miss Wellbeloved said, folding up her blouse sleeves to get some respite from the heat. "I thought we mentioned it when we were working on the Japanese spirit the other day."

"No, not a word. I'm presuming it's some sort of overnight thing, though?"

"Yes, that is correct," Dr Ribero interrupted. He finished his glass of Malbec with a flourish, then for some reason, positioned the empty glass directly over the hole in the centre of the table, where a sun parasol would normally stand. *He's a strange chap,* Kester thought, watching as he moved the glass a millimetre to the left to ensure it was evenly positioned.

"So, what do you observe then?" Kester asked reluctantly. What he really wanted to ask was, *Do you really need me there?* And, *Can I go to bed instead?* But he already knew what the response would be to those questions. Plus, he couldn't tolerate the thought of Serena's goading expression. He'd seen quite enough of her smug taunting already.

"That is what we need to discuss," Dr Ribero said. He finally let go of the glass, and pulled his handkerchief out of his pocket, dabbing his forehead. "Mike, are you having another go with this new machine or not?"

Mike shrugged. "I can give it another try, but I'm not convinced it'll do much. I'll bring along the interrupter though, that might be worth a shot. And the sonar emitter."

"Oh no, not the sonar emitter," Pamela said with a groan. "That thing goes quite through my head."

Dr Ribero nodded. "Good. I'd recommend bringing whatever you can, Mike. Anything is worth a shot. Especially as we're making no progress at the moment, yes?"

"I've got a few ideas how we might get the spirit to communicate," Miss Wellbeloved added. "A few might be a little radical, but I'm not too sure what other options we have."

"Sounds like it might be an interesting night," Mike said with a grin. He leaned back, placing his hands behind his head. "Jennifer, bake an extra cake would you? You know I always get hungry on the night jobs. Just don't stuff the cake with quinoa or chia seeds or any other weird health stuff."

"Well, it all depends if I get time."

"Oh, why not just pack a picnic basket and have done with it?" Serena snapped, exasperated.

"That's not a bad idea, actually."

"Er, do you really think you need me there?" Kester interrupted, growing more reluctant by the minute.

"Yes, we do," Dr Ribero said. He narrowed his eyes at his son. "How will you learn the tricks of the trade if you do not do the job, eh?"

"Well, I'm not actually employed by you, am I?" Kester pointed out.

Ribero considered. "I will get a contract created for you in the morning," he said, pressing his finger on the table and wiggling it around for good measure. "How is that?"

"Just go along with it, dear," Pamela said, rubbing his arm. "You'll soon get used to all the strangeness."

"I don't know, I've been working with you for five years and I'm not used to it yet," Serena said with a sarcastic snort.

"Well," Miss Wellbeloved said, raising her glass of water in mock salute. "Here's to another adventure then. Let's hope it's not too turbulent a night."

Kester looked up at the sky, noticing the first faint cumulous clouds slipping slowly across the vast sea of blue. They were ominous grey, a sign of the storm to come. He hoped it wasn't an omen.

Chapter 10: The Observation

Pamela pulled up outside the house just as the first rain-drops started to fall. The handbrake shrieked, cutting through the quiet. Kester watched with dismay as the rain pebbled against the windscreen, leaving water trails down the dirty glass. He peered out the window at Isabelle Diderot's front door. It appeared even more grim than before—a black, forbidding entrance that had more in common with a gothic castle than a Georgian-style property.

"Do you think the weather's a sign?" he said with a high-pitched giggle, which he hastily smoothed into a cough, hoping Pamela wouldn't notice.

Pamela laughed, pulling the door open. "Oh dear me, no. When you get to my age, you give up on fanciful notions like that. It's just a bit of rain, that's all. It might actually be a blessing, take the temperature down a little bit."

A vague, grumbling sound in the distance indicated that thunder was on its way. Kester frowned, opening the car door reluctantly. *Could the weather make it any more like a horror film?* he thought to himself, eyeing the darkening sky. The clouds glowered overhead, tumbling across the piercing moon.

"Excellent night for ghost hunting, isn't it?"

Mike's strident voice snapped Kester out of his daydream, and he turned, wincing. "I was just thinking the same thing," he said, as the rain began to fall more heavily. He noted the kitbag by Mike's side, bulging with equipment, and gulped. *What the hell has he got in there?*

Dr Ribero, Miss Wellbeloved, and Serena emerged from behind the van. Miss Wellbeloved was clutching a tin, which he presumed contained a cake. He brightened, hoping it was something tasty like chocolate cake, and not something healthy which contained hemp or seeds.

"Right," announced Dr Ribero, shaking the rain off his luxuriant hair and holding aloft a key. "Let us proceed. Mrs Diderot has now vacated the house, so we shall be quite alone."

"Let's do this!" Mike shouted, pumping his hand in mock salute. "If we don't bag us a Green Lady ghost by sunrise, I'll eat my cap."

"We better had," Serena grumbled as they walked to the door. "I had to cancel a hot date tonight."

"Oh, was it with that nice young man again?" Pamela asked, stepping into the house, then shaking herself off like a sheepdog after a bath.

"If you mean Gideon, yes it was."

Kester followed reluctantly. There were no lights on, and the long hallway, complete with its clinical black and white floor tiles, looked eerily like the entrance to a mental asylum. To his disappointment, things didn't improve when Pamela switched on the lamp. The orange bulb cast an insipid glow, casting long shadows across the walls.

"Oh, you're not still seeing Gideon, are you?" Mike sneered. "Honestly, his name alone should speak volumes about what he's like. Over-privileged toff."

Serena folded her arms. "For Christ's sake, Mike. He went to a state school."

"Yeah, that's what he says," Mike retorted, dumping the bag. "But let's face it, no kid called Gideon ever went to a state school ever. Plus, he's an Oxbridge type, isn't he?"

"There's nothing wrong with being Oxbridge!" Kester piped up. Serena gave him a tight smile.

"Mike doesn't like intelligent people," she explained, narrowing her eyes. "He only likes people he can talk to on his own, dim-witted level."

"Nah, I'm just not down with people who wear patent shoes and say 'jolly good' every five minutes."

"He only said that twice when you met him," Serena retorted. "Three times at most."

"More like twenty or thirty times. It was every other bloody sentence. Even the cup of tea I gave him was jolly good, wasn't it?"

Serena growled, stalking off into the darkness of the living room. However, she emerged only a second later, looking worried.

"Pamela, check it out in there," she said in a low voice. "I could pick it up, and I'm not even a psychic."

Pamela nodded, looking around her. "I know; I was picking it up from outside. It's not good, not good at all." She scuttled into the living room, then emerged just as rapidly as Serena had done, shaking her head. "Oh dear," she muttered. "Oh dearie me. Something tells me we're not in for an easy ride tonight."

A loud creak silenced them. Before Kester could detect where the sound was coming from, the living room door slammed shut with inhuman ferocity. He leapt back, pressing himself against the wall, mouth open.

"Who did that?" he squeaked, his heart thumping against his ribs.

"Who do you think?" Serena said.

"But, I didn't realise ghosts could do things like that!" Kester spluttered, looking around. "No one warned me that they did nasty things like slam doors!"

"Ah, come on mate, it could be a lot worse," Mike said, prising him from the wall. "It's just her way of making sure we know she's got a cob on. Typical woman."

The light in the lamp suddenly flickered, blinking haphazardly like an ineffectual lighthouse, before winking out entirely. They were left in darkness. Kester felt like crying. *What have I let myself in for?* he thought, feeling the contents of his stomach slosh around in a very unpleasant manner. *I didn't sign up for this when I agreed to come tonight!*

"Right, I'll get the torches, shall I?" Mike said. Kester could just about see his silhouette, groping around in the bag at his feet. "Though she'd better not mess around with those, that could really put a dampener on things, couldn't it?"

"I'm not too happy at the messages I'm getting here," Pamela hissed, a dislocated voice in the darkness.

"I'm not too happy about them either!" Kester squawked in terror.

"What are you worried about in particular, Pamela?" asked Dr Ribero.

"I think we underestimated this spirit's power," Pamela replied. "I'm picking it up much more strongly now. She wants us to know she means business."

"Yeah, well we mean business too," Serena said. "So this stroppy cow can sod right off. She's already getting on my nerves and the night hasn't even started yet."

"Serena, I would advise you to speak a little bit more carefully," Miss Wellbeloved ordered. "We've already talked about this. You must leave your prejudices about spirits at home, regardless of your past experiences."

Above them, the floorboards knocked and clanked. Then,

Kester heard a whispering noise, a scuttling, breathless sound, like velvet dragged across pebbles. It started from above, then moved closer, creeping slowly down the stairs, over the polished tiles. He felt every hair on his body stand to attention.

"I really don't like this!" he protested, once again trying to compress himself as tightly as possible against the wall. "There's someone else here, I can hear them!"

"Well of course there is," Serena said from the darkness. "It's her, sodding around and trying to get us scared, which in your case, is obviously proving highly effective."

An ice breeze tickled Kester on the ear. He screamed, running blindly in what he hoped was the direction of the door. However, much to his horror, he ended up banging straight into something solid and rather warm, which turned out to be Mike's chest. Mike patted him, before prising him off, like a fisherman prising a limpet off a rock.

"I tell you what," Pamela suggested, "why don't we try and switch on a few more lights. There's only so many lightbulbs this spirit can break, I'm sure." With a reassuringly confident step, Kester heard her pad off into the living room once more, where she not only switched on the ceiling light, but two lamps too, bathing the room in sudden, welcome brightness.

"Does anyone fancy a cup of tea?" Mike asked. "And a bit of cake wouldn't go amiss, Jennifer."

Miss Wellbeloved handed him the cake tin. "You may as well go and put the kettle on," she agreed. "I think we might all need the caffeine."

"In the meantime, I'm going to stay in here for a bit," Pamela called out. "I want to see what I can learn from her."

"Yes, okay, that is a good plan," Dr Ribero said, as though casually discussing the weather, rather than the appropriate course of action for dealing with a deeply malevolent ghost. "You come and let us know how you get on."

"Righty-ho then, leave me to it." Without any further ado,

Pamela closed the door behind her, seemingly unperturbed by the fact that she was shutting herself in a room with a very angry, unpleasant spirit.

Kester followed the others to the kitchen, and was relieved to see that the lights were working there too. Mike had already filled the kettle, which was already making a reassuringly jovial noise as it bubbled.

"Is Pamela safe in there?" he asked, looking down the hallway, half expecting her to come running out of the room at any second. He noticed that his hands were trembling.

"Yes, she will be fine," Dr Ribero said, settling himself at the table. "Remember Kester, this is no big deal for us. This is what we do."

"Though this is a particularly difficult spirit," Miss Wellbeloved said as she pulled a chair across the slate-tiled floor with a screech and sat down. "I can't make her out. Normally, spirits make it fairly clear what they want, but this one is giving us no clues at all."

"Does she actually want anything at all?" Kester asked. "Doesn't she just enjoy haunting people?"

"Absolutely not," Miss Wellbeloved retorted, shooting him a disapproving look. "No spirit just torments people for the sheer fun of it. There's always a reason."

Serena perched on the edge of the table, taking the mug of steaming tea that Mike offered her without even the merest hint of a smile, let alone thanks. She yawned, looking up at the wall clock.

"You always say that," she mumbled. "Kester, you should know that Jennifer is inclined to think the best of the spirit world. In her eyes, they can do no wrong."

Miss Wellbeloved narrowed her eyes. "Don't patronise me, young lady" she warned. "I know it's late and you're tired, but we're not going to get anywhere if we can't work together harmoniously."

"See, there you go again," Serena said before sipping her tea. "It's always this left wing, softie approach with you. I'm not trying to patronise you. I'm just saying that you've got this very idealistic view of spirits."

Miss Wellbeloved folded her arms, leaning across the table. "How many years have I been doing this?" she asked.

Serena shrugged.

"Let me tell you," Miss Wellbeloved went on. "It's been over thirty years now. Longer, in fact, if you count all the times I helped my father when I was a little girl. You seem to forget, Serena, that this agency was my father's too. Not to mention my grandfather's. I grew up playing with spirits. I knew all there was to know about them before I was even eighteen years of age."

"Yes, I know all that," Serena said, in the placating tones of a parent trying to mollify an unruly teenager. "I'm merely saying that—"

"You are merely insulting Jennifer's wealth of experience," Dr Ribero barked.

Serena crossed her arms, pouting. "I wasn't at all. You've taken what I said the wrong way."

"Can we have a bit of cake?" Mike said, ignoring them all completely and eyeing the enormous cake tin in the middle of the table. Miss Wellbeloved nodded, with a baleful glance at Serena, who pretended not to notice.

Suddenly, the bulbs in the mock chandelier over the table began to flicker. Kester, whose heart had nearly settled back into its normal rhythm, felt his chest go tight once more.

"What does that mean?" he asked, looking down the hallway in a panic. "Is the ghost annoyed again?"

"Yes, probably," Dr Ribero said as he watched the ceiling light carefully. "Still, it is to be expected. The Green Lady, as we know, does not like people investigating her."

"God, she's like someone with a permanent case of PMT, isn't she?" Mike said in a muffled voice, spraying crumbs all over the table.

Kester watched with fascinated horror as the chandelier began to slowly sway from side to side, gathering momentum with every pendulous movement.

"She'd better not break that bloody light," Mike said. He took another bite of the cake. "I'll bet that thing's expensive. It's a nice piece of equipment, that is."

Dr Ribero looked at the ceiling and narrowed his eyes. "Aha," he whispered. "I see what she is doing. Very clever. Very clever indeed."

"What do you mean, clever?" Kester yelped. "It just looks very demonic to me."

"I wondered how she was moving things, when she was tied into the painting," Ribero explained, as the light swung more ferociously and clanged against the ceiling with every movement. "Now, I see that she is exerting a powerful energy force. That takes a lot of effort, not to mention skill, yes?"

"I don't know, why are you asking me?" Kester said after moving away from the table. The chandelier looked about ready to fall down at any moment, and he didn't want to be anywhere near it when it did. The crystal droplets looked suspiciously like glass, and, given that there were at least one hundred now swinging with wild abandon above his head, it didn't look like the safest of situations.

He bit back a scream as a bang echoed through the hallway, then realised it was Pamela, who had slammed the living room door behind her.

"It's alright! I'm leaving the room now, you can calm down," she shouted, as she padded into the kitchen. Seeing the others, she shook her head. "Didn't get much out of her, I'm afraid."

Gradually, the light slowed its chaotic swinging, until it ceased movement with a tinkle of glass. Pamela pointed at Mike, then at the kettle. "Come on," she said breathlessly. "I need a cup of tea after that."

"Well, what did you manage to discover?" Dr Ribero asked, as he pulled out a seat for her to sit down. "Did you find out anything at all?"

Pamela slumped down like a sack of flour and massaged her temples. "Oh, it was all very jumbled. I picked up some indistinct words, but I've no idea what they could mean. She was clearly annoyed with me trying to access her thoughts, and once she realised what I was doing, she blocked me with everything she had. Pushed me clear across the room at one point."

"Gosh, that's awful," Kester breathed, wide-eyed.

"All part of the job," Pamela replied. "Anyway, Julio, all I got was a name. Well, a couple of names actually. Ransome. And Constance."

"Could she mean 'ransom' as in holding someone to ransom?" Serena asked, leaning closer. "Ransome isn't really a name, is it?"

"It could be a surname," Miss Wellbeloved said. "However, it doesn't give us much to go on. Whoever Ransome and Constance are, they're certainly not living in this house now."

"I got some other pretty nasty messages too," Pamela continued. She glanced at Kester. "Perhaps you'd rather I didn't say?"

Dr Ribero followed the line of her gaze to the quivering form of his son at the other end of the table, then slapped his fist on the table. "No, Pamela, the boy must learn if he is going to join this agency. Please, carry on." He nodded, as though daring his son to contradict him. Kester wisely remained silent.

"Well, I kept getting real venom from her. The phrase 'I'll hurt you' came up a lot, spat out like she was shouting, right in my head, like a steam train. Not to mention 'I'll cut you up' and 'I'll see you buried.'"

Kester bit his lip. He wished he'd protested when he had the chance. *I'll be thinking of that when I'm next lying in bed trying to get to sleep,* he realised with a sinking heart.

"See, this is exactly what I was talking about," Serena said, standing and pacing around the kitchen like a restless cat. "This is why you need to take a tougher approach! When you go in all softly, softly, you just let them walk all over you."

"Serena, don't start this again," Miss Wellbeloved snapped. "I don't want the entire night to turn into a debate about how best to handle spirits. You haven't got a clue what you're talking about."

"Yes. Instead, we need to focus on how to address the problem practically, right?" Dr Ribero said firmly. "No more silly bickering. I think it would be best if I take Kester in now, see how he gets on, yes?"

"Er, no," Kester spluttered, as he choked on his final mouthful of tea. He shook his head as resolutely as he possibly could without hurting his neck. "No, that doesn't sound like a plan at all. No, thank you."

"It was not a request," Dr Ribero stated, as puff-chested as a circus ringmaster. "It was an order. Come on, up you get. Then after we're done, Mike can see whether his equipment will do any good this time."

"I really don't want to go in there," Kester protested, even as Serena slid behind him and pulled out his chair. "Remember what happened last time? I was no use at all."

"Nice try," Serena whispered into his ear, making him jump. "You're not wriggling out of it. If you want to be one of us, you've got to do the job properly."

"But I never said I wanted to be one of you!"

"I do hope," Dr Ribero interrupted, his eyebrows bouncing up and down in a vaguely threatening manner, "that my only son in the world is not a coward. Kester, are you a coward?"

"Yes! Yes, I very much am!"

"That was not the answer I wanted to hear." Without any further preamble, he grasped his son by the armpit and pulled him out of his seat and into the hallway. "We have a job to do, and you do not need to be frightened, okay?"

"I really must protest," Kester trilled, looking over his shoulder plaintively, hoping one of the others would help him. "I'm not cut out for this type of thing at all, I can tell."

"Ah, go on mate, you'll be fine. Remember, she's just a woman," Mike said, with a grin. "Show her who's boss."

Kester just managed to catch the collective filthy looks fired in Mike's direction by the others, before he was dragged into the living room like a naughty schoolboy being hauled into the headmaster's office. He cowered, scarcely daring to look around him. His heart was pounding wildly, and he half-expected the spectre in the painting to leap out of the canvas at any moment. More than anything else in the world, he wanted to flee from the room, from the house, preferably from the entire city, if possible.

After a minute or so, he opened his eyes. In fact, he hadn't realised that he'd shut them until now. He'd instinctively squeezed them closed and curled in on himself, like a frightened hedgehog. Now he felt a bit silly for doing so, especially as nothing even remotely sinister had actually happened. He looked around, and saw Ribero glaring at him disapprovingly.

"See, nothing to be frightened of," the old man repeated, as he gestured around the room. Indeed, Kester could see that it looked gratifyingly bland. Even the painting seemed fairly mundane, though he didn't dare look directly at it, in case he caused a reaction. "Now please," Ribero continued, "shall we make a start?"

"What do you want us to make a start on?" Kester said anxiously.

Dr Ribero smoothed down his hair, before he settled on the opulent leather sofa. He looked instantly comfortable, like a lord relaxing in his manor, a super-abundance of refined limbs, curling moustache, and hair wax. "We arc going to look at her," he declared and patted the seat beside him.

"Just look at her?" Kester asked warily.

"Just so. Now come, sit down."

Kester twiddled his fingers. "What if I don't want to look at her?"

The doctor cleared his throat. His moustache looked even more authoritative in the artificial light of the room, curled pertly upwards like two attention-seeking caterpillars. "How are you going to help us then?" he enquired in a dangerously soft voice. "Your gift will not be much use if you continue to cower like a toddler afraid of his own shadow, will it?"

"I'd say this situation is a little different," Kester protested.

Ribero shook his head in an elaborate show of disappointment. He shook his hands at the ceiling as though entreating the gods themselves to assist him, and grumbled in Spanish. "I do not know what your mother would think of this," he said finally.

"I think she'd probably be very sympathetic!" he bristled. "After all, it's not as if you're asking me to pick up a spider or something. This is a dangerous ghost you're talking about here!"

"Ah, dangerous, dangerous," Dr Ribero said, waving at the painting as though it was a minor annoyance and nothing more. "This is not dangerous. We have had cases in the past that would make your hair stand on end, my boy. I remember the first time Jennifer's father took me on an observation, now that was something to be scared about . . ."

Suddenly, an icy wind gusted around Kester's ears. He froze, rooted with terror. Instinctively, his gaze travelled to the painting, then immediately he wished it hadn't. The painting had changed. It was as though the lady herself had come to life. Although she hadn't moved, her eyes burned out of the canvas, connecting with his own and pinning him in place, like a moth on a mounted board.

It was horrible—deadly horrible—though he couldn't say exactly why. He felt mouse-sized under her malevolent gaze. Yet, at the same time, her beauty was overwhelming, all-encompassing, angelic. It was too much to bear. He tried to shout

out, but the only sound that emerged from his throat was a half-strangled gurgle, like a baby choking on milk. Dr Ribero sat up straighter, his expression alive with excitement.

"Ah yes, now she is paying attention to us," he said as he slapped his thigh. "My dear spirit," he boomed, addressing the portrait as naturally as a real person, "thank you for joining us. Would you mind if we sat with you for a little while, yes?"

The answer was a horrible, rasping whisper that oozed all around them, seeping from the walls and through the air. Kester remained fixated upon the Green Lady, unable to tear his eyes away. She was beautiful, achingly beautiful, yet there was a mercilessness that chilled him. He began to think he might die here, pinioned in place by those terrible, irresistible eyes. *What a way to die,* he thought, half-transfixed, half-terrified. *To be killed by such gorgeousness.*

"Kester, are you seeing anything at all?" the doctor asked from behind him. "Can you see the door? Kester, look away from her for a moment. Look around her, look outside the painting. Is the door there?"

"I can't look," Kester whispered, tears streaming down his cheeks. "She has me. I can't look away."

Dr Ribero muttered something in Spanish under his breath. "Kester," he said in a louder voice. "I need you to look at me. Come now. Take your eyes off her, please."

Kester opened his mouth to reply, but nothing emerged. His lungs felt frozen, his throat narrowing, becoming more useless by the second. Although he was more scared than he'd ever been in his life, he also felt a strange sense of calm begin to wash over him, a sweeping tide of indifference that numbed his senses. *It's alright,* he thought serenely. *Everything will be fine.*

"Kester!" Dr Ribero shouted. Kester felt hands pulling at his face, mashing his cheeks, but he was unable to move. His head was fixed in place by an unseen vice, regardless of how hard the doctor tried to move him.

Dr Ribero cursed again, before pacing to the door. "Mike! Jennifer!" he shouted, though Kester was only dimly aware of the noise. The air felt as though it was thinning around him, making it difficult to breathe. Things were fuzzing at the edges, going greyer, and his ears began to ring, a torturous, high-pitched sound that squeezed out all rational thought.

A pair of arms seized him firmly about the middle, and he was yanked backwards. Again, he could just about make out the sound of someone shouting his name. As he was dragged out of the room, he closed his eyes, a desperate weight pressed against his chest. *I've lost her,* he thought as the living room door closed behind him. *They've taken me from her.*

A cacophony of voices buzzed around him as he slumped against the wall.

"Jeez, what happened?"

"I do not know! One minute he was fine, the next, he was crying and I couldn't move him, you see?"

"I did wonder whether it was a good idea bringing him tonight, Julio. For some reason, I think that spirit has selected him as a focus. That's not good. He has no experience with these things."

Kester allowed himself to be carried back to the kitchen, where he was lowered onto the nearest chair.

"What the hell happened to him? Don't tell me he had another silly little wobble."

"Serena, not now."

Kester suddenly felt a rush of cold air enter his lungs, piercing him back into consciousness. He wheezed, rearing backwards as though an electric current had passed through his spine.

"Ah!" he cried out, then promptly vomited his half-digested tea and cake on to the table.

Serena screamed, hastily side-stepping the drips of bile as they plopped off the tabletop. Even Mike looked lost for words as he surveyed the foul-smelling mix, his mouth a perfect circle of surprise.

"Oh my goodness," Pamela exclaimed, finally breaking the silence. She leapt up and reached for the kitchen towel. "Kester, what happened to you, my dear?"

"She . . . she had me; she wouldn't let me go," he rattled, feeling his lip start to tremble. "She pinned me with those eyes, oh they're terrible . . ."

"See, I told you he wasn't cut out for this," Serena said. However, when Kester looked up, he could see concern in her eyes, concealed behind her sneer.

Pamela started to mop up the mess, while Kester stared at the ceiling and struggled to understand what had happened. His stomach rolled, bringing a fresh wave of nausea.

"Why is she going for me?" he asked weakly, wiping his mouth with the back of his sleeve. "Why not Mike? Or someone else?"

As though in answer to his question, the lights above them flickered once more, and the chandelier began to swing.

"Oh, for goodness' sake, love, can't you just piss off?" Serena shouted. She glowered at the rest of them, shrugging. "I can't help it; this spirit is getting right on my nerves. Just let me go in there and try and drag her out. I'll bet I can manage."

"Serena, you absolutely cannot manage," Miss Wellbeloved snapped, eyeing the ceiling apprehensively. The lights dimmed, before sputtering out completely. Kester sobbed; he felt as though his mind was about to explode with the horror of it all. *This is the worst night of my life,* he thought as he struggled to stop himself from screaming. *This is like a nightmare, and it just won't stop.*

"I do not think we are getting anywhere tonight, are we?" Dr Ribero said reluctantly, a dislocated voice in the darkness. "I feel perhaps we should go home, review our strategy tomorrow, yes?"

"I certainly think we need to get Kester home," Pamela

agreed, placing an arm around his shoulders. "I think this spirit is locking on to him for some reason, and he hasn't got the skills to protect himself."

"I didn't want to come anyway," Kester said with a low moan, pressing his face into his hands. "I never want to do this again. Please, please let me go." Things seemed even worse than before, now that everything was dark, and felt eternally grateful for the solid presence of Pamela's arm.

Dr Ribero sighed, a protracted exhalation that pierced through the black. "Mike, you and I will stay here, see if we can have one last attempt at getting her out."

"I'll stay too," Miss Wellbeloved said. "I've got a few ideas that might work."

"Pamela, you get Kester back to your place, get him to bed. He has had a rough time of it. Serena, you go too. Call up your fancy man, see if you can get your hot date."

"Why do I have to go?" Serena flared. "I haven't had a go yet!"

"You are too angry, too aggressive," Ribero retorted. "You will only make things worse. Go. Have the evening off. I will still pay you overtime, don't worry."

"I don't care about that," she snapped back. "It's more the fact you're trying to get rid of me that's upsetting me."

"Serena, let it go," Miss Wellbeloved advised.

"It's always you guys, ganging up against me," she retorted. Kester could hear the click of her stilettoes, pacing across the kitchen tiles. "It's not fair."

"We will talk tomorrow," Dr Ribero said, in a voice that indicated that the conversation was closed. "For now, off you go. Go on."

"You're unbelievable," Serena muttered. Without another word, she stalked angrily towards the hallway. Kester could just about make out her silhouette, flouncing towards the front door.

Pamela eased Kester out of his seat, leading him, meekly as a lamb, down the hallway and out into the fresh air. It was raining, but this time, he welcomed the moisture on his face. It revived him, and he instantly felt more human.

"That was the worst experience I've ever had," he said as he staggered down the steps and towards the car. "How can you all do this for a job? I think the stress would kill me."

Pamela unlocked the car with a chuckle. "You'd be surprised," she answered. "Sometimes, even the most awful things aren't really that bad once you get familiar with them. Give it time, love."

Kester didn't reply, but silently vowed one thing. Whatever the consequences, he was never joining in a ghost hunt ever again.

CHAPTER 11: RESEARCH

Telling his father that he didn't want to join in any more supernatural activities was actually far harder than he had thought it would be.

Last night, lying in bed, watching occasional passing headlights trace beams across the ceiling, he had been adamant. Never again would he put himself through such a torturous experience. Dealing with the supernatural was obviously not his speciality, regardless of who his parents may be. His nerves simply couldn't cope with the pressure.

At around two in the morning, when sleep continued to elude him, he had started to plan out how to break the news to his father. Around fifteen minutes later, he had decided that the doctor would not be angry. After all, Kester had effectively managed to ruin the entire investigation, albeit accidentally, so Ribero would probably be relieved to hear that he no longer wanted to take part. By 2:45 a.m., he had come to the conclusion that the doctor would be positively delighted at the news, and, with the matter settled firmly in his mind, finally drifted off to sleep.

However, sitting in Ribero's office the following morning, trying not to breathe the nicotine-filled air too deeply, he realised he'd misjudged the old man's reaction. Ribero's face fell, much like a puppet whose strings had abruptly loosened, and he slumped in his armchair. The cigarette, forgotten in the ashtray, smouldered like a carbonised stick insect.

"Why not?" he asked eventually, meeting Kester's gaze. "Can you tell me that?"

Kester shifted on the swivel chair. "I'm not cut out for it," he said, deciding to be as frank as possible. "I think last night proved it, didn't it?"

"How?"

He was taken aback by the question. "Well," he began slowly, "I made a mess of things, didn't I?"

"You made a mess of the kitchen table, that is true," the doctor said. "I think that smell may linger for quite some time, even though we used quite a lot of disinfectant. But you did not make a mess of the observation. These things happen from time to time."

"Well, I don't think it's the career for me," Kester persisted. "I was terrified last night. I couldn't cope with that stress on a regular basis. It was awful."

The doctor exhaled and scratched his chin. The alarm clock ticked quietly. For a while it was the only noise in the room: a tiny, ominous sentinel to the growing awkwardness, which swelled like an over-stretched vacuum cleaner bag.

"What, you are planning to run away again, is that it?" Dr Ribero barked, looking up. "Is that how you normally deal with problems? Run away and hope they don't follow you, yes?"

"No," Kester said defensively. "Anyway, I never said I wanted to run away. I just don't want to see any more ghosts."

Dr Ribero clucked like a nettled bantam hen. "But this is a

supernatural agency! What else are you supposed to do? That's like working in a restaurant and saying you never want to smell food, no?"

"I haven't actually signed a contract," Kester muttered, "so technically, I don't work here yet anyway, do I?" His father's thunderous expression made him wish he'd kept his mouth shut. *This isn't going well,* he thought. He held his hands up placatingly, trying to avoid any confrontation. "Isn't there anything else I could do?" he suggested. "Admin work? I'm good at sorting through paperwork."

"Admin? Admin?" Dr Ribero's face grew more purple by the moment. "No son of mine will do a woman's admin work!"

"This is the twenty-first century," Kester pointed out. "Men do admin jobs too, you know."

Ribero shook his head, struggling to maintain composure. "No, that will not work. That will not do at all."

The entire office was still musing over the problem come lunchtime, which was a quiet affair, as each member of the team tucked into sandwiches behind their computer screens. Kester started to wish he'd never brought it up. There was a distinct air of disappointment in their dealings with him; a sense that they'd expected better, and that he'd let them down. Feeling rather guilty, not to mention a huge failure, he huddled in the corner of the room, trying to make himself as unnoticeable as possible.

It was Pamela who suddenly came up with the solution at just past three, right after Dr Ribero's nap had ended.

"Research!" she exclaimed suddenly, whirling a finger in the air like a mini tornado. The others peered over their computer monitors, and looked at her as though she'd gone temporarily mad.

"What on earth are you wittering on about?" Serena asked, resting her chin on her hand. "What the hell is 'research' meant to mean?"

"That's what Kester can do!" Pamela said excitedly.

"Research! He's an academic, it'll come naturally to him!"

Serena rolled her eyes at the others. "Research what, exactly? The theory of relativity? Holidays in Spain? How not to throw up on someone's kitchen table? What's he meant to be actually researching?"

"Well, he could start delving into the history of this bloody Green Lady painting, for starters," Pamela continued. "That might come in useful."

"I really don't see how," Serena said. "Does anyone else?"

Kester sat up straighter. "I do like research," he said. "And I am very good at it. When I was at university, I got the highest marks in my year for my dissertation. My lecturer said I was like a dog with a bone."

"More like a lemming with a cliff," Serena muttered.

"Well, there you go then!" Pamela said. "Jennifer, what do you think?"

Kester waited anxiously to see what Miss Wellbeloved would say. He felt oddly excited. Research was something he felt comfortable with. Research was something he could do. In fact, he loved it. Nothing filled him with more enjoyment than rifling through old books and hunting out secrets. *I could bury myself in the nearest library and never meet another spirit ever again!* he thought, with deep satisfaction.

"Do you know," Miss Wellbeloved said slowly, scratching her head. "I think that's quite a good idea."

"That's great!" Kester exclaimed.

At that moment, Dr Ribero swept out of his office, resplendent as a lion visiting his pride. "What is great?" he demanded, hands on hips. "What has been decided in my absence, eh? What are you all plotting out here?"

"Kester. Research job," Miss Wellbeloved explained. "He's good at research apparently. He can start investigating this painting, see what he can find out." She looked at the doctor, then shrugged. "It can't hurt to try, can it?"

Dr Ribero twirled his moustache as he pondered. "It might work," he admitted. "This is a strange case. Perhaps delving into the history of that Green Lady portrait might assist us, that is true." He scrutinised Kester's face, then pointed a finger in his direction. "But we cannot pay you much, okay? This is a very basic job, so you earn basic wages, yes?"

"Suits me," Kester said. He didn't really care much about what he earned. Apart from books, he never spent much anyway.

"You can carry on living at mine for free anyway," Pamela said kindly. "If you just give me a little amount towards food and bills each week, that would be more than enough."

"That's brilliant!" Kester smiled. "Can I do that then? Can I start researching the case?"

The others looked at each other, then at Ribero.

"Ah yes, why not," Ribero said, a hint of a smile playing under his moustache. "If that is what you are good at, then let us see how you get on. And if you don't find anything, perhaps you can start again as a proper member of the team." He caught Miss Wellbeloved's eye and added, "I mean, someone who goes on observations and deals with spirits. You know what I mean."

Kester knew exactly what he had really meant, but he wasn't too bothered. *I'll show him,* he thought, with sudden energy. *I'll prove that I'm not just a useless lump.*

"When can I get started then?" he asked.

"No time like the now," Dr Ribero said, looking at his watch.

"No time like the present," Miss Wellbeloved automatically corrected. "The library is still open, and it is only five minutes from here. You just walk down Gandy Street, turn the corner and you're there."

Kester scooped up his satchel and rose to his feet. "Leave it with me!" he declared, a beaming smile on his face. Mike chuckled and saluted him, and Pamela and Miss Wellbeloved smiled. Even Serena managed to offer the ghost of a forced grin.

"You go find something good, okay?" Dr Ribero said, with a big thumbs up.

Kester nodded. *Oh, I certainly will,* he thought with sudden determination. *If mum managed to be a success in this bonkers agency, I'm going to make sure I am too. Just in a totally different way.*

"Kester," Miss Wellbeloved called out as she scurried to catch up with him. "Might I have a quick word? I'll walk over to the library with you, I could do with some fresh air."

"Yes, of course," Kester held the door open for her. *I wonder what she wants to chat about?*

Miss Wellbeloved waited until they were outside to begin speaking. "I wanted to ask you how you were finding everything," she said, as she started to cross the car park. "How has it been for you?"

"Um, fine, I suppose," he said. He wasn't quite sure which part she was referring to: the supernatural side of things or his relationship with Ribero.

She coughed, looking concerned. "It must be difficult for you. Finding out that you have a father."

Kester followed her along the alleyway and nearly tripped over a sleeping cat as he passed. "I suppose so," he said, then paused. "I suppose it's been difficult for you too though, hasn't it?"

There, now it's been said aloud, he thought, studying Miss Wellbeloved's expression. The older woman grimaced, then nodded.

"I wasn't sure whether you knew or not," she whispered, aware of a pair of students walking in the opposite direction. Kester waited until they'd passed before continuing.

"I found some letters, back at my old house. From Dr Ribero to my mum. They said that you and my dad were going to be married."

Miss Wellbeloved took a deep breath, patting at her

chignon. "Yes, that's right. But that was a very long time ago." They stepped out on to the main high street, and she picked up her pace. "Gosh, it must have been over thirty years ago. It's terrifying how fast life slips away from you."

"It must have been horrible at the time."

"Yes. Yes, it was."

Kester didn't know what else to say. He felt sorry for the older woman, who had shown him nothing but kindness, in spite of his dubious origins. *My mother stole her husband-to-be,* he realised, *and there's not even a hint of resentment towards me. How does she manage it?*

"Do you mind me asking something?" He caught up with her, keeping pace with her long strides.

"Of course not. Fire away."

"Why did your father give the agency to Dr Ribero? I could understand it if you and he were married, but—"

Her mouth twitched, and she looked up at the sky, as though seeking inspiration. "Everyone thought we were going to get married," she started. "The venue was booked, I'd bought my dress, I think we'd done the table plans. That's why my father signed the agency over. He believed that the wedding would go ahead."

"And when it didn't?"

Miss Wellbeloved's jaw tightened. "Regrettably, my father was very ill at that time. He died shortly after it all happened. So he never changed the name on the business deeds. It automatically became Julio's."

"But that's awful!" Kester stopped in his tracks, open-mouthed. "That means my father basically stole your family business!"

Miss Wellbeloved chuckled, tugging him out of the path of a woman steering a pushchair. "It wasn't like that at all, don't worry. Julio was . . . very apologetic. He wanted me to have the business back. But my father was rather old-fashioned. He didn't think women were capable of running companies. So I respected his wishes and let Julio keep it."

Kester shook his head. "Wow," he breathed. "You are far more forgiving than I would have been in those circumstances."

"Oh, make no mistake," she said, her eyes hardening. "I found it very hard to forgive. Remember, your mother was one of my best friends. We'd all met at university; Gretchen and I had shared a room. She knew how much I loved Julio."

He swallowed. "I'm so sorry. I feel so awful about it all."

She leaned against him and squeezed his arm. "Don't be silly. It's not your fault at all. Believe it or not, I don't really blame your mother either. Or Julio. Love does strange things to us all."

"I wouldn't know about that," he laughed. "Girls tend to take one look at me and retch."

"I very much doubt that." Miss Wellbeloved stopped across the road from a steep concrete ramp. "Here we are. Time to get researching, Kester."

His eyes followed the line of the ramp to the building above. As indicated, the library was a huge, ugly concrete and glass construction, which Kester thought looked a little bit like a building made of children's blocks.

"It's not a natural beauty, is it?"

"Ah, never judge a book, or library, by its cover, Kester." Miss Wellbeloved smiled. "Enjoy your research."

Kester said goodbye before he climbed up the steep ramp to the automatic glass doors at the top. He wasn't expecting much, judging by the exterior. However, to his surprise, the inside was an oasis of calm, pristine white and filled with his favourite thing in the world—books. He felt the tension of the previous night ooze out of his system like resin from a tree and basked in the serenity of the surroundings.

After enquiring where the local history books were, he made his way up the polished spiral stairs, into a smaller room, lined with shelves of earnest-looking academic texts. Desks ran down the centre of the floor, each filled with a person studiously peering at a computer screen or scribbling away in a notepad. Kester sighed with pleasure. This was his sort of place. He belonged in these types of buildings. In fact, he loved nothing more than breathing in the scent of old literature, thumbing through delicate pages, eyeing rows of antique book-spines and leather-bound covers.

He sat at the nearest available computer, and started to search online. *Coleton Crescent. That's a good enough place to start.* He scanned web page after web page, varying his search every ten minutes or so. "Portraits of ladies in green dresses." "Local painters." "Hauntings in Exeter." Before he knew it, an hour had passed, and the crowds of people around him had started to thin.

"10 Coleton Crescent." "Hauntings at 10 Coleton Crescent." "Exeter ghosts in Coleton Crescent." "Female ghosts in Exeter." It was starting to become frustrating. No matter how many pages he trawled through, he couldn't find anything remotely relating to the case, though he did read through some fascinating tales of hauntings in other parts of the city. It made him wonder how many of them were actually true. *Perhaps all of them,* he thought with a smile. *Perhaps every ghost story ever told is true, and people just don't know it. Now there's an alarming idea.*

Suddenly, he had a thought. It struck him with the internal force of a battering ram, and he sat back with a low whistle. "What were those names Pamela mentioned last night, after she'd been in the room with the Green Lady?" he whispered to himself. The girl sitting beside him, a waif with a riot of green dreadlocks and a lip piercing, gave him a wary glance. He tapped his finger against the keyboard, fighting to remember.

Handsome? Why is the word "handsome" coming to my mind? he thought with frustration. The name had definitely been something like that. In fact, he vaguely remembered the others saying what a strange name it was. He sighed, leaning back and staring at the ceiling for inspiration. For a while none came. Then the name came to him like a thunder bolt.

"Ransome!" he chorused triumphantly, smacking the table. The girl beside him frowned, edging her chair away. He didn't care. He'd remembered it: *Ransome*. Ransome and someone else, but he couldn't remember the other name at all.

"Ransome, 10 Coleton Crescent," he typed into Google. Leaning forward, he scanned the results. "Exeter property prices on Coleton Crescent." "Exeter memories—Coleton Crescent." "Coleton Crescent on Streetmap." Nothing of any real interest. He scanned the second page of results, then the third. Still nothing. Kester felt his excitement begin to dwindle, like smoke escaping from a window.

However, an entry on the fourth page caught his attention, "Robert Ransome, An Exeter History."

"Aha, what's this?" he whispered. He double-clicked, praying it wouldn't be another dead end.

The website looked depressingly dated, with spindly fonts, ancient graphics, and poor layout. Indeed, it looked as though someone had created it a couple of decades ago, then promptly forgotten all about it. Kester felt his heart sink, but ploughed on regardless, speed-reading through the content. It seemed to be a long list of past residents of Coleton Crescent, dating back to the early 1800s. Unfortunately, it wasn't in alphabetical order.

Finally, he found the name he'd been looking for. Robert Ransome. *Bingo!* he thought with glee. He felt like standing up and punching the air like a goal-scoring footballer. Ransome's address was listed as 10 Coleton Crescent. *This could be our man,* he realised. *It must be. It's too much of a coincidence for it not to be.* The listing was spartan, refusing to give away too much, merely outlining his address, full name, and date of death: 12th of March, 1861.

So, thought Kester, cracking his knuckles and staring at the screen. *The question is—how was he related to the Green Lady?*

He recorded the name of the website on his phone, before going back to Google and trying another search: "Robert Ransome, 10 Coleton Crescent." As he had anticipated, the first few entries were not related, and the website he'd just been reading was also listed.

Come on, come on, he silently willed. *Give me something fresh, something that I can work with.*

At the bottom of the page, he found another website that looked vaguely interesting. He clicked through, finding details of an out-of-print book, called *Devon Painters of the Victorian Period.* Kester felt his heart begin to pound, and he readied himself to take more notes. *A painter!* he thought with excitement. *Is Ransome the painter of the portrait?*

After jotting down the book's details, he searched for it online, praying that someone, somewhere would have a copy. To his surprise, there were a few copies around, mostly in America for some reason, though a couple were in Italy. Rather depressingly, they all cost at least £200 or more. *Dr Ribero's not going to like that,* he thought, feeling himself return to earth with a bump. *There's no way his budget will extend to buying a book, when it might not even contain the right information.* He puffed out his cheeks, leaning back in the chair once more.

Gazing round the room for inspiration, his eyes rested on a hunched old woman, diligently feeding books on to the shelf from a mobile trolley. She shuffled along the shelves with the care and effort of a straining tortoise, squinting at each book before rustling it back into position. Seemingly aware of his stare, she turned, catching his eye. Kester smiled, a polite expression that diminished as the old woman ambled over to his computer.

"Are you alright there, dear?"

Kester blushed, wishing he'd never turned around. The old woman leaned close to his shoulder, peering at the screen. The muffled odour of peppermint and lavender seeped from her in a pungent cloud, making his eyes water, and he noted that her teeth were disturbingly brown, long and blunt as gravestones. She wore a name tag, which announced that her name was Doris, on her lilac cardigan.

"Oh, I'm fine, thank you," he said hastily, feeling somehow embarrassed. "Sorry, I didn't mean to call you over." The green dreadlocked girl sniggered, before burying her head even deeper in the enormous book in front of her.

"Ah, *Devon Painters of the Victorian Period.* That's an interesting book," Doris commented, poking at the screen.

"Yes, I suppose it probably is," Kester replied. "Please, do feel free to continue what you were doing, I don't want to disturb you."

"No, I mean it is an interesting book," Doris persisted. "It really is."

"I'm quite sure you're right," he said, fighting to remove his impatience from his voice. His mother had always taught him to be respectful of older people, no matter how deaf, loud, or generally mad they might appear to be.

She cackled, slapping his back. "You're not understanding me," she said. "I mean it is an interesting book."

Oh dear lord, Kester thought, rolling his eyes. *I really could do without this at the moment.* The girl next to him let out a snort, then turned it into a cough.

"I can't say whether it's interesting or not, because I haven't read it," he replied.

"I'm sure you haven't, dearie. But I have. That's what I'm trying to say. It's a really interesting read. If you like Victorian art."

Kester gawped at her. "You mean, you have the book?" *Surely not,* he thought, examining the woman in more detail. No, he decided. He couldn't possibly trust her judgement. She looked distinctly short of a few marbles, and couldn't be a day under eighty. How she was still managing to work was a miracle in itself.

The lady chuckled, pointing at the shelf. "The library has it. Not me personally. I just work here, love. Anyway, I'll leave you in peace."

"No, no! Don't go away!" Kester said, pushing his chair out. "Do you really have the book?"

"Yes, I know we have, because I only read it myself about a year ago. Or was it two years? It could have been three, actually. Time does go very fast these days, and it's ever so difficult to keep track of things, it really is."

"Where is it?" Kester interrupted.

"Where's what?" Doris asked, raising her glasses a little higher on to her nose.

"The book!"

The old lady laughed, a hoarse, rasping noise that swiftly descended into a fit of inarticulate coughing. "My, my," she said finally, when she'd hit herself several times on the chest and got her breath back. "You are keen, aren't you?"

"Yes," Kester confirmed. "Yes, I am. I thought this book would be impossible to get hold of. If you actually have it in this library, I'd love to borrow it."

"Oh, you wouldn't be able to get it out, it's a reference only, my love."

Kester sighed. "That's fine," he said. "As long as I can look at it, that's the important thing. Please, would you show me where to find it?"

"Probably in the art section," the green dreadlocked girl offered sarcastically, waggling her stubby pencil towards the back of the room.

"I was about to say that," Doris interrupted. "It'll be in local art, dear."

Kester gave both of them a grateful smile, before striding down the room. He felt invigorated, filled with momentum, and triumphant at his success so far. *See,* he thought, side-stepping out of the way of a man walking in the opposite direction. *This is what I do. You can keep the ghost hunting. Research is my thing.*

He ran his fingers along the book spines, bumping a path along plastic-wrapped books and hardback monstrosities, which only just fitted on the shelf. Soon, he found what he was looking for, nestled close to the end, next to another book on artists of the region.

Unable to stop himself from grinning, he tugged it free, cradling it in his arm. It was smaller than he had imagined, more innocuous. *Perhaps it will yield nothing at all,* he thought, frowning. *But on the other hand, perhaps it'll help solve this mystery.*

He rifled to the index. There it was: *Ransome, Robert. Page 182.* His heart quickened as he skimmed back through the brittle pages. Expecting to see the portrait of the Green Lady herself, he was mildly disappointed to see only three of Ransome's paintings printed in the book, and all were rather tedious landscapes. He began to read.

Robert Ransome, born 15*th* April, 1819 in Exeter, was perhaps best known for his landscape compositions of the local area. In particular, Ransome focused on the scenic tors of Dartmoor, and the woodlands close to his native Exeter. Ransome received an education in the Classical Arts and, almost immediately, began to make a successful career of his work.

His most celebrated work, *Haytor by Twilight*, was exhibited in the Devon County Museum in 1845, shortly after his return from Italy. Ransome had resided by Lake Garda for four years, before returning to Exeter to marry his childhood sweetheart, Miss Constance Pettifer. Regrettably, Ransome's life was cut prematurely short in 1861, by an unidentified illness.

Constance! Kester thought with triumph, slamming the

book shut. *That was the other name that Pamela mentioned the other night at the house! Ransome and Constance!* He now felt convinced that Robert Ransome was their man. Could the portrait of the Green Lady be the ghost of Constance, mourning her husband? There had to be a connection.

He looked at his watch. It was close to five in the evening, and he knew Pamela would be heading home soon. However, he felt that he'd found out a lot of information in a short space of time. He couldn't wait to relay it to the others.

Chapter 12: Coming to the Rescue

The following day, he and Pamela arrived at the office early in a state of excitement. After he'd left the library the previous evening, he'd outlined his findings to Pamela whilst driving home, who had shown so much enthusiasm she'd nearly driven the car off the road. He'd been up most of the night, planning out how to tell the others, and he was greatly looking forward to seeing their faces, especially Serena's. *That'll show her,* he thought with a gleeful rub of the hands as they bounded breathlessly up the stairs. *Time to prove I can do something right, after all.*

However, as he entered the office, the expression on Miss Wellbeloved's face stopped him in his tracks. Her bony features, normally severe and carefully composed, looked somehow out of shape, and there was a puffiness to her eyes that suggested she might even have been crying. Kester stared gormlessly open-mouthed, the wind blown entirely out of his sails.

"Is everything alright?" he said, blinking in confusion.

"Nope, it's definitely not alright," Serena barked. She was

slumped over her keyboard, her head propped in her hands like a wilted flower. "We've had some really bad news."

Pamela stepped forward, ushering Kester to one side. "Not the Bournemouth case?" she asked. Miss Wellbeloved nodded.

"That bastard Higgins got it," Mike piped up from the corner.

"No!" Pamela squeaked. "You're joking me? Larry Higgins got it instead?"

Mike shook his head, flicking a balled up piece of scrap-paper on to the floor. "I kid you not," he said. "Julio's been ranting and raving about it since he got in, and now he's stormed off into his office."

"It's really bad news for the agency," Miss Wellbeloved said. "We needed this contract. Badly."

"I just can't believe that pompous git got it over us!" Mike said, thumping his fist on the desk. "Higgins doesn't know his arse from his elbow! He's a bloody accountant, for god's sake!"

"He's an ex-accountant, to be fair," Miss Wellbeloved said. "And he's always worked within the supernatural field."

"Yeah, doing the financial side of things, which makes him an accountant," Pamela clarified.

"A fat moron, with zero expert knowledge of the supernat-ural, that's what he is," Mike thundered. "He's blagging it, that's what he's doing. He'll totally mess this project up, and then the government will have to think twice about hiring him."

"Yeah, we may only have basic equipment, but at least we know what the hell we're doing," Serena added.

"I very much doubt he'll mess the project up," Miss Wellbe-loved said, sitting down. "Larry Higgins and his team are doing very well at the moment, as you all know."

"Why is it such bad news?" Kester asked, edging forward. "Aren't there other contracts?"

Mike leaned back in his chair, folding his hands behind his head. "We worked on the bid for this one for ages. We thought we were going to get it, to be honest. It's in our area, after all. It's a great project—a poltergeist in a Bournemouth arcade. Causing right panic, it is. Would have been a lovely, easy one to do. But that git has got it instead."

"Despite the fact he's up in Essex and shouldn't be bidding for work down here anyway," Serena concluded.

"That's what they're all like though, in the southeast, isn't it?" Mike said ominously. "Greedy, money-seeking bastards. It's all about the cash, nothing about the expertise. Honestly, if I had Higgins in front of me now, I'd bloody—"

"Mike, that's enough," Miss Wellbeloved snapped. "You wouldn't do anything to Larry Higgins, because he's perfectly within his rights to bid on the project. He won it, fair and square. Aiming your anger at him isn't going to change the situation."

"I don't understand," Kester said, following Pamela to her desk. "You bid on jobs then? How does it work?"

Pamela sat down, gesturing at Kester to perch on the edge of her desk. "All supernatural incidences are recorded on the government website."

Kester laughed. "Hang on a minute," he said, "that can't be right. Anyone can look at the government website."

"It's an Swww.co.uk address!" Serena shouted from the other side of the room. "Don't you remember anything?"

"It's a special website address," Pamela clarified. "It can only be accessed by approved people; namely people like us."

"So they post jobs on their site, and you bid on them, is that right?" Kester was bewildered. It all sounded very mundane and business-like, which was rather at odds with his preconceived notions of the supernatural.

"Basically, yes. They'll have regional jobs, national jobs; that type of thing."

Ribero's office door swung open with a bang and startled them all. Dr Ribero stood, framed by the doorway, shaking his hands to the ceiling, as though personally offended by the wooden beams and plaster.

"Ah, it could not be worse!" he announced. "This is surely our ruin! How can we keep running like this, eh? We are only winning small contracts. We need the big jobs, otherwise we will go under, yes?"

"Yes, but the problem is that we have the reputation for being a small-time agency," Serena emphasised. "If we could build our reputation, as I've said a thousand times before, we would be able to get the better contracts, no problem. After all, it's not like we don't have the talent."

"Yes, but how can we build our reputation, when we cannot even handle very simple jobs?" Ribero growled back. "Look at how we've performed recently! Even that Japanese spirit was more tricky than we thought, right? And as for this Green Lady painting, ah, don't even get me started! A simple case, we thought, yes? But now, we are no closer to finding the solution, and we're wasting valuable time!"

"Not to mention money," Mike added.

Kester stuck his hand up, then remembered he wasn't in a classroom and put it down again. "I found something out," he said. "Something that might help us."

Ribero's head jerked round, as though magnetised in his direction. "Seriously?" he asked incredulously. "But I thought you were just going to read at the library, I didn't think you'd actually do anything useful."

"Thank you very much!" Kester squeaked indignantly. "Actually, I'll have you know that I did a lot of research, and I think I'm on to something."

"Something that's actually going to be of genuine use, or something completely irrelevant that we might just find interesting for five minutes before forgetting about it entirely?" Serena enquired, raising an eyebrow to emphasise her scepticism.

"Something useful!" Kester retorted. *Well, I hope they think it's useful,* he added silently. *Now that I'm wilting under Serena's scornful gaze again, I'm not so sure.*

"Yes, it absolutely is," Pamela confirmed before nudging him forward. Kester told them everything he'd found out the previous day. He hoped they'd be as impressed as he wanted them to be.

"Well now," Ribero said, scratching his chin. "That is very interesting. So it seems you've solved a little mystery about our enigmatic Ransome and Constance. Well done."

"I wonder why our Green Lady was so fixated upon them?" Miss Wellbeloved mused, leaning on her elbows. "Obviously those two people were important to her. If Ransome is a painter, as you suggest, then he may be the one responsible for creating the painting in the first place."

"That's what I thought!" Kester said. "I wondered if Constance died, and was angry with Ransome, then took revenge by entwining herself in the painting."

Serena laughed. "Spirits aren't dead people, idiot. They come from an entirely different world."

Miss Wellbeloved shot a warning look in her direction. "It's a common misconception," she said. "Humans are an entirely different matter, and they're not the same as spirits at all."

"So it's not Constance doing the haunting then?" Kester felt disappointed. He was sure he'd been on to something.

"No, definitely not," Miss Wellbeloved said, frowning up at the ceiling. "It's difficult to conclude anything with the limited information we've got. But it's a good start, a surprisingly good start."

Kester beamed. He couldn't help himself. He was delighted at the prospect of being regarded as something other than a useless creature who kept puking and passing out. Pamela gave him a wink before switching her computer on.

"Yes," Serena persisted, "but how is that information actually useful?" She waved her hands in the air, anticipating the protests before the others had a chance to open their mouths. "Look, it's impressive that Kester found that out, but still, I don't see how it helps us. So we know that the guy's name was Robert Ransome and that Constance was his wife. That still doesn't tell us how they relate to this cow-bag of a spirit, does it?"

"Give me time, and I might be able to find out more," Kester said.

Dr Ribero leaned on the doorframe with a sigh, like a gallant hero in a silent movie. "Time is the thing we do not have," he said softly, looking around the room. "We are in trouble. Big trouble. If we do not get a successful case under our belt soon, we may as well close our doors, right?"

"That's probably true," Miss Wellbeloved agreed reluctantly. "And that cannot happen. This company was set up by my great-grandfather. My grandfather made it flourish and my father turned it into one of the finest agencies in the south. We cannot let it go under." She flushed, bringing unusual colour to her thin cheeks, and her eyes blazed. "I won't let it," she concluded.

"How much time do I have?" Kester asked.

"A week?" Dr Ribero suggested. "Less, if you possibly can?"

"Blimey," Kester said, puffing out his cheeks. He took off his glasses and polished them on his shirt. "Well, I'll do my best. After all, that's all any of us can do, right?"

Miss Wellbeloved suddenly smiled. It changed her appearance entirely, bringing a glimmer of beauty to her stern features, like a ray of sunlight through a cloud. "You sounded just like your father when you said that," she said with surprising fondness.

To his surprise, the comment made Kester feel oddly proud.

"Tell you what, you have my computer," Pamela said, unfolding herself from her chair and gesturing to the unoccupied space. "I can easily busy myself in the storeroom, there's a few reports I need to write up, plus I need to phone Infinite

Enterprises to arrange our next inspection."

"Oh Christ, I'd forgotten about that," Mike groaned, clapping his forehead. "Last time was a disaster."

"Well, just make sure your equipment doesn't blow up when you switch it on," Pamela replied, bustling across the office. "If you can manage that, I'm sure we'll pass inspection this time. Anyway," she said, turning confidingly back to Kester. "You do your thing. Internet's a bit slow, but it should do the job."

"Okay, I'll do my best," Kester promised. "Leave it with me."

After only a few minutes, he swiftly realised that Pamela hadn't been exaggerating about the internet. It trudged through pages with the speed of an arthritic mole digging through particularly hard soil, which was rather frustrating.

To begin with, Kester focused his searches on Robert Ransome, then Constance Ransome, though neither brought up anything of particular interest. He tried to find out more about the history of 10 Coleton Crescent, though again, he failed to find anything that would help them. Eleven o'clock came and went, and he felt his frustration begin to rise. *Come on,* he thought. *There must be more information out there somewhere, it's just a matter of locating it!*

After a while, he reached for his phone, bringing up the brief notes he'd made the previous day. He tried a search based on Ransome's date of death, but couldn't find anything new. *Obviously, this artist wasn't particularly well known,* he concluded, *otherwise there would be much more on him.*

His finger hovered over the notes, lingering on one in particular. "Italy, Lake Garda, four years, back 1845." The book had suggested that Ransome had lived there, before returning to get married to his childhood sweetheart, Constance.

I wonder what he was up to in Italy, he pondered, rapping the keyboard rhythmically with his pen.

He typed in "Robert Ransome, Lake Garda, 1841." The first entry on the list made him lean backwards in his chair, omitting a low whistle of surprise. "By Jove," he muttered. "That looks like something interesting."

"What have you found, mate?" Mike asked, peering round the side of his computer. He was only just visible amidst the usual pile of messy electronic equipment. *"Something good?"*

"I'm not sure yet," Kester said, clicking through to the link. "I'll let you know in a minute." *Or make that five minutes,* he thought in exasperation, as the website struggled to load.

Finally, the page appeared, a website dominated by stark black, complete with pale, ghostly fonts and spectral images floating around the perimeter.

"Fantasmi del Lago di Garda," he read out loud. *Fantasmi. That sounds suspiciously like Phantom.* Quickly, he hit the translate key in the corner.

"What's that?" Mike asked, standing to get a better look.

"Hauntings of Lake Garda," Kester said. He hit his fist on the desk in excitement. "Hauntings of Lake Garda! I don't believe it!"

The others looked at him blankly.

"Well, as long as it's exciting to you, that's the main thing," Mike said as he returned to his seat. "Because I'll tell you now, that doesn't mean a thing to me. Is that a lake in the Peak District or something?"

"No, you ignoramus, it's in Italy," Serena snorted. "Why is that relevant, Kester? What has Italy got to do with anything?"

"It relates to Robert Ransome. Let me dig around a bit more, I'll update you properly in a minute." He scanned the page swiftly, too excited to pause his investigations. It was a vast, unwieldy webpage with a wall of text, so he had to scroll through the content. The web page featured a series of ghost stories from the region, each complete with its own small image and brief blurb, which, when clicked on with the mouse, took him through to the tale in full.

Towards the end of the huge document, he finally found

what he was looking for. The title of the story was "The Haunted Studio," which mentioned Ransome directly in the introductory paragraph. *Yes!* he thought, clicking through, and sighing with frustration as the page took its usual five minutes to load up.

"Listen to this!" he announced, waving for attention. "This is it! This is what I've been looking for!"

The others gathered round. Even Ribero emerged from his office, still smoking the remainder of a cigarette. They formed a silent semicircle around the desk, gazing at the screen.

"The haunted artist's studio at Gardone Riviera was a tale that fuelled fear among the locals and is still told to this day," Kester began to read, feeling his heart stir with a thrill. "Even now, investigators of the paranormal claim to feel energy in the building, and some say that the cries of a woman can still be heard, late in the night, when the moon shines over the neighbouring lake waters."

"Oh, I really do hate people who call themselves paranormal investigators," Serena said, clicking her tongue in exasperation. "They're always complete charlatans."

"It's a bit of a waffling story, isn't it?" Mike said, with a hint of incredulousness.

"Remember it's been translated from Italian," Kester said. "Sometimes the translation isn't terribly smooth. Shall I carry on?"

"Yes!" everyone cried in unison.

He coughed, pausing for dramatic effect, before continuing. "The small property, situated on the grounds of the Palazzo Grassi, was once the home of the groundsman and his family. In 1841, an English painter, Robert Ransome, took up residence, using the building as both a place to live and a painter's studio. Local accounts claim that Ransome was a handsome young man, only in his early twenties, who swiftly charmed the people living close by, not to mention their daughters. He was fluent in the language and was initially very welcoming, allowing people to see his work. Ransome had patrons in the area who commissioned him to paint large landscapes. However, one day, everything changed, and Ransome painted landscapes no more.

"Ransome started work on a portrait, a portrait he referred to only as 'my lady'. He claimed that he was inspired by a great muse, a beautiful creature who visited him nightly, helping him create his finest work. However, when pressed, he refused to show the painting to anyone. Locals said he became obsessed with the image, hiding it in the attic of the building, where it could not be seen. People walking by the property began to report strange noises, a whispering sound that floated down to the lake waters. Some said they saw blue lights glowing in the windows, quite unlike the lights of an oil lamp or candle. Soon, people began to believe the artist's studio was haunted."

"My word, are you all thinking what I'm thinking?" Pamela said excitedly.

"That portrait sounds rather like it might be our Green Lady, doesn't it?" Miss Wellbeloved added, squeezing Kester's shoulder in an uncharacteristic show of emotion. "Goodness me, I never would have thought it would have come all the way from Italy. This is quite remarkable, well done for finding it."

"Let him carry on, will you?" Mike said, squinting at the screen. "Go on, you were doing a good job of telling it."

Kester smiled. "Okay, I'll get on with it," he said, taking a deep breath.

"Soon, people began to believe the artist's studio was haunted," he repeated. "Ransome himself, who had been so popular in the community, was seldom seen. Instead, he was only briefly glimpsed, peering behind the shutters of his windows, or pacing silently in the gardens at midnight. Those who did see him described him as a changed man—wild-haired, wild-eyed, and muttering strange incantations. They believed him to be possessed. The baker, delivering bread one day, heard him calling out a woman's name—Mary. He cried, 'I dare look

in the mirror no more, I see her there . . . Mary! She is there.'
After a year or so, Ransome moved away, leaving the house in a
state of terrible disrepair. On inspection, the owners found that
mice and rats had taken over the building, red paint covered the
walls like blood, and that there were scratch marks across the
walls and doors. Every mirror in the property had been smashed.

"Nobody knows what happened to Robert Ransome during
his time at the house on the grounds of Palazzo Grassi. However,
there are enough strange events associated with the building to
believe that he was haunted by a terrible spirit, who still haunts
the house to this day."

He finished with a flourish, and they all stared at the screen
in silence.

"Well," Pamela said, in awe. "That was a bit of a ripping
yarn, wasn't it?"

"So I think we have a much better understanding of our
painter, don't we?" Dr Ribero said, stroking his moustache. "And
a few clues about our spirit too, it would seem."

"Yes, I think it might be worth using her name, if indeed
the story has it right," Miss Wellbeloved said. "Knowing a spirit's
name is a powerful thing and can assist with negotiations. If I
refer to her as Mary, it may well help."

"*If* the story is right," Serena raised a sceptical eyebrow.
"Don't get me wrong, it's impressive detective work, Kester. But
most of it could be made up, for all we know."

Kester nodded. "It could be," he acknowledged, scrolling
through the page to check there were no more details. "As a
researcher, it's always important to mistrust your source, unless
you know it to be 100% reliable. But it's certainly interesting,
isn't it?"

"Interesting, but not much else to go on," Serena said. "I
guess when we go back there this afternoon, we can try using the
names Mary and Ransome, see what her reaction is. But that still
doesn't tell us how to get her out of that sodding painting, does

it?"

Kester puffed out his cheeks, leaning heavily against the comforting coolness of the leather chair. "There's something about that story that's bugging me," he said, rubbing his eyes. "I don't know what though. I'll need to have a think."

"I know what you mean," Pamela said. "It's a bit like there's more to it, I've just not noticed it yet."

"Yes, exactly!" Kester agreed. He spun round on the chair to face the others. "What time are you going back to the house?"

"After lunch," Dr Ribero declared, looking at his watch. "It is inconvenient, as I will have to miss my siesta, but we need to get moving with this project as soon as possible. If we do not generate results soon, the government will start questioning our ability to do the job."

Kester looked up. "Who exactly in the government oversees your line of work?" He couldn't imagine the Prime Minister calling Dr Ribero, asking why he hadn't fulfilled his quota of supernatural investigations for the month.

"Bernard Nutcombe," Ribero replied.

"Don't you mean *Lord* Bernard Nutcombe?" Mike added. "Let's not forget his title, eh?"

"His name rings a bell," Kester muttered. "Don't know why though."

"He's MP for Scunthorpe, and was involved in a bit of a scandal with public spending a few years back," Mike said. "He looks like a melted candle with a black loo brush glued on top."

Serena laughed. "That's a pretty good description, actually."

"He's MP for Scunthorpe, and also Minister for the Supernatural," Dr Ribero concluded. "Though obviously, he keeps his official title quiet, yes?"

"So what does he actually do then?" Kester asked. "How does it all work?" It was all fascinating to him, an entire ministry that he had no knowledge of until today.

"Well, his team basically monitors all supernatural activity,"

Miss Wellbeloved explained patiently. "It's often the police who are first called out if something supernatural happens. They contact the government, who get the supernatural agencies to sort out the problem."

"So the police know about the supernatural too?"

"Of course," Serena said, "it's part of their basic training."

"How the heck do you all keep it a secret, with that many people knowing?" Kester couldn't get his head round it.

"It may seem like a lot of people," Miss Wellbeloved explained, resting against the window ledge. "But actually, it's not that many at all. For every person who knows about the spirit world, there's about ten thousand who don't."

"And if someone does start opening their mouths and talking about the supernatural, no one believes them," Mike concluded.

"It's all very odd," Kester said, stretching with a yawn. "The whole idea that there's all these supernatural things, happening all over the country, and most people are completely unaware. It's weird."

"It's important people remain unaware!" Serena said earnestly. "Imagine what chaos there would be if people realised they were sharing their planet with spirits from another world?"

"Yes, I suppose it would be mad," Kester said, eyeing his satchel with desire. His stomach had started to rumble, and his thoughts wandered to the cheese and pickle sandwich nestled inside his bag.

"Not if the situation was handled correctly, and people learned to live with spirits," Miss Wellbeloved tutted. "Like they used to in the old days."

"The problem is spirits and technology," Mike said. "Ghosts and tech don't mix."

"What do you mean?" Kester asked.

"They bugger the electrics up," Mike explained. "They mess around with the lights. They distort mobile phone signals. And when they slip inside a WiFi signal by mistake—carnage. All the computers in the near vicinity crash. It's an absolute bloody nuisance, I can tell you."

"It's true, the modern world and the world of spirits is a problematic mix," Miss Wellbeloved acknowledged with a rueful smile. She glanced up at the clock on the wall. "When do you think we need to head over? Now?"

"Yeah, but let's eat lunch on the way," Mike agreed. "I don't want to spend too much time there. I need to get back to work looking at that sonar machine again. It's still emitting completely the wrong pitch."

"Will you be joining us today?" Dr Ribero asked Kester. "It might be a little better in the daytime, yes? Not so scary."

Kester frowned. "I don't think it's a good idea," he said. "For some reason, she seems to pick on me. I don't know why. But I don't think I help much when I'm there."

"You need to keep trying until you get used to it," Dr Ribero argued with narrowed eyes. "Do you not imagine that we were all scared when we went on our first jobs?"

"Yeah, I actually broke my ankle the first time I went out on an observation," Mike said. "I was so busy sprinting out the front door, I forgot about the steps, and ended up falling down them all."

"Wish I'd been there to see that," Serena said, smirking. "Bet you looked a right prat."

"Yes, but the point Kester is trying to make," Miss Wellbeloved interrupted, "is that this spirit latches on to him. If he's inexperienced, he simply hasn't got the skills to deal with it. I'm not sure I'd have the skills to deal with it either, to be honest."

"Okay, okay," Ribero said crossly, his hands up in defeat. "But we will get you back on the job soon. In the meantime, you keep looking for things on the internet. You have done a good job so far."

Kester sighed. "Thanks. If only I could work out what's

bothering me about that Lake Garda ghost story, I'd be a lot happier."

He left with the others, but instead of clambering into the van, he strolled along the street towards the cathedral. There was a nice green space directly outside, and it was the perfect place to not only eat his sandwich, but muse about the things he'd discovered.

Firstly, he called his estate agent back in Cambridge, only to find that the one viewing on the house hadn't been a positive one. The house had been too old-fashioned, apparently. Kester bristled a bit at the comment. He liked his house the way it was, outdated décor and all.

Then, he settled down by a tree, unwrapping his lunch with anticipation. Pamela had cut the bread as thickly as possible, creating an almighty brick of a sandwich that only just fitted into his mouth, which was exactly the way he liked it. He began to eat, idly scrolling through the notes on his phone as he did so.

When he reviewed everything he'd discovered so far, there wasn't much to go on. As far as he could see, the artist had been born in 1819, had travelled to Italy when he was twenty-two, stayed there for four years, where he presumably painted the haunted picture, then returned to get married. Judging by his date of death, he hadn't experienced any major problems on his return to England, and had lived there perfectly happily for several years.

Hmm, he thought, tapping his phone. *There's a lot of questions that haven't been answered. What did Ransome do when he got back to the UK? We know he got married, but what about his wife? Was it a happy marriage? We know he still had the painting, as it was found in the attic of 10 Coleton Crescent by our diary-writing Emmeline. Did the painting continue to haunt him? Why? Why would it want to? And, who is this Mary person anyway?*

There were so many mysteries, and frustratingly limited ways of uncovering the truth. The name Mary was an intriguing discovery, but also an irritating one. He was fairly sure that in the early 1800s, it must have been one of the most common names around, which made researching it fairly pointless.

There was also something about the Lake Garda story that unsettled him, firing some distant alarm in his brain, which he couldn't quite access. Opening the internet browser on his phone, he visited the Italian haunting site again, clicking through to Ransome's tale. However, after reading it through twice again, he felt none the wiser, though if anything, the unsettling sense that he was missing something had grown.

What are you trying to tell me? he wondered, shutting the browser down with a sigh. He stuffed the last piece of sandwich into his mouth, still pondering. *There's a message here, and for some reason, I'm missing it.*

He sat in the sun for a while, enjoying the laid-back atmosphere. Students laughed and chatted on the lawns, and toddlers scurried away from their mothers. It was an idyllic scene. On a day like this, it was almost impossible to believe that the supernatural existed—that just across town, a vicious spirit haunted someone's home.

Should I bother going back to the office? he wondered, plucking at a clump of daisies beside him. There didn't seem much point. The internet was painfully slow, and the room unnervingly silent without the others there. Not to mention the fact that there were all manner of spirits locked away in the storeroom, and he didn't much fancy the prospect of being there alone with them.

He decided to return to the library instead, to see if he could uncover anything else interesting there. *Not that I have any idea where to start looking.* It was unlikely that there would be any further art books on Robert Ransome, and trying to track down a spirit called Mary seemed completely hopeless. *Still,* he thought, trundling down an alleyway and looking longingly into a pub window at people eating huge, steaming jacket potatoes, *at least the library internet is a bit quicker.*

Pausing to purchase a Cornish pasty from a local bakery, he continued on his way, making the most of the sunny day before arriving at the library. He wolfed down the last remaining piece of pasty, then felt a bit ashamed. It probably had been a bit excessive. But he always needed food when he was thinking hard. His brain simply couldn't function unless his stomach was completely full.

The electric doors of the library slid open with a hiss, permitting him entry into the cool haven inside. He lingered for a moment by the café counter in the entrance hall, then swiftly marched past. *You don't need a chocolate bar,* he told himself sternly. *Maybe have it as a reward, if you find out anything good.*

Climbing up the stairs, he arrived at the room where the academic and local texts were situated. It was less crowded than yesterday. Kester moved to the furthest end of the bookshelves, intending to browse through the entire row until he had found something useful.

However, an hour later, he had reached the end, and hadn't found a single book to help him. He pursed his lips in frustration. *Normally books don't let me down,* he thought, glancing over to the other side of the room. *There must be more information here somewhere.*

An hour after that, he'd browsed the shelves on the other side, and still found absolutely nothing. *What a waste of an afternoon,* he thought, looking at the sunbeams filtering through the blinds. *There were probably at least a hundred better things I could have been doing with my time than sifting through useless books.*

As a last-ditch attempt, he walked over to the information desk, where a young lady was busy piling books onto a trolley. She saw him and stood up quickly, smoothing down her skirt.

"Can I help?" she asked, in a heavily accented voice. Judging by her blonde hair, height, and generally rather attractive appearance, he presumed she must be from northern Europe, possibly

Sweden or Denmark. Her nametag announced that she was called Anya. He blushed.

"Oh, I'm looking for something," he began, shuffling his feet. "And to be honest, I don't have a clue where to start."

Anya giggled, tucking a loose strand of hair behind her ear. He noticed she was wearing a rock band t-shirt; some group that he was vaguely aware of. *Oh no, she's way cooler than I am, despite working in a library,* he thought, his anxiety increasing by the second.

"Why don't you tell me what it is you are looking for, and we can go from there?" she suggested, with a sympathetic look that was rather similar to how someone might view a particularly dopey puppy. "What's the name of the book?"

"Well, that's just it," he said. "I don't know the name of the book. I don't even know if there is a book. I'm trying to find something out about a local artist called Robert Ransome."

"Do you want me to try searching on our system?" she asked, gesturing at the computer on her desk, which looked as though it hasn't been replaced for at least twenty years.

"You could try, but I'm not sure it will bring anything up," Kester said. "I've already been through all the shelves. I just wondered if the name would mean anything to you."

Anya wrinkled her nose, then shook her head. "No, I am sorry," she said. "I've never heard of that artist before. Is he famous?"

"Not really," Kester said, feeling glum. "An old lady pointed me in the direction of one useful book the other day; I think her name was Doris or something? Is she in today?"

Anya giggled again, covering her mouth. "Doris, she doesn't really work here. Well, she used to, you see. But then she retired. And she didn't like being retired, so she volunteers to work here instead. It is funny, isn't it?"

Kester agreed that it was quite funny, trying not to melt as the librarian gave him a beaming smile. He suddenly panicked that he might still have Cornish pasty stuck in his teeth from earlier, and pulled his lips tightly shut again. *Oh great, now I don't dare open my mouth again,* he thought, feeling even more idiotic than before.

"I am very sorry I cannot help you," said Anya. She sounded as though she really meant it. Kester smiled, remembered, then clamped his mouth shut again.

"That's okay," he said, running his tongue over his teeth as surreptitiously as he could. "It was very nice to meet you." He glanced down at the books she was stacking into the trolley. "Ah," he said, pointing at the top one, which happened to be *The Diary of a Nobody*. "That's a bit of a classic, that one is. I've always rather related to that."

The librarian laughed again. She held up the next one in the pile, which had a sensational front cover of a demon, covered in blood, rather unimaginatively called *The Monster in the Mirror*. "As long as you don't relate to this one, right?" she said with a wink.

"Quite!" Kester agreed jovially as he walked away. "Though in the mornings, I probably relate to that one too, if I'm honest. I'm an absolute fright until at least midday." As the librarian laughed again, he felt rather pleased with himself. *I just had a conversation with a girl!* he realised with almost euphoric disbelief, giving her a little wave as he left. *And she didn't look repulsed at the sight of me either!*

He went outside, resisting the urge to skip. His day had suddenly got a lot better, even though he hadn't really achieved much. He reached the concrete ramp then suddenly stopped. His mouth dropped open, and he clutched the railing for support.

"That's it!" he exclaimed, oblivious to the strange looks of the people around him. "I've got it!"

An elderly couple eyed him with alarm, side-stepping to avoid coming within a ten metre radius of his person. He could tell they thought he was completely mad, but he didn't care.

"The Monster in the Mirror," he muttered, grinning. "Mirrors! That's the connection!"

CHAPTER 13: MIRRORS . . . AND MARY

Kester hared back to the office with more speed than he'd probably managed in the last ten years. When he reached the back door, he was red in the face, sweating profusely, and feeling as though his ribcage might pop open at any moment with the exertion of it all. However, he hardly noticed his physical discomfort. Instead, he bounded up the stairs, and ploughed through the darkness of the landing without a second thought.

Thankfully, the others had left the door unlocked, and he walked straight into the soothing airiness of the office, striding over to the storeroom. Under normal circumstances, it wouldn't have been his ideal choice of location, but in this instance, the occasion called for it. He turned the key in the door, which Pamela had carelessly left in the lock, and stepped into the blackness beyond.

Trying not to look too hard at the three water bottles sitting on the shelf, with their shifty, cloudy contents, he went over to the table in the corner, which was covered in books, paperwork, and various cardboard boxes, containing all manner of junk and strange items.

"Yes!" he whispered with delight, spotting what he was looking for: Emmeline's diary. Fortunately, Pamela had tossed it casually on top of one of the boxes, making it easy to find. He scooped it up, rubbing the worn leather cover speculatively with his fingers.

Taking it out to the main office so he could read it properly, he carefully locked the storeroom behind him, then pulled open the book. Flicking through with trembling hands, he located what he was looking for, in the entry dated the 20th April, 1892.

Here we go, he thought, re-reading Emmeline's words. "Even Margery agrees with me," he read out loud, following the spidery words with his finger. "She told me that the Green Lady has started to haunt her dreams; she now sleeps with the candle burning. She said that she had nightmares of the lady reaching out of the very canvas itself, grasping out with skeletal hands, trying to pull her in. She says she can no longer look at mirrors . . ."

He skipped forward a couple of pages, to an entry written on the first of June. Soon, he found another reference, a further indication that his instinct had been right.

"It is a house under a curse, I believe that most strongly. It is haunted. I have smashed the mirror in my room. At least that will stop her watching me while I am asleep."

"The mirrors," Kester breathed, looking around the room in wild-eyed wonder. "It's something to do with the mirrors!"

He paced over to Pamela's computer and wiggled the mouse until the screen lurched to life. Slamming the diary onto the desk, he typed in the URL of the Lake Garda site, drumming his fingers in irritation as he waited.

Finally, the page loaded, and he whizzed down until he had found Ransome's story again. And there it was, translated on the screen. The connection that he'd been looking for. The thing that had been niggling him, from the moment he had found the site in the morning. He read aloud.

"The baker, delivering bread one day, heard him calling out a woman's name—Mary. He cried, 'I dare look in the mirror no more, I see her there . . . Mary! She is there.'"

"He saw her in the mirror," Kester concluded, stunned into silence. Scrolling down, he looked at the final description of the house, after Ransome had left. "Red paint covered the walls like blood. Scratch marks across the walls and doors. Every mirror in the property had been smashed."

Every mirror smashed, Kester thought, his head reeling with excitement. *Ransome saw her in the mirror. He then smashed the mirrors. Emmeline, fifty years later, sees her in the mirror. Then she smashes the mirror. There's our connection.* He pulled out the chair and sat down heavily. His brain was speeding like a racing car, threatening to spin off the track at any moment, and he knew that he desperately needed to organise his thoughts. "It's history repeating itself," he muttered. "But why?"

Rubbing his eyes, he opened up Google, and without much hope, typed in "Ransome mirrors." Unsurprisingly, nothing came up, just a long list of unrelated websites. Tutting anxiously, he typed in "Coleton Crescent mirrors," then "Coleton Crescent haunted mirror." Again, nothing. He wasn't surprised.

What else can I try? he wondered, looking up at the ceiling as though desperately seeking inspiration there. *Or is it pointless? After all, trying to search for anything related to mirrors is a huge topic, it's unlikely that I'll be able to find anything.*

He typed in "Mary mirrors" and leaned back, flinging his hand off the mouse in frustration. It was a last-ditch attempt, but he couldn't bear to admit that he'd hit another dead-end, especially after discovering such a significant connection.

"What on earth?" he muttered, reading what appeared on the screen with widening eyes. He leaned closer, squinting at the results, then started to laugh. "I don't believe it," he said, grabbing the mouse again. "I just don't believe it!"

The page was filled with results about ghosts. Or, to be more precise, one ghost in particular. Bloody Mary.

He clicked through to the first site, which happened to be Wikipedia. "'Bloody Mary (folklore)'," he read aloud, scanning quickly through the content. "A folklore legend . . . ghost, phantom, or spirit . . . appear in a mirror when her name is called three times."

That doesn't sound quite right, he thought, scratching his head. *Why would Ransome or Emmeline have tried to summon her by calling her name?* He quickly moved to another site, hoping to find one with more specific information on the matter. However, this one was clearly an urban legend, narrating the gory tale of a young girl who had been discovered with her throat slit, after having said the name "Bloody Mary" three times in the mirror.

A further site linked Bloody Mary with Queen Mary I, claiming the ghost caused miscarriage, as the queen herself had suffered so many miscarriages of her own. *And of course, Emmeline lost her baby,* he thought, stroking his chin. *And she blamed it on the Green Lady. Could that be another connection, or just a red herring?* However, the beauty of the lady in the portrait didn't match too well with the portraits Kester had seen of Queen Mary in the past, who, in most instances, looked rather pug-nosed and plump. Not to mention the fact that Miss Wellbeloved had told him earlier that spirits weren't dead humans.

He browsed another site, claiming that the ghost of Bloody Mary latched on to men, whilst deliberately hurting women. Indeed, there were a number of tales featuring the repeating motif of the ghost emerging from the mirror to hurt the woman standing the other side. In some instances, this was only a scratch on the face. On other occasions, the stories narrated her dragging women down the corridor by their hair, gouging their eyes out, or pouring blood over them.

"She sounds like an absolute charmer," he said aloud, with a rueful smile. He was now even more relieved that he hadn't gone to Coleton Crescent with the others.

A muffled thump startled him, until he realised it was the door downstairs, which was closely followed by footsteps echoing steadily closer. He looked at his watch, noting with surprise that it was just past three-thirty. *Well past Ribero's nap time,* he thought with mild amusement, watching the door. A few moments later, it swung open, slapping against the wall with a bang.

Serena stormed in, her face as livid as a thundercloud. She threw her handbag on the desk, before throwing herself down into her chair.

Miss Wellbeloved scuttled in after her, sharp and angular as a metal ruler. "Serena, can you please calm down! This is not helping anything!"

Kester watched with bemusement as the others followed. He gave Pamela a questioning look and she shook her head, a mute warning not to ask.

"Well, that was a complete bloody waste of time," Mike grumbled, piling the equipment bag into the corner of the room. He folded his arms, glowering in Serena's direction. "I've seriously had it up to here with you. If you keep ruining jobs like this, then I'll—"

"What will you do?" Serena spat, circling on her chair. She glared back at him, spearing him with her pixie-green eyes. "Go on, I'm listening."

"It doesn't matter," Mike rumbled, lumbering towards his desk. "Just drop it."

"No, I won't drop it! You've just accused me of ruining the job, so have the balls to back up your comments!"

"Oh, don't even get me started," Mike shouted. "You don't want to get me going on this one, believe me!"

"Oh yeah? What exactly do you want to say, Mike? Spit it out!"

"I think you damned well know."

"Do I? Do I really?"

"Will you be quiet!" Miss Wellbeloved shrieked. Her voice pierced the room like a skewer, and everyone fell silent, shocked into speechlessness. To their even greater surprise, Miss Wellbeloved walked to her desk, sat down, then buried her head in her hands and began to sob.

Immediately, Dr Ribero was at her side, wrapping an arm around her heaving shoulders. He glared at Serena and Mike, who looked abashed.

"Just sit down and get on with some work!" he hissed. "You've caused enough problems for one day, the pair of you!"

He prised Miss Wellbeloved from her chair, guiding her into his office as carefully as a tiger leading its cub. With one last furious glance over his shoulder, he slammed the door behind him, leaving the rest of them in shocked silence.

"That was your fault," Mike growled, pointing a finger at Serena.

"Like hell it was," she snarled back.

"Pack it in, the pair of you," Pamela said warningly. "You both need to learn when enough is enough."

"What happened?" Kester asked, still recovering from the shock of seeing the normally composed Miss Wellbeloved reduced to tears.

"Ask her," Mike said sullenly, jacking a thumb in Serena's general direction. She scowled, burying herself deeper into her chair.

Pamela ignored them, perching on the desk next to Kester. "Well," she began, carefully choosing her words, "things didn't go quite according to plan, put it like that."

"You can say that again," Mike added. "It was a total shambles. We're screwed on this case. Absolutely screwed. We'll have to give it to Higgins or someone else. There's nothing else for it."

"Why are you screwed?" Kester asked. "What was the

problem today?"

"Do you want to tell him?" Mike snapped at Serena. She shook her head sulkily, her jaw tightening.

"Serena decided to try to do things her way today," Mike continued. "Despite the fact that Ribero and Jennifer both said not to do it, she carried on regardless, because of course, Serena knows better than everyone else, doesn't she?"

"Mike, calm down," Pamela warned. "It's not helping."

"I don't care if it's not helping!" Mike shouted. "I'm hopping mad about it, and I don't mind who knows it! Serena only bloody tried to damage the picture. She went completely mad, started screaming at it and trying to slash it with her finger-nails, then the spirit started hurling things round the room. It's smashed a lamp, and I bet it was an expensive one. That'll come out of our payment, mark my words."

"I thought it was worth a shot!" Serena mumbled, folding her arms. "No one else was trying anything new. They were just wasting their time with useless words. At least I tried to take action!"

"You made the situation a bloody fiasco, because you couldn't control your temper, that's what you did."

"And what did you do?" Serena said, standing up and pointing furiously in Mike's direction. "What was your contribution today? Oh yes, that's right, you brought another of your knackered machines to the house." She clapped her hands in mock applause. "Oh well done Mike, what an achievement. No wonder Infinite Enterprises didn't want you."

"Serena, please, can you stop shouting!" Pamela pleaded. "Calm down, both of you!"

Mike swore at Serena, then stomped into the storeroom. Serena stared in his direction for a moment, lip wobbling, before bursting into violent tears. Before Kester could react, she spun on her heels and tore out of the door.

Pamela sighed, massaging her head with her hands.

"I don't know what's happened to this agency," she whispered, looking as though she was about to cry too. "It's all gone downhill, and I don't think any of us know how to make it better."

Instinctively, Kester reached over and patted her on the leg, which felt oddly soft to the touch, like a creamy Victoria sponge. "For what it's worth," he said, "I think you all do an amazing job. Whenever I see you all working, I'm just in awe. I couldn't do what you do in a million years."

Pamela peered up at him, then broke into a beam, lighting her pudgy face like a beacon. "Oh Kester," she exclaimed, "I think that's the nicest thing anyone's ever said to me. Bless you."

"That's okay," Kester replied. He looked at the door, which still seemed to be vibrating from the force of Serena's departure. "I wish there was something I can do to help." Suddenly, he glanced back at the computer screen, remembering. "Actually, there is! There is something!"

Pamela followed his gaze to the monitor, eyeing the websites with confusion. "What on earth have you been looking at while we've been out?" she asked, raising a quizzical eyebrow. "Demonic ghosts in mirrors? That doesn't sound like very pleasant reading."

"No, it's all relevant!" Kester stuttered, getting to his feet. "I've found out something, something really important. It might help."

Pamela gave a small smile. "I'm not sure how, love," she said. "Unless you've found a way to get that spirit out of the painting and into one of our water bottles. We've got serious problems."

Kester rubbed his nose, staring at the computer screen.

"Maybe I have found a way of getting her out," he said, mulling over the beginnings of an idea in his head. Even as the words tumbled out of his mouth, he doubted himself. However, there was a seed of something there, hatching slowly into a plan, and he wondered if it might just work.

"Kester, dear," Pamela said, as kindly as she could, "we know you want to help, but really, I think it's impossible. We've tried everything, and we feel like we've hit a dead end. I think we'll have to pass the case to someone else."

"But I really do believe I'm on to something here," Kester persisted. "I know I'm no expert, but it might be of use . . ."

Pamela patted him, before hefting herself to her feet like an aged elephant. "Save it for later, perhaps? I think I need a good strong cup of tea right now. How about you? The usual three sugars?"

"Make it two, I'm trying to cut down," said Kester, remembering the Cornish pasty. "Well, two and a half, perhaps."

"Right you are, love," Pamela said, before waddling to the storeroom to put the kettle on. Mike was still in there, messing around with some equipment probably, but whatever he was doing, he was keeping quiet about it. In fact, the whole office was disturbingly silent, as though someone had entered, sucked all the atmosphere out, then departed again.

Kester sighed, looking again at the information on the screen. Although a lot of it was sensationalist and didn't relate specifically to the case, there was something in the myth that made him suspect he might be on to something. *If only I could piece it together,* he thought with frustration. *There's something here that might be of use, but I don't know how to grasp it.* He shut down the webpage, his brain whirring at a maddening pace, clicking through ideas and theories like a machine on hyperdrive.

A loud creak diverted his attention, and he looked up to see Miss Wellbeloved emerging from Dr Ribero's office, her thin face even longer than usual. Ribero came out directly after, a hand still draped over her shoulder.

"Miss Wellbeloved is going home to have a rest," he announced, as though addressing everyone, even though Kester was the only one in view. "Go on, Jennifer, you take the rest of the day off. I will figure something out, don't you worry. Okay?"

Miss Wellbeloved nodded, a worn-out gesture of reddened eyes and blotchy cheeks. She attempted a smile as she passed Kester, who gave her a sympathetic smile in return. In spite of his initial opinion of her as a cold, austere woman, he'd grown surprisingly fond of her in the short time he'd been here. There was something about her that reminded him of his own mother at times, a certain vulnerability and gentleness that only showed itself on rare occasions.

Dr Ribero watched her leave, leaning against the door frame with an expression that was hard to interpret. He accepted Pamela's offered cup of tea without a word, and gulped it down, as though hoping to find something alcoholic hidden at the bottom.

"Bit of a mess, isn't it?" Pamela said, cupping her own mug for comfort.

"Yes, it most certainly is," Ribero agreed, studying the floor, then kicking at it, scuffing his polished shoe against the floorboards. "It is more than a mess, it's a disaster. Where is Serena? And Mike?"

"Mike's right here," Mike answered, lumbering out of the storeroom. "Serena's flounced off in a huff."

"Serena and Mike had a fight," Pamela explained. "And Mike was a bit unkind, weren't you, Mike?"

Mike shifted his weight from foot to foot, picking up a piece of wiring from his desk and wrapping it round his fingers. "I was perhaps a little hard," he admitted. "But she really made a cock up of things in there. It made me so cross. This case is hard enough as it is, without her behaving like that. It was like watching a toddler lose their temper."

"Yes, but Mike, she is enthusiastic," Dr Ribero said, finishing his tea with a slurp. "I was once the same. Remember, she is still young."

"She's only two years younger than me!" Mike said.

"Really? Are you only two years older?" Dr Ribero asked. "That is most surprising, I had thought you were already over forty."

"Bloody cheek!" Mike huffed. "I'm thirty-six!"

Dr Ribero grinned weakly. "It is this silly bushy beard of yours," he said, reaching over and giving it a tug. "It is very ageing. You need a nice little moustache like mine, you see?"

"Yeah, if I want to look like Salvador Dali," Mike muttered, folding his arms.

"Better than looking like a big, hairy yeti, yes?"

"It's my style, alright?" Mike protested. "I like the yeti look. And I don't think it's ageing at all."

Kester cleared his throat. "Dr Ribero?" he said. *I'm going to have to get used to calling him Dad sooner or later,* he realised. However, it still felt far too odd to refer to him in such a familiar way just yet.

Ribero looked over, as though only just remembering he was there. "Yes?"

"Can I have a chat?" Kester asked.

Dr Ribero looked perplexed. "Yes, of course," he said. "Please, go on."

"Would it be possible to talk in private?" Kester clarified.

At once, the old man's face darkened. "Now, if this is you telling me you want to quit again, just say it now, alright?" he growled. "I have had a very bad day as it is, and I do not want any more nonsense, no? So spit it out now, if you must."

"I wasn't going to say that," Kester stuttered, feeling suddenly rather nervous. "It was about something else actually."

Dr Ribero looked mollified. "Oh. Okay. As long as it is no more bad news. I am not in the mood for more bad news. Tell you what—why don't we all shut up the office early, and Kester, you come with me for a nice walk? We can chat then, and it will be much nicer than standing in this stuffy office, yes?"

Mike punched the air. "Excellent, early doors down the

pub!" He linked arms with Pamela and performed a gentlemanly bow. "You up for a pint or two of Devon's finest ales, my love?"

Pamela giggled. "Oh Mike, you are silly," she said. "Go on then. After a day like today, I could do with it."

Dr Ribero straightened his collar, then gestured to the door. "Shall we?"

Kester trotted after him, struggling to keep pace with the doctor. He moved with surprising speed, striding with the fluidity of a cantering horse. *In his youth, he must have been a really imposing man,* Kester supposed, watching him with envy. Although Ribero's shoulders had started to slope with age, Kester could see the ghost of his youthful musculature, outlined in the graceful curve of his neck and the slender lines of his waist.

"Where are we going?" he asked, panting a little as he scuttled to catch up. Although the high street was relatively peaceful at this time of day, it still wasn't quite the location he had in mind for a quiet chat.

"We are catching the bus," Dr Ribero said, flashing Kester a smile. "I believe it is a P that we want. Or is it an R? I do get muddled from time to time."

"I suppose that happens with age," Kester suggested. "Your memory starts to go."

"No, it is nothing to do with that, thank you very much," Dr Ribero snapped, glowering in his general direction. "It is a case of too much on the brain, and not enough time to think about it all, right?"

Well, if you didn't have a two-hour long siesta every day, you'd probably have more time to think about things, Kester thought, but chose to keep this suggestion to himself.

After further fretting and debating over buses, they finally leapt on a P bus, which proclaimed to lead them up to Crossmeads, wherever that might be. Kester balanced himself on the closest seat, watching with fascination as the bus bobbled out of town and into the suburbs.

They passed rows upon rows of red-brick terraces, tumbled on top of one another like endless geometric brushstrokes, before rising steadily up a hill, into a more rural area. Finally, Ribero leant across, pressing the button, then shimmied to the front, maintaining his balance perfectly, in spite of the lack of suspension and general bumpiness of the road.

"Time to get out in the fresh air," he announced with a flick of the wrist, gesturing at the fields beyond. Aside from a few 1970s style suburban properties, they were surrounded by greenery: a narrow stream, dense woodlands, and sloping hills. It seemed quite remarkable that nature could sit so snugly on the perimeter of a city.

"This is nice," Kester said, stepping off the bus. The air felt cleaner and a lot less humid. A gentle breeze carried the scent of distant pine with it, drawing his attention to the tree-covered hillsides. Again, he imagined the land before the arrival of people, before the construction of higgledy-piggledy houses and suburban streets. The thick trees huddled together like plotting men, looming over the meadow below, and the stream scampered through the middle of it, a ribbon of sparkling grey in the greenery.

"I come here when I need to think," Dr Ribero stated, gesturing for them to proceed. "It reminds me of home. I mean my proper home, back in Argentina."

"Does it?" Kester asked. He hadn't imagined Argentina to be anything like Exeter. Instead, images of rugged gauchos, endless pampas grass, and sexy tango dancers sprung to mind. *Not many of those around here,* he thought with a wry smile.

"Yes," Ribero continued. "I grew up near the Andes. The pines, they crawled down the mountains like wild animals hidden by thick, swirling clouds. It was very beautiful. I miss it, even now."

"That does sound lovely," Kester said wistfully. He'd never been travelling. In fact, the furthest he'd ever been from home was here in Exeter. "When did you come to England?"

With a small skip, Dr Ribero jumped over the stile, saun-
tering into the next field. "Ah, it was a long time ago. I was so
young! Younger than you are now, yes? Such a boy. I hardly
spoke any English."

"Then why did you come to England?" Kester asked with
interest, tripping over a fallen branch in the process.

Dr Ribero scratched his nose, pondering the question. "I
had a bit of trouble in Argentina."

"Gosh, what sort?"

"Some people, they thought I was dangerous, because I saw
spirits," Ribero explained, waiting for Kester to catch up with
him. "So they threatened to chase me out of the country. My
mama, she was so ashamed. It was a bad time, Kester, a bad
time."

"So why come to England?"

"I came here because it was famous, right? The celebrated
home of the world's best ghost hunters. I couldn't think of
anywhere I would rather have headed. So I begged my papa to
lend me the money to get here, and I came. That is all there is to
it."

Kester sucked in his cheeks and let out a low whistle.
"Weren't you terrified, leaving your home country and coming
somewhere new, all by yourself?" Kester asked. He couldn't
imagine doing the same. He liked things to be as familiar as
possible.

Dr Ribero shrugged. "Perhaps a little. But I got lucky. I got
into university, then met Jennifer."

"And then you fell in love with each other?" Kester said,
without thinking. Dr Ribero blanched.

"Love . . . it is always a complicated thing," he said, after a
brief silence. "I know you probably think I am bad, that I used
your mother and did not treat her with respect. But that is not
how it is, Kester. I thought very highly of your mother, and still

do."

"I know," Kester answered. He looked up at the surrounding woodland, at the sun, glinting over the treetops. "I know you do."

"You miss her very badly, right?" Dr Ribero said quietly.

Kester sighed. "I sometimes feel like she's the only person who ever believed I wasn't completely useless," he said, shaking his head.

"I don't think you are useless, if that counts for anything," Ribero replied. "I know we don't know each other so well, but I certainly don't think you are useless."

"Isn't that just because you believe I can see this door into the spirit world?" Kester asked, unable to stop cynicism from creeping into his voice.

Dr Ribero rubbed his moustache. "Perhaps it was, at one point," he said. "But now . . . now I have gotten to know you, I think differently. I like that you are positive about things. I like that you are caring, that you are respectful of people around you. These are admirable qualities, and you should be pleased to have them."

"But I'm a complete coward," Kester added. "And I've disappointed you on a number of occasions. I can tell."

The doctor shrugged. "I suppose," he said, with a little more honesty than Kester would have liked, "but it is not really my place to judge you."

Kester took a deep breath, and tapped his father on the arm. "I want to go back to Coleton Crescent with you tonight."

Ribero stopped beside a tumbledown fence. He leant against the splintered wood, wiping his brow. "Why?"

"I think I've got an idea about how to deal with the Green Lady . . . and, I want to show you that I'm not a coward."

Dr Ribero paused, licking his lips. His eyes narrowed, scanning Kester's face like a lizard surveying a wandering fly.

"Well," he said eventually, placing his hands on his hips. "Of all the things I expected you to say, that was not one of them. What made you change your mind?"

"That's what I wanted to talk to you about all along," Kester continued. "I know that you're all feeling desperate about this case, and I want to help."

Dr Ribero scratched his chin, looking up at the deep blue sky. "But Kester," he muttered, "we know that you can't help. The Green Lady, she latches on to you, she controls you, and it is not good, it is not healthy. I don't think you can help, not really."

Kester felt himself slump inside, the air rushing out of him like a deflating balloon. *So he really doesn't have any faith in me, does he?* he realised. *In spite of all his kind words a moment ago, he does just believe I'm useless.*

"Will you just let me try?" he asked, trying to hide the quiver in his voice. "Please?"

Dr Ribero frowned. "I do not understand you," he said. "One minute, you are telling me that you will never go on a ghost observation again. Then, just a day or so later, you're telling me that you must. It is strange, isn't it?"

"My idea . . . it might not work," Kester said. "But I think it's worth a go. If I mess it up again, then that'll be it. I won't do any more ghost observations again. But if I don't try, then I'll never know if I can do it, will I?"

Dr Ribero smiled, his lips stretching into an expression of pure delight, like a child. "You know," he said quietly, "you looked just like Gretchen then. That determination. That strength. And now you make me miss her." He wiped his eye, reaching for his immaculately pressed handkerchief. "Good for you, boy," he concluded.

Kester beamed. It felt good to be told he was determined and strong, even if it wasn't true. "However," he went on, as they continued along the path, "It'll need all of us to make it work." Quickly, he filled the doctor in on what he'd found out so far, particularly about the Bloody Mary myth and the mirrors. Ribero said nothing throughout, only nodded occasionally, looking at the ground.

"What do you think?"

"That would be quite something, if it was a Bloody Mary." Ribero frowned, rifling in his pocket for a cigarette. "But that is impossible. The Bloody Mary spirits are extinct. No one has seen one for decades. Centuries perhaps."

"What do you mean, a Bloody Mary? Don't you mean *the* Bloody Mary?" Kester asked. "Isn't it just a single ghost?"

Dr Ribero laughed, slapping him on the back. "Goodness me, no," he said, flicking his lighter open with a metallic click. "The Bloody Mary, or Bloodied Marié, as we supernatural experts like to call them, were just a class of spirit. But I do not think this spirit can be one. Surely not."

"But it does kind of make sense, doesn't it?" Kester pressed on. "I mean, everything I've found out points towards it. Perhaps people were mistaken. Perhaps they're not extinct after all."

His father mused for a little while, surveying the dense congregation of trees that surrounded them, as though seeking the answer there. "It is possible," he said finally. "Anything is possible, I suppose." Slowly, he started to chuckle, his dark eyes twinkling with merriment. "It never would have occurred to me to think our Green Lady might be a Bloodied Marié. That is excellent detective work, yes!"

"Why are they called the Bloodied Marié?" Kester asked. "It didn't say anything about a different name on the websites I was looking at."

"No, it wouldn't, would it?" Ribero said with a frown. "The less the public know, the better. It's better to give this type of spirit a spooky name, turn them into a myth, a story, something not to be believed, yes?"

"Why the name then?"

"Bloodied Marié, it comes from the French word 'to marry'. This type of spirit, they fall in love with human men. So it kind of makes sense that our spirit is one of them. Kester, you are a genius, right? If, of course, you are right. It still seems a little crazy."

Kester blushed, burrowing his hands in his trouser pockets. "Oh, I don't think I'm a genius," he said. "I think I just got lucky, stumbling on some good information."

"Some people think that the name also comes from the French word for 'tide'," Ribero continued, "making her name literally 'the blood tide', you see?"

Kester blanched. "I know which version of the name I prefer," he said. "I don't really fancy the idea of a sea of blood."

"Well, some experts believe it's related to menstruation too. The Bloodied Marié, they apparently had a nasty habit of causing women to miscarry if they are pregnant, because they are jealous, you see?"

"I'm not sure I wanted to know that," Kester replied, cringing. *Perhaps that explains why Serena gets so ratty around the Green Lady,* he thought uncharitably.

"So, what is your plan?" Dr Ribero asked. "Do you really think you've got a way of getting rid of this nuisance spirit? To be honest, she is threatening the entire business. If we don't get her out of that painting and back in the spirit realm, we will become a laughing stock. No one will want to hire us. I'm willing to try anything."

"I know, I heard about the problems from the others," Kester said. "That puts a bit of pressure on us to get it right, doesn't it?"

"It certainly does," Dr Ribero said with a sigh. He scooped up a branch from the floor, and started swiping it through the tall blades of grass, still puffing at his cigarette. "I do not mind so much for myself. It is Jennifer I do not want to let down. It is her family's business, you see."

Kester nodded. "I understand," he said. "Let's act quickly then." *Before I change my mind,* he added silently, thinking back to the eerie house, the swinging chandeliers, those horrible eyes, boring into his. Revisiting the property wasn't an appealing thought. Still less appealing was the thought of revisiting the kitchen table where he'd managed to humiliate himself by vomiting all over it.

"Well, you will have my help, plus all the rest of the team, except not Serena," Dr Ribero said. "But I am sure we can manage."

"Why not Serena?" Kester asked. "Is it just because she stormed out of the office earlier?"

Ribero shook his head, giving the grass one last cursory swipe before flinging the stick into the air. "No," he said. "She cannot handle this job. She is too unmanageable. I have lost my trust in her."

Kester stopped. "But we need her there," he said, grabbing Ribero by the arm. "If she's not there, I don't think my plan will work."

Dr Ribero looked down at Kester's hand, then patted it with his own, a lion's paw resting briefly on his chubby fingers. "Good luck convincing her," he muttered. "Because I do not think she will want to return to that house either."

Kester gulped. "You'd better give me her address then."

Dr Ribero grinned wolfishly. "Now you're being brave," he concluded.

"It'll be fine, I'm sure," Kester said, gulping. His father strode on ahead with a laugh.

I'm not sure which prospect is scarier, he thought with a frown, watching Ribero's back heading into the distance, dwarfed by the surrounding hills and trees. *Facing the Green Lady again, or facing Serena.*

CHAPTER 14: SERENA'S HOUSE

"No." Serena folded her arms over her chest and glared in his direction. Kester fidgeted on the small leather sofa, trying not to look too uncomfortable.

"Is that a no, as in, 'I might consider it when I'm in a better frame of mind,' or is it a definite no as in, 'I absolutely won't do it in a million years'?" Kester asked.

Her eyes narrowed. "It's a *no*," she replied, ice dripping from every syllable.

Kester coughed, looking around the room. Serena's flat, situated right in the heart of the city centre, was small, sleek, and fairly unwelcoming—much like the owner herself. Although the lounge was only just big enough to swing a moderately sized mammal in it, the ceilings were high, and a large sash-window looked out onto the busy street below.

"Can I ask why not?" he ventured, averting his eyes from her ferocious glare.

"No, you bloody can't," she said.

Kester nodded. Then shook his head. Then nodded again, feeling a little confused about what message he was trying to convey.

"Shall I leave then?" he said eventually. The sofa squeaked under his bottom, sounding horrendously as though he'd accidentally passed wind. He repeated the movement swiftly, to try to emphasise that he hadn't, but frustratingly, couldn't get the sound to occur again. Serena rolled her eyes.

"Why did you even come here?" she demanded. "I suppose Ribero sent you, now that you're his favourite little lapdog?"

"Steady on, that's a bit harsh," Kester said, offended by her tone. "I didn't come here to have a fight. I really would like you to join us at Coleton Crescent tonight."

"Who died and left you in charge?" she spat, slamming her mug down on the coffee table. "Since when did you get to ask me to join you on a job? Last I remember, you completely screwed things up by going all soppy over a spirit then puking all over the table!"

Is she ever going to stop going on about that incident? he thought crossly. However, he knew that getting into a fight would get them nowhere. He took a deep breath and subsided back into the brick-like wedge of the sofa cushion.

"You're right," he agreed.

Serena looked surprised, then muffled the expression with a frown. "I know," she retorted. "You screwed up good and proper."

Kester twiddled his thumbs in his lap, feeling rather like he was in a cage with a somewhat unpredictable animal.

"I did screw up," he continued, "because I'm not very good at this spirit-catching lark." He leant forwards. "The truth is," he said, "I watch all of you, doing what you do, and I'm just in awe. When you caught that Japanese spirit in the wood, I thought it was incredible. I realised I could never be that brave."

Serena snorted, though she looked vaguely mollified.

"The truth is," he carried on, getting into his stride, "I've realised that we all have a talent. You're remarkable at what you do. The rest of the team are great at what they do. And I believe I'm pretty good at detective work. But that's why we need you there tonight, Serena. Detective work isn't enough to sort this Green Lady out. We need your skills to pull her out."

She stared at him, eyes wide as a cat's in headlights, then shook her head. "I can't do it," she said, shrugging her shoulders and gazing out of the window. The sunlight hit her cheekbones, making her look like a Grecian statue, all angles and smooth, strokeable surfaces. "I tried and I failed. Don't you see? I'm not that good at what I do after all. So there's no point asking for my help."

"But you are," Kester insisted, edging forward. "You're exceptionally good. You know you are, you told me so yourself . . . quite a few times."

Serena shook her head. "The others are angry at me," she mumbled. "And I can't blame them. I messed up earlier today. I lost my rag. And now I've made things worse. Your dad is probably going to sack me, I should think."

"He's definitely not," Kester reassured her.

"Well, Mike hates me anyway," she sniffed, before adding, "not that I care about that, of course."

"Of course," he agreed.

"So there's really no point me being there," Serena concluded, pressing her lips together. "Okay? I'm sorry that you came all this way, but I've already shown I'm unable to stuff that spirit in a water bottle, so I can't help you, alright?"

Kester took a deep breath. "What if I told you that you didn't need to stuff her in a bottle?" he said, letting the words hang in the air. "What if there was another way to get rid of her?"

Serena shook her head. "There's no other way. We need to store them in something, to take to the official spirit drop-off at

Infinite Enterprises."

"What if I could get the spirit door open again?"

Serena snorted, her nostrils flaring. "You can't though, can you? I mean, it only happens every so often. It's not like you have any control over it." She sighed theatrically, grabbing a red cushion and pressing it against her narrow stomach. "I really don't know why you're bothering to pursue this. Just give up. I know I have."

"You haven't really though, have you?" Kester stated, meeting her eye with a level gaze. *I've had enough of this nonsense,* he thought. *I know you're not the mega-bitch you pretend to be, and I know you desperately want to get this Green Lady out as much as the rest of us.*

"Well, you can think what you like," she replied, fiddling with a bit of fluff on her leather leggings. "It doesn't really make a difference. We can't get her out of that painting, and that's that. I've never seen a spirit that's so good at keeping itself hidden."

"I think I know a way we can extract her, and we're going to try tonight. In an hour or so, in fact," Kester announced, rapping his watch.

Serena groaned, slapping her forehead. "Oh dear lord!" she exclaimed. "One week working at the agency, and you think you're an expert!" She leaned forward, eyeing him dangerously. "Go on then," she goaded. "Tell me how it's done."

Kester leaned forward too, feeling a little like a chess player, about to move his queen into a supremely clever position. He smiled, perhaps a little smugly, but he couldn't help himself. "It's all about the mirrors," he said.

"Oh I see," Serena said with a sigh. "And there was me, thinking you were going to say something to completely waste my time. Well, I'm ever so glad you proved me wrong."

"Hear me out!" Kester said, holding a hand out to pacify her. "She can be summoned. She's a Bloody Mary spirit. Or a

Bloodied Marié. Whatever. I'm not sure which. But she can be summoned using a mirror."

Serena started to laugh. The laughter bubbled up until she was nearly hysterical, and had to go and get a tissue to dab her eyes. In fact, she seemed to be hamming it up to a certain degree, just to emphasise the sheer comedy of it all. Kester waited, feeling a little bit silly, which was probably her intention.

"That's utterly ridiculous!" she exclaimed eventually, clutching at her stomach to calm herself. "Oh Kester, you really are funny. Don't you realise those spirits are long gone? They don't exist anymore. It's like saying that a dinosaur is roaming around outside."

"Dinosaurs went extinct millions of years ago," Kester said, feeling nettled. "Whereas Dr Ribero told me that Bloody Marys only went extinct a few hundred years or so ago."

"So you do acknowledge that they're extinct then?" Serena said, leaning back and placing both feet on the coffee table. "In that case, why would you suggest that the Green Lady is one? Can't you see how preposterous that is?"

"What if they weren't extinct?" he suggested, his cheeks reddening. He didn't like his ideas to be referred to as preposterous, and her ridicule was starting to make him doubt himself. "What if they've just been lying low for a bit, and now they're back? Or what if this is the last Bloody Mary left in the world?"

Serena stood up, startling him. The cushion fell to the floor, bouncing like a ball to her feet. "Do you realise how silly you sound?" she barked.

Kester rose instinctively, feeling threatened. "No, I don't actually," he said, as coldly as possible. "Because I don't think I sound silly at all."

Serena eyed him. "Well, you do," she said. "This conversation is over. I won't be helping, okay? Not that your plan would work anyway. So you go ahead, fail miserably. It doesn't matter to me either way."

"You really are unpleasant sometimes, do you know that?" Kester flared, placing his hands on his hips. "You put on this act of being mean, but I don't think that's really you. Actually, I think deep down you're just as insecure as I am. I don't think you really hate me. I don't think you hate the spirits either, even though you're always going on about it."

She stood straighter, eyes blazing. "Don't presume to know how I feel about spirits. You have no idea."

"I presume something happened to you as a child or something, but I don't think—"

"A spirit plagued my house and drove my mother mad. She killed herself. So don't tell me I don't really hate them, because I do."

He winced. "I'm sorry, I didn't know that. I wouldn't have brought it up if I'd—"

"No, you don't know much, do you? Despite pretending that you know it all."

He faltered, before finally finding his feet and making for the door. "If you don't want to help," he concluded, "that's fine. But don't pretend it's because you think my idea is silly."

"Why else would it be?" she retorted, her expression unreadable.

"It's because you're scared of what the others think about you," he said. "You think they're angry at you, so you're afraid to show your face. But the mad thing is, they'd be happy to have you back, if you could calm your temper a bit."

"Oh, just leave, will you?" she shouted, marching over to the door. She waved down the narrow hallway, staring stonily at the floor. "You don't know me at all, Kester. So go and pass your judgement on someone else, you stupid little boy."

"Fine," he snapped. "It's a shame, because we do need you. We need you if this plan is going to work. But I can see I'm getting nowhere here."

"Quite," she hissed, her pointing finger quivering. "Time to leave, I think."

"I was going anyway," he muttered. "I wish I'd never come. Goodbye, Serena."

Her expression flickered for a second, before returning once again to ice. "Goodbye."

Kester marched down the staircase, clutching hold of the bannister, worried that his emotions were going to overcome him. *She called me stupid!* he thought, stamping down the stairs. *She's the stupid one! And now she's going to spoil everything, because we really do need her for this plan to work!* He had no idea what he was going to tell Dr Ribero. How could he admit that he'd failed miserably, before they'd even arrived at Coleton Crescent?

Storming out onto the street, he paced down the hill, heading towards the river. He still had some time before he was due to meet the others at the house, and he desperately needed to come up with another plan.

But what? he wondered, panic rising in his chest. *I've given Ribero some hope, how the hell am I going to deliver what I promised, if the person we need the most won't show up?*

Lost in a trail of despair, he continued his march onwards, oblivious to the rush hour traffic crawling miserably alongside him. Although it was close to six o'clock, the sun still shone over the hills in the distance, bathing the surrounding rooftops in a warm, golden glow. It was a beautiful evening, but he couldn't take any pleasure from it, not at the moment. He had an overwhelming sense of impending doom, and suspected that he was going to screw everything up royally.

Just like I always do, he thought, stepping off the pavement and onto the river path. *Oh Mother, you always thought I could achieve something, but now look at me. I've messed it up again.*

Serena's angry expression, her quivering finger pointing at the door, still loomed in his mind, making him feel even more frustrated. He kicked at the gravel, nearly lost his footing, then wished he hadn't bothered, especially when he spotted a pair of teenagers sniggering at him from higher up the riverbank.

Maybe I could just leave, he thought, looking at the steep hill ahead. He could see Coleton Crescent even from all the way down here; an austere curve of pristine white houses, glistening in the gentle sunlight. The sight filled him with dread. *Maybe I could just go to the train station instead. No one would realise until it was too late. I could just go back to Cambridge, and never come back.*

It was a tempting thought. *After all,* he reasoned, *what could I offer now? My plan has already failed. If indeed it would have worked anyway, which I very much doubt. At least if I leave, I won't have to face them. I won't have to see their disappointment, when they realise that I really am as utterly useless as I look.*

Kester sank down on to the grass with a sigh, startling the swans nesting down by the waters close by. He didn't have a clue what to do. He rested his head in his hands, keen to block out the world, if just for a little while.

Suddenly, a wet ball wedged its way into his palm, snuffling around like an insect. Kester squeaked, startled out of his morose daydreams, and looked around, trying to identify the culprit.

"Ugh, it's a rat!" he squawked with fright, recoiling as he spotted the thin brown creature, which was currently still nosing around his trousers. He hated rats. They filled him with utter revulsion, with their nasty little dark eyes and slippery fur. He bit his lip, edging away from the squirming creature, which seemed to have developed a dreadful obsession with his leg.

"Oh my goodness, I am so sorry!"

He followed the source of the female voice to an equally female person, who was presently perfectly silhouetted by the sun at her back, framed like an ancient goddess in front of the fierce light.

"Er, that's quite alright?" Kester grunted, scrambling to his feet. He looked down at the rat, which rather confusingly was on a lead. Even more confusingly, it looked as though it had been stretched to roughly the same length as a ruler. Then he realised, with considerable embarrassment, that it was a ferret.

"I hope Thor didn't scare you!" she said. Her voice sounded vaguely familiar. Kester squinted harder, then smiled.

"You're the girl from the library!" he exclaimed. "Anya, wasn't it?"

She nodded, then stepped to the side when she realised the sun was making him squint. "That is right. I am surprised you remember. You must have a good memory!"

"You've got a ferret," Kester commented, aware that he was stating the obvious. He pointed at the creature on the ground, which was still sniffling around at his feet, as though convinced he was stashing away a delectable treat in one of his shoes. "Not a rat. Sorry about that. I just noticed it was small and brown, then jumped to conclusions."

Anya giggled. "That's okay. He looks quite like a rat, I think."

"Did you say he was called Thor?" Kester said, raising an eyebrow. "That's a big name for a little fellow like that."

She giggled again, a sound that edged its way into Kester's ears, tickled his heart, then nestled in his belly like warm butter. She really was rather pretty, in a quirky kind of way. *Why is she bothering to talk to me?* he wondered, suddenly feeling self-conscious. He was fairly certain that he was a bit sweaty, and started to panic that he had moist patches under his armpits. Quickly, he crossed his arms, then realised that it made him sweat even more, so unfolded them again, keeping his arms pinned tightly to his torso.

"What are you doing down here?" she asked, looking out over the river. "Are you going for a walk?"

Kester shrugged. "I was thinking about going home, actually."

Anya smiled. "You live round here, then?"

"No," he continued, "I meant, going back home to

Cambridge."

She frowned. "Oh, but that is a long way away, isn't it? Is that where you live?"

"I think so," he said sadly, gazing back up at Coleton Crescent.

"That's a shame." Anya grasped his hand, then pumped it energetically. "It was nice to have met you. It's nice talking to someone clever. I hope your journey back is okay, right?"

Hang on, did she just say that it was a shame I was going? he thought, blinking with confusion. *Why would she say that? Maybe she didn't mean it. She was probably just being polite.*

"That's very kind of you," he said aloud, removing his hand. The warm press of her palm still lingered in his own. "I'm not sure I'm very clever though."

"Well, you should let me know if you ever decide to come back to Exeter," she said. "I'm part of a book club, we are looking for new people to join us. Perhaps if you ever move here for good, you could join?"

Kester gawped. The ferret started to run up his trouser leg, but he scarcely noticed. "Um, yes," he agreed, fighting to get his brain to function properly. At present, it seemed to have turned into some sort of gooey mush. "Yes, that would be nice. I'll let you know."

"Do you think you might come back then?" she asked.

He paused. *Will I be back? Should I even go?* His gaze travelled up to Coleton Crescent, then back to Anya. He nodded. "It might happen."

She smiled, then started to walk in the opposite direction, dragging Thor out of his trousers.

"In fact, I might not go back at all," he called after her, in a moment of bravery. She looked over her shoulder and grinned, giving him a wave. Kester started to grin himself, feeling a lot better than he had done five minutes ago.

Maybe she just felt sorry for me, he thought, with a little smile. He carried on walking towards Isabelle Diderot's house, without really realising he was doing so. *But it's still nice that a pretty girl pities me. At least she noticed me. That's a start.*

It was only after he'd passed the iron footbridge and started to head up the narrow steps that he realised what he was doing. Turning the corner, he saw the house standing in the middle of the elegant terrace, so seemingly innocuous on the outside, concealing the creature that lurked inside with a veil of normality.

I appear to have decided to stay after all, he thought to himself with a rueful nod. *That's somewhat surprising.*

It was still early. He leant against the iron railings, eyed the black door across the road, then settled himself in for a wait. He was glad he was early. It gave him a valuable twenty-five minutes or so to think of a new plan. However, if the blankness of his mind at present was anything to go by, inspiration was highly unlikely to come.

Oh boy, he thought, casting a glance down to the river below, which twinkled in the sun like a sparkling silver road. *I'm in trouble.*

CHAPTER 15: CHAOS AT COLETON CRESCENT

"What do you mean, the plan's gone a bit wrong?" Pamela said, placing the mug back on the kitchen table, which definitely still had an unpleasant odour of Kester's stomach contents about it, despite its innocent appearance under the light of the chandelier.

Kester swallowed. He'd put off telling them straight away, hoping that an alternative plan would spring to mind. But the fact was, without a young, unmarried woman to lure the Green Lady from her painting and into the mirror in the hallway, he didn't know what else to do. All the sites he'd looked at indicated that it needed to be a young woman, though he supposed they could try it with Pamela, and see if it worked. Not that he held out much hope. Pamela was definitely the wrong side of fifty, and didn't look like the marrying kind, plain and simple. And from what he could tell, the Green Lady wasn't stupid.

"We kind of needed Serena to get the Green Lady to go into the mirror," he offered lamely, as the hot tea misted his glasses.

"And Serena wouldn't come. She said I was being ridiculous."

Mike paced up and down the tiles. "Well, it is a bit farfetched, mate," he said, as tactfully as possible, which in Mike's case, wasn't very tactfully at all. "I mean, it's like saying a dinosaur has come back to life or something."

"Why does everyone keep saying that?" Kester snapped, running his hands through his hair. "It's not the same at all."

"No," Dr Ribero agreed. "It's more like saying Queen Victoria isn't actually dead. More like that. The Bloody Marys have been extinct for about a couple of hundred years, that's all."

"A couple of hundred years is bad enough," Mike said. "At the end of the day, extinct means extinct. It doesn't matter if it's a few hundred years or a few million."

Kester sighed. "I'm sorry," he said. "I've messed it up again. I feel really awful about it. And I haven't got a Plan B either. Sorry."

"To be honest, you never really had much of a Plan A, either," Mike added, patting him sympathetically on the back. "But I can see why you got excited. The mirror connection was a bit of a red herring, I think."

"You do not know that for sure," Dr Ribero berated, rapping at the tabletop with a fingertip. "Stranger things have happened, you know?"

"Yeah, I know. We deal with strange for a living," Mike said with a gruff laugh. "But no one's seen sight of a Bloody Mary for centuries. And they were the kind of spirits that really didn't like to lie low. It seems unlikely that they'd have managed to remain hidden for so long."

Pamela gave a low whistle. "So," she said seriously. "What are we going to do?"

Miss Wellbeloved, who until then had been sitting quietly in the corner, raised her head. "Perhaps we should just go home again," she suggested, staring out of the window. "There's not much point being here, is there? I'll call Infinite Enterprises in the morning, ask them to arrange for their team to come and sort it out."

"No," Ribero barked, pushing his chair back and rising to his feet. He prowled across to Miss Wellbeloved and placed a hand on her shoulder. "No, we are not giving up, Jennifer. Come on. We have been running this agency too long to just give it all up."

She looked up, giving him a weak smile. "Exactly," she said. "We're probably at retirement age anyway. So, what does it matter now? Perhaps it's easier just to admit defeat."

Ribero retreated a little, eyes widening. "I don't think you really mean that," he said. "I think you are just feeling a bit tired, yes?"

"I'm utterly exhausted," Miss Wellbeloved answered, with a humourless chuckle. She reached out, taking him by the hand. "I think perhaps it's just time to know when to quit. Let's face it, we've been struggling for years now."

Kester coughed, feeling utterly wretched. "I'm so sorry," he mumbled again. "I feel responsible."

"Don't be silly," Miss Wellbeloved said, shaking herself. "You've tried to help, and I'm grateful to you. You even gave us a bit of hope for a while, and that was nice while it lasted."

Kester gulped, feeling even worse than he had done previously. *Gosh,* he thought, *I've only known them all for a few days, and already I've completely ruined their business. That must be a record.*

"Shall we go then?" Mike said. "Doesn't seem like much point sitting in here, does there?" He glanced at his watch, before adding, "and *Chef Maestro* has only just started. If I leave now, I'll only miss a few minutes."

"Can't you just watch it on catch up?" Pamela suggested.

Mike shook his head. "It's not the same," he said, lifting up the equipment bag and throwing it over his shoulder. "It's the live finals tonight. I want to see if Sheena manages to win."

"She was doing very well, wasn't she?" Pamela agreed, hoisting her considerable bulk off the chair. "That cake she baked last week was amazing, a real work of art. I loved those little chocolate flowers she added."

"Yes, anyway," Dr Ribero interrupted, glaring from under his heavy eyebrows, which were twitching in their direction. "I have not yet said we are going home. You are jumping over the gun a little, yes?"

"There's no point us staying, is there?" Mike said, looking around them, as though an answer would present itself from one of the kitchen cupboards.

"Well, that depends whether or not you have given up, doesn't it!" Dr Ribero said, his voice rising.

"I was rather under the impression that we all had," Mike retorted. "Haven't we?"

"I think we might as well go home," Miss Wellbeloved agreed, standing up.

Dr Ribero's shoulders slumped. He turned, fixing his gaze on Kester. "Have you any other ideas?" he pleaded, reaching out and resting a hand on Kester's arm. "Any other plans that we could try?"

"I did wonder if we could use Pamela to lure the Green Lady into the mirror," Kester offered, without much conviction. The others all looked at Pamela with varying degrees of scepticism, depending on how polite they were. Pamela didn't seem to object. Indeed, she looked fairly sceptical herself.

"No, that will not do," Ribero muttered. "It needs to be a young woman, someone who the Bloody Mary will believe is looking to marry."

"Oh, that definitely isn't me." Pamela shook her head. "I never liked the idea of getting hitched. Far too much hassle."

"Hear hear," Mike echoed.

"Well," Miss Wellbeloved said, plucking her handbag from the back of the chair and walking towards the door, "I believe that's that then. Shall we?"

They started to troop down the hallway, as despondently as a group of children heading into an examination room. Kester felt so depressed he didn't even notice the lights flickering overhead, nor the eerie hissing from the living room.

I've really blown it this time, he thought. *I wish I'd just gone to the train station instead. Anything would have been better than feeling like this.*

Pamela swung open the door. "Well, I'll see you all tomorrow morning."

"Yes, have a good evening," Dr Ribero said, stepping outside, into the golden glow of the early twilight. "Let's all have a sleep on it. You never know, one of us might get some sudden inspiration."

"A few beers would probably help," Mike added. "Can you give me a lift home, Pamela?"

"What, are you going already?" A sharp voice pierced the still air, and they all turned as one, like a pack of startled flamingos.

Kester's mouth fell open, leaving him gawping like a breathless goldfish. *Serena! But what is she doing here?*

"We were told you weren't coming," Pamela said, in an unusually tight voice.

"Yeah, thought you'd deserted us," Mike grunted, crossing his arms and staring out over the river, deliberately avoiding her gaze.

Serena fidgeted, adjusting her t-shirt unnecessarily. "I fancied getting out of the house," she muttered, keeping her eyes fixed on her shiny stilettoes. "Change of scenery. You know."

Kester stared, then slowly broke into a smile. Instinctively, he reached out, enveloping her in a hug of pure relief. Serena stiffened against him, then relaxed a little, patting him just the once on the back, as though rapping on a bongo. "I'm so glad you came," he said quietly. "Seriously. You don't know how brilliant it is that you're here."

She gave him a weak smile. "Just because I'm here, doesn't mean I think you're right. In fact, for what it's worth, I think you're very wrong indeed, and I don't think your plan is going to work." She paused, watching Kester's grin falter. "However," she continued, "it's worth a shot. And we are a team, after all. I could hardly leave you all stranded, could I?"

Dr Ribero strode over, punching her on the arm. "Good for you," he beamed. "Yes, you may have messed up badly the last time, but you are ready to try again. Well done."

Serena grimaced, unsure how to take the comment. "Quite," she said finally. Standing back, she took in the length of the house, narrowing her eyes. "Shall we get to work then?" she asked. "Or are you still planning on going home?"

Pamela chortled, linking her arm through Serena's. "Not a chance," she said, tugging her towards the front door. "I know it's the *Chef Maestro* finals, but this is more exciting."

"Nothing is more exciting than the *Chef Maestro* finale," Mike declared, looking horrified at the suggestion. "Apart from the *Chef Maestro* finale and a pint in my hand. But I'm game to have a go if you all are."

Dr Ribero laughed out loud, slapping his thigh in delight. "This is good!" he said. He patted Miss Wellbeloved on the back, who looked a little brighter now. "See?" he added, giving her a quick hug. "I told you not to give up."

Miss Wellbeloved shook her head. "We haven't got rid of her yet," she replied seriously. "And if she's not a Bloody Mary spirit after all, we're no closer to getting rid of her than we were before."

"Nothing ventured, nothing to be gathered up!" Ribero replied, with a jaunty wiggle of his hips.

"Gained," Miss Wellbeloved automatically corrected. "The word is gained."

"Ah, whatever," he retorted. "It means the same. Let us get

on with the task at hand."

They stepped back into the house, shutting the door behind them. The sound echoed around the hallway, before leaving them in silence.

"Honey, I'm home!" Mike called out, giving the others a wink. "Well, I know I only left two minutes ago, but I'm back again!"

The house made no response, but the air seemed suddenly heavier, and more watchful.

"She knows we're up to something," Pamela whispered, casting her eyes to the ceiling as though searching for something in the coving. "I can sense her. We've got her attention now."

"So, how is this going to work?" Serena asked in a low voice after she nudged Kester. "You still didn't really explain what you wanted me to do. You were rambling on about mirrors when you came to visit me earlier, but I didn't get much else out of you. Well, nothing that made any sense, anyway."

Kester coughed, and tugged at his collar. "Serena," he whispered, looking around them, feeling horribly as though they were being overheard by unpleasant, unseen ears. "You and I will wait out here. In the hallway."

Serena nodded to the opposite wall, where the large mirror was hanging. "Because of that?" she said.

"Yep," Kester confirmed. "The others are going to be in the lounge. They already know what to do, we discussed it before you arrived."

"Can you run me through it?" Serena said, looking interested. Suddenly, an icy breeze ran through the length of the hall, chasing around their heads like a mini whirlwind, before departing again.

Dr Ribero coughed, nodding meaningfully at the others. "Perhaps we should relax first," he said pointedly. "Let's not discuss work now. Why don't we go to the garden, have a drink?"

Serena looked at him as though he had gone completely

mad, then grasped his meaning. "Oh, yes, yes of course," she answered, raising her voice to ensure the spirit would hear. "That's a great idea. There's nothing for us to do in here at the moment, is there?"

They looked at Pamela, who paused for a moment, sniffing at the air in a disturbingly dog-like way, before nodding. "That worked," she whispered. "Let's go."

They trooped through the kitchen, following Ribero to the small cloakroom at the back, which opened out into the walled garden. The setting sun reflected piercing beams off the Victorian greenhouse, and a set of deckchairs were laid out on the carefully mowed lawn, as though awaiting their arrival.

"Is it safe to talk now?" Dr Ribero asked Pamela, easing himself into the nearest one.

Pamela wrinkled her nose, then nodded. "Yes," she said in a louder voice. "She doesn't like to venture too far from that painting of hers when we're around. But careful everyone, she's on to us. She must have detected our emotions when we came back into the house."

"God, just like a bloody woman," Mike grumbled, kicking at the base of the ornamental birdbath. "Always listening into conversations and jumping to the wrong conclusions."

"In this instance, it was actually the right conclusion though, wasn't it?" Kester pointed out.

Mike grunted, refusing to acknowledge the point.

"So talk me through it then," Serena said, perching next to Ribero. "What's the plan?"

Kester sat down next to her. Unfortunately, the chair buckled beneath him, clamping shut on his bottom and wedging him in an awkwardly folded position until Pamela prised him free. He bounced up, deliberately avoiding both Serena and Mike's expressions, which he could already sense were filled with poorly concealed amusement.

"Anyway," he began, mustering up as much dignity as

possible. "The first step will be the mirror. I've been reading up on it, and Bloody Marys cannot help but be summoned if a young woman calls to them in a mirror."

"And that's where I come in?" Serena asked.

Kester nodded. "Then," he continued, looking up at the house, "it's Mike's turn to destroy the painting, while she's out of it."

"What one of your fancy pieces of machinery are you going to use for that?" Serena asked, sneering at his equipment bag.

"Blow torch," Mike replied with a grin. "I'm going to enjoy flaming that painting to bits, the amount of trouble it's caused us."

"It's at this point," Kester continued, "that I'm predicting we'll have the most trouble. The Bloody Mary will be out of the painting, unable to get back in, and we don't know how she'll react."

"Yes, and we all know what the legends say, don't we," Miss Wellbeloved said, leaning on the back of Ribero's chair. "These types of spirit can be vicious if agitated. We'll be dealing with a highly volatile creature here, make no mistake."

"Is that where I come in and trap her in a water bottle?" Serena asked, looking excited.

"In theory, yes," Ribero concluded. "Pamela and Jennifer will attempt to connect with her and soothe her so you can gain better control. Then we have her trapped, yes?"

"When you put it like that, it sounds nice and easy," Mike said, scratching his beard.

Kester frowned, studying the windows, which looked ominously black and empty, despite the warmth of the sun at their backs. "Let's hope it will be," he muttered. There was something about the plan that was worrying him, but he couldn't quite put his finger on it. *Am I missing something?* he wondered. *If so, I need to find it fast. This isn't a situation we want to mess up.*

"And what if it's not a Bloody Mary?" Serena asked. "Which,

let's face it, it's unlikely to be. What then?"

"Then we are back to where we started," Miss Wellbeloved said. "We're no better or worse off than we were before."

"But we must give it a try," Ribero said, clapping his hands together, then gesturing to Mike. "Here, help me up. I am an old man, right?"

Mike snorted, but hoisted him out of the deckchair nonetheless. "Come on then," he muttered. "Let's do this. I've had it with this miserable git of a spirit, I want her out of my hair. She's keeping me from my favourite TV programmes."

As they walked back towards the house, Kester fell back in step with Serena. "By the way," he said in a low voice, "when you summon her in the mirror, you know there's a chance she'll show you your future husband, don't you? After all, that's what Bloody Marys do, isn't it?"

Serena gave him the most scathing look she could muster. "I hardly think I need be worried about that," she retorted, stepping into the cloakroom. "I have no intention of ever getting married."

"Okay," Kester said with relief. "I just thought I'd better warn you."

"No need," she snapped. "I already know the legend. To be honest, I think it all sounds like complete and utter rubbish anyway."

"Oh, absolutely," he agreed, following her in after meticulously wiping his feet on the mat.

The house was still eerily silent and still, and Kester had the distinct impression that they were being watched, as intently as bugs under a magnifying glass. He could feel the weight of the heavy, scrutinising stare, radiating from the walls and ceilings, observing their every move. *She really dislikes us,* he realised, with a shiver. *She wants us gone, every bit as much as we want her gone.* It wasn't a comfortable feeling.

"So," Dr Ribero boomed, as they entered the living room.

"Shall we just sit here for a while instead, as the garden wasn't so comfortable for my old bones?"

Miss Wellbeloved shot him a look. "Why not," she said, nodding to the others. "I'm not in the mood to carry on this investigation, are you?"

Mike caught her eye and gave her a wink. "Oh no, me neither," he said deliberately, launching himself into the armchair and putting his feet up on the coffee table. "Let's just chill out here for a bit, then head home."

"Are you ready?" Kester whispered to Serena. She nodded and gave the hallway a grim look.

"Shall we go home then?" she said out loud. "As there's nothing else for us to do here?"

"I think that's a great idea," Kester replied, fighting to keep the nerves from his voice. *Please let this work*. His mother came to mind, and he closed his eyes. *Let me have the strength to do this,* he added. *If you're listening anywhere, Mother, please help me.*

They moved towards the front door, pausing by the large mirror. Serena adjusted her hair, meeting his gaze. "Are you ready?" she whispered.

"Ready when you are," he stuttered.

She nodded, then turned to face the mirror.

"Bloody Mary, Bloody Mary, Bloody Mary!" she shouted, clutching the frame with both hands. To begin with, there was nothing. Then slowly, the mirror began to darken, as though someone was pumping black smoke into it from behind.

"My god," Serena whispered, her eyes widening in shock.

My god, Kester thought, staring. *I was right. I was actually right.*

The mirror continued to darken, until the surface was jet-black, shiny and empty as a black hole. Serena gasped.

"Kester, what's happening?" she hissed.

"You've done it, you're summoning her!" he replied, half terrified, half fascinated.

"I don't mean that," she stammered. "Why can't I move my head?"

Kester looked at her with confusion. "What do you mean?"

"I can't move my head!" Serena repeated, her voice tight with panic. "And my hands are stuck to the mirror!"

He opened his mouth, then shut it again. "I don't know," he whispered, still transfixed on the shifting surface of the reflection. "Do you want me to try to move your head for you?"

Serena began to say something, then suddenly stopped. Her eyes widened, and she swallowed hard.

"What? What can you see?" Kester asked, looking over her shoulder. He could see nothing but blackness.

"Mike?" Serena whispered. "Is that you?"

"No, it's Kester here, not Mike," he replied, confused. Serena looked dazed, as though she'd only just woken up. Then suddenly, her head reared back, as though she'd been slapped. She winced, pulling away.

"She's there!" she cried out. "She's in the mirror, Kester!"

Kester peered over her shoulder, but couldn't make anything out, only the darkness, which seemed to be shifting, like a brewing storm.

"I can't see her," he replied, squinting. "Are you sure?"

"Yes, I'm bloody sure!" she yelled back. "Tell the others to get started, quickly! Hurry up, she's trying to hurt me!"

Kester gasped, then leapt towards the lounge door, galvanised into action. He thrust the door open with a bang, jabbing his fingers in the direction of the painting.

"Now!" he cried out, feeling light-headed with nerves, excitement and raw terror. "Mike, get on with it, for goodness' sake! She's hurting Serena!"

"Bloody hell," Mike exclaimed, flicking on his blow torch. The flame burst out immediately, a fierce blue tongue that he directed at the base of the painting. "Here goes nothing," he muttered, concentrating on the task at hand. The flames licked the corner of the frame, blackening the gilt edges.

"Is Serena okay?" Miss Wellbeloved asked, eyes creased with worry. She peered out the doorway, then looked back at Kester, her slate-grey eyes like circles. "Does this mean your idea has actually worked?"

"I rather think it might have done," Kester breathed, feeling faint. "I'll go and help Serena. How about you get ready for the next stage?"

The flames were now starting to travel across the base of the picture, caressing the brushstrokes almost indecently, sending the aged canvas curling and spitting with fury. Once they had taken hold, they spread rapidly, snaking upwards, turning the bright green dress to a murky shade of black. Kester gulped as the flames reached her face, and forced himself to turn away.

"Er, anyone have any thoughts about how we put the fire out?" Mike commented. No one replied. Kester closed the door behind him, preferring not to know the possible solutions to that particular problem. He switched his attention to Serena, who had gone deathly white.

"Oh my goodness," he muttered, reaching towards her. "Serena, let go of the mirror, quickly!"

"Can't . . ." she whispered, eyes roving across the mirror's surface. "Can't move. Hands. My hands are melting."

Kester frowned, studying her hands, which were clasped tightly around the ornate frame, knuckles white as limestone pebbles. He touched them, then leapt back with a shout. *She's on fire,* he thought irrationally, looking at Serena's face, half expecting her to burst into flames at any moment. *Dear Lord, is that what this Bloody Mary spirit does to people?*

Steeling himself, he grabbed her by the wrists, and started to pull. Serena screamed, closing her eyes with pain.

"I'm sorry, I'm sorry!" he shouted, cringing at the noise. "Oh god, Serena, I'm so sorry. I didn't know this would happen."

"Get Pamela," she whispered, head pitched backwards at an

unnatural angle. Kester realised that she was close to passing out. "Quickly."

"Righty-o," Kester replied, in a voice that was verging on hysterical, then pulled open the lounge door with a bellow of desperation. "Pamela! A little help here please!"

"We've got a bit of a situation of our own here, love!" Pamela called from somewhere by the sofa. Kester looked upwards, to see large pieces of ash flying around the room, not to mention the wallpaper behind the painting, which was now burning merrily.

He tried not to think too hard about it. Sometimes, he reasoned to himself, it was counter-productive to think about things too much. Instead, he focused on the main priority, which was helping Serena.

"It's absolutely 100% urgent that you help me now!" he said, in as authoritative tone as he could muster. Pamela looked at him with surprise, looked back at the fire, then shrugged.

"You guys have got this one, right?" she said to Mike and Dr Ribero, who were desperately trying to stamp the fire out with some particularly large velvet cushions.

"Yeah, got it covered," Mike said, looking completely unconvinced. He ducked as a section of frame collapsed, spraying him with sparks. "No problems here."

Pamela scuttled after Kester, rolling up her sleeves. "What's happening here then?" she asked, then faltered at the sight of Serena, who had now passed out, and was leaning crazily against the mirror, suspended only by her hands, which were still stuck tight to the frame. "Jesus," she whispered. "What has that horror done to her?"

"I don't know," Kester said, scooping Serena up to ease the pressure on her arms. "But you've got to help her, Pamela. I don't know how."

Pamela peered into the mirror, examining the fretful swirling shadows. Then she nodded grimly. "Only one thing to stop this cow doing any more damage," she declared, placing her hands on her ample hips. "Bloody Mary! Listen to me now! Your painting is on fire, and you've nowhere else to go. Better get out of this mirror now, whilst you still can!"

A low, sickly thrum began to emanate from somewhere deep within the mirror's surface, spilling out like poisoned treacle. It grew louder, rising in volume until it started to rattle the ornamental vase on the hallway table, sending it teetering from side to side. Kester brought his hands to his ears, taking the weight of Serena's frail frame against his chest.

"What's happening?" he shouted above the noise. "What's she doing?"

"She's getting royally hacked off, that's what's happening," Pamela announced, with grim pleasure. "Go on, you old devil, you! Out of the mirror before we trap you!"

The humming noise rose, turning into a shrill, eardrum-bursting whistle. Then suddenly, it stopped. The darkness seeped out of the mirror like smoke pouring out of a window, leaving the surface clear once more. Serena's hands fell from the frame, and she slumped to the floor like a broken puppet.

Kester crouched down, lifting her head. Her eyes rolled back, showing nothing but the whites of her eyes. He swallowed hard. *God, what have I done?* he thought, searching her face for signs of life. *Is she okay? What happened to her?*

A noise from the living room caused him to look up, startled. Pamela shook her head, gesturing to the door.

"It's kicking off in there now," she announced with an ominous nod. "I can feel her anger. She's realised what's happened." Without warning, she reached over to the mirror, pulled it off the wall, and smashed it against the door frame. It shattered with a piercing crash, spraying shards across the hallway.

"What did you do that for?" Kester squawked, surveying the mess. He brushed some stray glass off Serena's lap.

"She'll be looking for another place to hide in a moment," Pamela said grimly, as she strode into the living room, wading through the puddle of broken glass at her feet. As she entered, a wild breeze tore out through the door, whipping around Kester's head with such power that it nearly knocked his glasses off.

"Oh boy," he heard Pamela mutter, before the door slammed behind her with a deafening bang, leaving Kester alone in the hallway, with Serena still unconscious on his lap.

"Serena, please wake up!" he murmured, prodding her as hard as he dared on the stomach. Taking her chin firmly between his finger and thumb, he moved her head from side to side, searching her eyes for signs of wakefulness. However, her eyes remained white, rolled back as far as they would go. It was a hideous sight, and were it not for her chest, rising and falling in shallow, rasping breaths, he would have thought she was dead.

Now what are we going to do? he wondered, looking up at the lounge door, which hulked over them both like an impenetrable fortress. *Serena's a vital part of this plan. I didn't imagine she'd end up being knocked out cold!*

Gently, he moved her on to the floor, then rose to his feet.

"Everything alright in there?" he asked in a quavering voice, rapping at the door politely.

"No it bloody isn't!"

Kester grimaced at the declaration, grasping the door-knob in an agony of indecision. He didn't want to go into the room. Every cell in his body was rebelling against the idea. But he knew he had to. Even the excuse of being the world's worst coward wouldn't cut it now. He owed it to the others to at least try to do something. After all, he was the one who had come up with this awful plan in the first place.

Slowly, he poked his head around the door, trying very hard to not see the pandemonium inside.

"Need my help at all?" he asked quietly, keeping his eyes firmly fixed on the floor. Even there, he could see feet leaping anxiously from place to place, not to mention charred pieces of canvas littering the carpet.

"Yes, that might be nice, dear!" Pamela replied, straining to be heard above the noise. The room oozed diabolical sounds, quite unlike anything Kester had ever heard before—low, throbbing, moaning that needled right into his eardrums.

"Where is Serena?" Miss Wellbeloved asked, staggering across the room. Her normally immaculate hair was a wilderness of steel fuzz, and her hollow cheeks were flushed.

"She's still unconscious!" Kester shouted. A wind buffeted against him with hurricane force, sending him reeling towards the sofa. He tottered, fighting to steady himself against the side-table.

"She keeps doing that," Mike mentioned, still trying to stamp out the flames on the wallpaper. "It's a right pain in the backside. Any ideas what to do now then, mate?"

"No!" Kester whimpered. "In the original plan, Serena wasn't unconscious at this point!"

"At least we've got her out of the painting," Pamela said, as brightly as possible, before being thrown across the room like a hot air balloon in a storm. She landed on the armchair in the window, bouncing like a beach ball and looking rather dazed.

"Kester, we need to come up with something," Ribero shouted, reaching across to him. "This is bad. This is very bad indeed. This spirit, she is so powerful, we need to get her locked up in a water bottle quickly. Can Serena be woken up?"

Kester thought back to the shallow breathing and the whites of her eyes. *Not a chance.* He shook his head. "I wish she could," he answered, clasping the edge of the sofa as another whirlwind crashed into him, "but she's out cold. The Bloody Mary did something terrible to her, I think."

"That evil cow," Mike spat. He glared up at the ceiling, searching for the spirit amongst the wind and chaos. "Yeah, I'm talking to you, you nasty piece of work. I don't care how powerful you are, you've been a nightmare from the start, and I, for one, am sick to death of you."

"That probably won't achieve much, Mike," Miss Wellbeloved suggested, before being lifted off her feet and tossed like a wayward twig on to the sofa next to Pamela.

"What are we going to do then?" Mike shouted, running a hand through his hair. "Seriously. Are we totally screwed here? Have we just unleashed a complete monster into the world, without any means of bringing her under control? Is that what we've done?"

Kester thought it was very kind of him to use the expression we, when, in fact, it had been all his idea. His shoulders slumped, and he clasped his forehead, wishing that he had never come tonight. He'd thought that the worst outcome would be that he'd been wrong, and that the spirit hadn't been a Bloody Mary after all. He now realised that the ridicule and disappointment of the others would have been a lot easier to deal with than this.

"Kester?"

He looked up to see Ribero's face, only a few inches from his own.

"What?" he murmered. "Don't ask me, I've got no idea. I've messed up again, haven't I?"

Ribero seized him by the shoulders. To Kester's great surprise, he smiled at him. It was an incongruous gesture, given the madness of the moment, but for the briefest moment, he felt as though everything would be alright.

"I don't think you have messed up," Ribero whispered, pulling him closer. "I think you have achieved something marvellous. Something that none of us managed, and we've been doing this for years, yes? And I think you can solve this. I believe you can do it."

Kester looked up at the old man, blinking with confusion. The wind continued to hurtle around them, smashing against them from all angles, but for a moment, he hardly noticed.

"But I don't know how to," he replied, rubbing his eyes. He felt like a child again—confused, bewildered and scared. "I don't know what to do. I wish I did."

"Think what your mother would have done."

"But what would she have done?" Kester fretted, clutching Ribero. "That's just the problem! I don't know what she would have done. It turns out I didn't really know her at all, did I? She had this whole life with you, and I knew nothing about it!"

"She would have been brave," Ribero replied, lowering his arms. "She would have been brave, and nothing else."

Kester bit his lip. *Is that true, Mother?* he thought, fighting back a sob. *Would you have known what to do, in this situation?* An image of Gretchen came to him, not as she had been as she was dying, but before that, when she had been strong, full of energy and purpose.

Yes, she would have been, he realised. *I understand now. You would have been scared, but you would have solved the problem. Because that's what you did, your whole life. You solved all my problems. And that's what I've got to do now.* His eye widened, as he looked around him. It was as though everything had slowed down, as though he was watching a scene that he'd seen before. He took it all in: the ashes blowing in crazy circles, Mike desperately beating at the flaming wall, the two women clutching one another on the sofa, and his father calmly watching him. It didn't seem real. *I'm not afraid,* he thought. *I'm not afraid at all.*

And just like that, the door appeared.

Initially just a tiny hole in the air, Kester watched with detached fascination as it tore itself wider, becoming a thick line of darkness that stretched downwards, until it formed a ragged doorway. The air around his head screeched even more loudly, in protest.

"I can see it!" he shouted, pointing. "The door! The spirit door! It's appeared!"

He heard Ribero laugh with delight, and felt a hand clapping him on the back, but his attention was centred on the hypnotic sight of the doorway, shifting and slithering in the air like a living thing.

"Hang on, hang on, let me get my phone out!" Mike announced for some inexplicable reason, but Kester was too focused to give it much thought. The screeching rose into a deafening crescendo, sending a monsoon of wind tearing around the room, until it began to be sucked away, through the spirit door.

Kester continued to fix his gaze upon it, terrified that if he looked away, it would disappear. The winds gathered in front of him, rippling and rolling in the air like two fighting dogs, before shaping into a shadowy, bony form. He gasped, horrified by the sight of it—the ugly, jutting limbs; the dome-like head; and the mouth, open in a maw of rage.

"You are doing it!" Ribero bellowed behind him. "I see her! I see her now!"

Kester winced, then focused all his energy on driving the spirit backwards through the door. She howled, an inhuman sound of fury, scratching at the air by his face, trying to stop him. Then, as he felt he was about to collapse, the door sucked her through, and closed completely.

The wind dropped. The howl ceased, giving way to silence. The swirling ashes dropped to the floor like pieces of parchment. Kester fell to his knees, rested his head in his hands, and promptly passed out.

Chapter 16: Celebrity Status and Wedding Bells

It took Kester several days to recover from the events at Coleton Crescent. He remained cocooned in the sunny confines of Pamela's back garden, cossetted away from the rest of the world, where he promptly made himself at home amongst her considerable book collection. He ignored Ribero's agency—at least, for a little while.

Serena, after a brief but panicked trip to A&E, was declared in perfectly good health, and after a lot of grumbling, agreed to take some time off too. Quite what she was getting up to in her flat, Kester had no idea, but he suspected she might have taken down a mirror or two, just to be on the safe side.

On the fifth day, he finally dared to venture out, at the special request of his father, to a dinner party at Ribero's home. Kester's curiosity was naturally piqued. So far, he hadn't seen his father's house, and hadn't even the whiff of an idea what it might look like. Did Ribero live in an elegant manor house, to match his own smooth Argentinian style? Or did he live like an impoverished artist, in a cramped little basement apartment in town? He wasn't sure what to expect at all.

At half past seven, Pamela drove them through the centre of the city, then out the other side, past the river, and down through the terraced houses and cluttered local shops. She kept on driving, up another hill and along a narrow, winding road, which seemed to lead to nowhere. The road narrowed, until it wasn't really a road anymore, but more of a dried out mud-track, and the car began to bounce about, as though it was being repeatedly electrocuted.

"Where on earth does he live, a farm?" Kester said, peering out of the window and bracing himself against the car door.

Pamela chortled, swerving to avoid a huge pothole. "You'll see," she tittered, as the car kept bobbling along. Kester surveyed their surroundings with great interest, as the thin line of firs flanking the road thickened into impenetrable woodland. Finally, Pamela pulled on the handbrake, bringing the car to a jittery halt.

Kester looked up at the house, then started to laugh.

"What's so funny?" Pamela asked, opening the car door. A tang of pine and dry earth drifted in on the breeze.

He shook his head, still chuckling. "Well," he said, taking his glasses off and giving them a polish, "of all the places I expected him to live, I didn't predict it would be like this. But of course, this makes perfect sense!"

A sprawling, rickety wooden house stood at the end of the driveway, which would have looked perfectly at ease amongst the pampas plains of Argentina. The worn-out porch leaned a little to the left, and there was a rocking chair positioned by the front door. Kester half-expected to see a gaucho's hat, slung over the fence, or a horse tethered to one of the posts.

"Let me guess, he had this house built specially," Kester said, taking in the entirety of the building.

Pamela smiled. "You're half right," she said. "Actually, he and Jennifer's father had it built many years ago."

"Miss Wellbeloved's father?" he asked, raising an eyebrow. "Why?"

"It's probably best if your dad explains that one."

"You mean, when Miss Wellbeloved and he were engaged to be married?" Kester guessed.

"Oh, so you knew about it already?" Pamela looked surprised.

Kester nodded, "Yes, don't worry. It's not news to me. I found some letters in my mother's bedroom a while back."

Pamela nodded, squeezing herself out of the car like a large schooner pulling out of a particularly narrow harbour. "Come on then," she called, gesturing toward the house, which in fairness, could only really be referred to as the world's most incongruous ranch. "In we go!"

Kester pressed the doorbell, which released a plodding, melodious tune that continued for about a minute longer than it should have.

"Please don't say that was the Argentinian national anthem," he said, looking at Pamela.

She giggled, then rapped at the door. "Kester, you need to be a little bit more patriotic," she said with mock severity. "After all, you're half Argentinian yourself, remember?"

I hadn't actually really thought about that, he thought. *Gosh. I suppose I am. Half German and half Argentinian. Well, there's a mix. Why I look 100% like a plump English academic makes even less sense now.*

The door swung open, revealing Dr Ribero, who greeted them like the lord of a manor, gesturing inside with a sweep of his arm.

"Aha, you are finally here!" He ushered them in, giving them no time to respond. Kester struggled to fight back a giggle. His father was wearing what could only be described as a smoking jacket in brushed burgundy velvet, and had even taken the trouble to add a pristine white handkerchief to the breast pocket. Kester couldn't decide whether or not he looked like the world's most debonair old gentleman, or a rather overdressed idiot.

He was instantly entranced by the pictures that surrounded him. A sea of black and white photos lined both sides of the hallway—the pictures full of serious-looking people, wearing all sorts of fascinatingly dated outfits.

"That one is your grandmother," Ribero said, pointing. "*Mia madre*. My mother."

"She's very beautiful," Kester commented, struck with the woman's strong jaw and fierce, dark eyes, so like Ribero's own.

"Yes, yes she was," Ribero agreed. He looked momentarily confused, then suddenly remembered himself. "Come on, come on! Serena, Mike and Jennifer are already here, and we have some big news."

"Big news?" Kester repeated, following Ribero through the house. It was every bit as wood-dominated inside as it was out, with polished floorboards and wood-panelled walls. *It must feel like living in a tree,* he thought, but he rather liked it, nonetheless. The wood exuded a natural warmth that made him feel at ease.

They stepped into an open-plan room, with floor-to-ceiling windows overlooking the woodland beyond. Serena, Mike, and Miss Wellbeloved waved, lost in the huge leather sofas by the fireplace.

Mike raised his glass in salute. "Good to see you again," he said with a wink. "Thought you'd sodded off back to Cambridge, it had been so long."

"It's only been a few days," Kester replied, looking round the room in awe. It really was a remarkable living room, and the amber twilight emphasised its beauty. "I just needed a bit of recovery time. Speaking of which," he said, suddenly remembering, "Serena, how are you?"

Serena sipped her wine before answering. "Fine," she replied pertly. "Completely recovered. It was lucky the Bloody Mary managed to knock me out cold, because if I'd been conscious, I would have seriously kicked her head in, I can tell you."

"I'm just really glad you're okay," Kester said. "It was horrible seeing you like that. Probably even more horrible than seeing the Bloody Mary herself."

Serena's expression softened, just for a moment. "Heard you did a rather good job of dispatching her," she said, fingering the rim of the wine glass. "So it seems you can control when the spirit door appears, after all?"

Dr Ribero sidled up behind Kester, patting him on the back and thrusting an over-full glass of wine into his hands. "Oh yes!" he beamed. "Kester saved the day, he really did. What talent! I knew you had it in you."

"It honestly wasn't that big a deal," Kester replied, feeling embarrassed, especially with Serena's scornful gaze scorching holes into the side of his face. "I can't really take much credit."

"Yes you can," Miss Wellbeloved interrupted, getting to her feet. Without warning, she pulled him into a hug, with a ferocity that quite took him by surprise, not to mention made him spill red wine all over the floor. No one seemed to mind though, nor make any attempt to clear it up.

"I didn't thank you properly on the night," she continued, placing her hands on his shoulders. "So I want to thank you now. Kester, you were amazing that evening. Your mother would have been so proud of you."

"And your father is very proud of you too," Ribero said, whipping out his handkerchief and dabbing at his eye. He beamed round at everyone, then gestured to the dining room table, an enormous oak affair flanked by carved benches and a pair of antlers on the wall. "Ladies and gentlemen," he announced grandly. "Dinner is served. And you had all better be hungry, right? I've been cooking for three hours now."

"You've been cooking?" Miss Wellbeloved exclaimed, placing her hands on her bony hips. "I did most of the work, if you remember? Marinating the steaks doesn't really count."

"Ah, but that is the most important part!" Ribero barked, scuttling off to the kitchen. "Sit down, sit down!" he shouted, in such an authoritative tone that they all scurried to the table.

A few minutes later, Ribero returned, complete with plate-fuls of sizzling steaks, which were releasing the most deliciously spicy smell. "This is how we eat in Argentina," he announced, slamming the plate down in front of Kester. "This is your heritage, yes? Right here, in front of you. Now enjoy."

Kester got started with great enthusiasm. As his father had promised, the marinade was particularly good, and he was quite disappointed to realise that he'd eaten it all. Even though it had been an enormous slab of meat, he felt as though he could quite happily eat at least the same again.

"It's good, isn't it?" Mike said, nudging him forcefully with his elbow. "The magic's in that sauce. What's it called again? Chiggichanka or something like that?"

"It is *chimichurri*!" Ribero snorted. "You just get it wrong to make me get cross, don't you?"

Mike sniggered. "Whatever it's called, it's a doozy," he concluded, leaning back with a belch.

"It is a traditional Argentinian sauce," Ribero corrected, wagging his finger. "Not this doozy, whatever a doozy may be."

"Anyway," Miss Wellbeloved interrupted, "why don't we stop discussing the merits of *chimichurri* sauce, and tell Kester the exciting news?"

"If Pamela hasn't let the cat out of the bag already," Mike added. "I know what you're like with a secret, Pam."

"No, I haven't given it away at all!" she protested, scooping up the last of the sauce with her finger. "Thank you very much. The cheek!"

"Given what away?" said Kester. "What's happened?"

"Thanks to my amazing genius, not to mention my super-cool head in the face of adversity, I've managed to single-handedly rescue this agency," Mike announced, scooping up his wine glass and raising it as a toast to himself.

"You did?" Kester said, blinking. He looked round at the others.

"No, he really didn't," Serena snipped, leaning over and pressing Mike's wine glass back down like a deflating balloon. "Mike, stop taking all the credit. You really are a moron at times."

"Steady on," Mike slurred, placing the wine glass down in an uncertain manner. "If I hadn't filmed the Muddy Blairy, then the agency wouldn't have been saved, and that's a fact, thank you very much."

"Did you just say 'Muddy Blairy'?" Serena replied, arching an eyebrow. "How many wines have you had?"

"Bloody Mary, whatever," Mike rambled. "I'd call her Bloody Nuisance instead, only you've bagged that nickname for yourself."

"Hang on, when did you film the Bloody Mary?" Kester interrupted. "I didn't see any film cameras."

"Film cameras?" Mike exclaimed, slapping the table. "Film cameras? What decade are you living in, mate? I used my mobile phone, didn't I!"

Kester thought back to the evening at Coleton Crescent. Now, come to think of it, he did vaguely remember Mike mentioning his phone. He hadn't given it much thought at the time, given that he'd been busy battling with a centuries-old spirit, but now it did make rather more sense.

"So how did filming the Bloody Mary save the agency?" he asked, perplexed. "I can't see the link between the two."

"Oh just wait," Serena drawled, "I'm sure Mike will illuminate you. He's been bragging about it all day."

Mike grinned and sat up in his chair, clearly enjoying the limelight. "Well," he began, stroking his beard, "thanks to my lightning-quick reflexes and good thinking—"

"Oh, get on with it, Mike!" Ribero interrupted. "We have had enough of the bloating for now."

"Gloating," Miss Wellbeloved automatically corrected.

"Dunno, he looks pretty bloated with smugness from where I'm sitting," Serena commented.

"Can I please carry on?" Mike said huffily, glowering at the rest of them. "Right, where was I? Ah, yes. I had the clever idea of filming the Bloody Mary, when you were busy stuffing her back into the spirit world, where she belonged. So, the next day, I downloaded the film on to SpiritNet, and—"

"Hang on a moment," Kester interrupted. "SpiritNet? What the hell is that?"

"It's the online network for supernatural investigators and whatnot," Mike said impatiently.

"Another Swww.co.uk address, in case you were wondering," Serena added. "Registered users only."

"Anyway," Mike carried on, shushing her with a finger. "I loaded it onto the forum, and sure enough, it went completely viral."

"Hang on a minute," Kester interrupted. "I'm still getting my head round that. The online network of supernatural investigators has a forum?"

"Yes!" Mike trilled like an enraged parrot, flapping his arms and nearly knocking over his glass. "Yes, just like any other industry, we've got websites too. Can we move on?"

"And the video went viral? Are there actually enough paranormal investigators in the country to make anything go viral?" Kester asked, scratching his head.

"Oh for goodness' sake," Mike exclaimed, slapping his forehead against the table in mock-frustration. "Look, we're not talking just the UK, we're talking the world. Everyone was going completely nuts about it, leaving comments about how it was a miracle, seeing a Bloody Mary again, not to mention the spirit door. Most paranormal investigators out there haven't ever seen one in action."

"So people were actually interested all over the world?" Kester asked in amazement. He couldn't imagine it. *Why would anyone be interested in me?* he thought. *I'm about as much of a non-event as it's possible to be.*

"You're actually trending on SpiritNet," Serena added. "Mike totally hammed your achievements up to the max, and now most of the paranormal world thinks you're the next bloody Messiah."

"Oh, that's terrible," Kester said, biting his lip.

"What do you mean, terrible?" Mike squawked. "It's absolutely bloody fantastic! We've never had so much attention! You've put Dr Ribero's Agency of the Supernatural right back on the map, you have!"

"Really?" Kester squeaked.

"Really," Miss Wellbeloved confirmed. "But there's even better news."

"Gosh," Kester muttered, feeling rather overwhelmed by it all. "What's that then?"

"We've only gone and been nominated for a GhostCon award!" Mike shouted, nearly falling off his chair. "We've been nominated for the top prize: 'Spirit Removal of the Year'! Do you know what that means?"

"Er, no. I don't even know what GhostCon is."

"GhostCon is an annual industry awards event," Pamela explained. "It's the most prestigious awards ceremony by a mile."

"It means," Mike continued, carrying on as though Pamela hadn't spoken, "that if we scoop the prize, we not only get a big fat gold award and serious recognition, but we get a grant of ten thousand pounds!"

Kester's mouth dropped open. "Really?" he said.

"Really, really," Pamela cut back in, with a beaming smile, "even if we don't win, you've made people take us seriously again. We've already had job offers come flying in, without us even having to bid for them!"

"They all want the miracle agency that can open spirit doors," Dr Ribero added, with a proud nod. "And that's where you come in, my boy."

"Oh," Kester said, now realising where this was going. "Oh, I see."

He looked around the table, at the five smiling faces looking back at him, and saw an energy and joy in them all that he'd never seen before. Ribero raised his glass, delivering him a smile of pure, unadulterated pride.

But I swore to myself I'd never go on another paranormal investigation, he thought to himself, as he nervously raised his own glass. *I hate doing it. It's the most terrifying, horrible thing I've ever had to do! Am I really agreeing to do this as a full-time career?*

"To Kester!" Dr Ribero declared, raising his glass and clinking with the rest. "To my boy."

"And to me too," Mike barked, raising his own glass again and nodding at the rest of them. "And to me, come on! I'm the one that filmed it and got it online."

"Well, if you're toasting him, you can jolly well toast me too," Serena added. "I'm the one who got her out of the painting and nearly got myself killed in the process."

"You are right," Dr Ribero said. He raised his glass once more, taking the time to meet each of their eyes in turn. "To you all. To our fantastic team, who have stood together through tough times. To our future."

"To our future!" they all agreed, clanking their glasses and spilling copious amounts of red wine over the table.

"And to the prospect of winning that award and knocking Infinite Enterprises right off their perch!" Mike bellowed. The others cheered. "And can you imagine the look on Larry

Higgins's face if we win?"

Ribero rubbed his hands together with glee. "That would make my life complete," he said. "Seeing his fat face looking so disappointed would be a wondrous thing, yes?"

The others nodded.

After a while, they retreated to the comfort of the sofas once again, which Kester was rather relieved about, given that his trousers were uncomfortably tight after all the steak. Ribero threw open the patio doors, letting the warm evening air float in, then lit some candles in the garden, creating little bubbles of light in the darkness. It was a beautiful location, and for the first time in a long while, Kester felt truly contented. Well, as long as he didn't think too hard about his future job as a paranormal investigator. That rather put a dampener on things.

To save himself from nodding off on the sofa in an intoxicating stupor of good food and pleasant wine, he ventured out into the garden, leaving the others chatting away in increasingly loud, inebriated tones.

The air was fresh and cool. Kester took a deep breath, closing his eyes. He wondered, not for the first time, whether or not his mother was somewhere out there, watching him. *I suppose I might be in the right sort of job for meeting her again one day,* he thought, deftly flicking a mosquito off his arm. *Even if spirits are totally different to human ghosts, there must be some sort of cross-over.*

A tap on his back startled him, and he turned to see Serena, standing in the darkness, framed by the glow of the light from indoors.

"Didn't mean to make you jump," she said. "Though you are rather skittish, aren't you?"

"Ironically, not before I met you guys," Kester replied, grinning. "There's something about dealing with ghosts on a daily basis that does make one a little jumpy, I suppose."

She chuckled. "Fair point. I keep forgetting you're still new to it all. Especially now you're Ribero's golden boy."

Kester studied her expression, unable to tell what she was thinking. "I think he rather thinks of you as a bit of a golden girl too, you know," he said finally. "You were incredibly brave with that Bloody Mary. I've never seen anything like it."

Serena smiled, giving the grass a slow kick with her feet. "Ah, it's just what anyone would have done," she said, with uncharacteristic modesty. "I'm just sad that I didn't get to give that Bloody Mary a good kick up the arse."

"If it's any consolation, the Bloody Mary really didn't look very happy about it all," Kester said.

"Speaking of which, Isabelle Diderot, the owner of the house, wasn't very happy either," Serena added.

"Why not?" Kester asked, feeling indignant. "She got what she wanted, didn't she?"

"Yes," Serena said, looking up at the sky. "But she probably wasn't expecting to have half her lounge burnt down in the process. Not to mention the priceless antique mirror smashed to bits. And I think you might have broken one of the deckchairs in the garden too."

"Oh," Kester said. "Oh dear."

"That didn't stop Ribero charging her full price for the job though," she added with a laugh. "But anyway, that wasn't what I came out here for. I wanted to talk to you about what happened. When I looked into the mirror, you know. When you were next to me."

"Oh, it's okay, you don't have to thank me," Kester said, placing a hand on her arm. "I honestly only did what anyone else would have done."

Serena raised an eyebrow. "I wasn't actually going to thank you," she said, plucking up his hand and dropping it like a dirty puppy that had just left a muddy paw on her. "I was actually going to ask you not to say anything."

"About what?" Kester asked. "What should I be saying

anything about?"

"About who I saw in the mirror when I summoned the Bloody Mary, of course!" Serena snapped. "You really are slow on the uptake at times, aren't you?"

"But you didn't see . . ." Kester began, then suddenly faltered. His face broke into a grin of realisation. "Oh my goodness. So *that's* why you said Mike's name, because you were being shown your future—"

"Yes, that's quite enough, thank you!" Serena said, peering over her shoulder to check no one was listening. She leaned towards him, placing her mouth directly by his ear. "If you breathe a word of this to anyone," she whispered fiercely, "you're dead. Okay?"

Kester fought to keep a straight face. "Yes, of course," he said. "You have my word. Not a word to anyone."

Serena studied his face, then relaxed. "Thank you," she said finally. "And, for what it's worth, I am grateful for your help when I was facing the Bloody Mary. I heard you helped keep me upright when I'd passed out. That was kind of you."

"Quite alright," Kester replied. He gestured back to the others. Mike had just fallen off the sofa, much to the amusement of the others, and was flailing around on the floor like a giant, upended tortoise. "Shall we go back in?" he suggested.

Serena looked in at Mike. Her expression curdled with derision. "Yes, I suppose so," she sighed.

Just before they stepped back into the room, Kester tapped her on the shoulder. "Oh, and Serena?" he whispered.

"Yes, what?" she said, preoccupied by the sight of Mike, who had now somehow managed to pull both the coffee table and Pamela on top of himself, much to the hilarity of the others.

"I'd just like to be the first to say," he started, unable to stop himself, "congratulations." He nodded at Mike, who was roaring like a bullfrog, drunkenly pulling himself back onto the sofa. "I'm sure you'll both be very happy together."

He skipped into the house before Serena had a chance to reply, but could feel her eyes, daggering into his back as he went.

"You can shut right up with that nonsense!" she shouted after him, a note of desperation in her voice. "It's just an urban myth! There's no truth in it at all, and there's no way I'm marrying that—"

"Of course, of course," Kester replied. He grinned at Mike, who was in the process of trying to give Pamela a piggy-back. It was a bit like watching a grizzly bear balancing on a spectacularly wobbly ladder. They teetered for a few moments, then Mike tripped over the rug, sending the pair of them sailing over the back of the sofa.

Kester turned and winked at Serena, gesturing to Mike's kicking legs. "You can't deny it though—he is a catch."

Hearing the snarl of rage, he ran to the downstairs toilet, locking himself in before she had a chance to catch up. Pressing his head against the door, he laughed until his glasses misted up.

Perhaps it wouldn't be so bad after all, he thought, taking a moment to compose himself. For the first time in his life, he actually felt like he belonged somewhere—that people wanted him around, and didn't just think he was a pale, plump idiot. He thought of the others. His father. The spirit door. Exeter. It was a different life to the one he was used to—a strange, frightening, completely stark-raving insane kind of life. But it might just work.

Maybe I could get used to this, he realised.

ABOUT THE AUTHOR

Lucy Banks grew up in provincial Hertfordshire, before fleeing to the wilds of Devon, where she now lives with her husband and two boys. As a child, she spent a disproportionate amount of time lurking in libraries, and prowling car-boot sales to feed both her hunger for books and her book collection. It's fair to say that she's bypassed being a bookworm, and become a book-python instead. Today, most of the available space in her house is stuffed to the brim with literature, which is just the way she likes it.

After teaching English Literature to teens, Lucy set up her own copywriting company and turned her love for the written word into a full-time career. However, the desire to create never went away, so Lucy turned her insomnia into a useful tool—penning her novels in the wee small hours of the night and the stolen moments of the day.

Lucy has enjoyed inhabiting worlds of her own creation from a young age. While her initial creations were somewhat dubious, thankfully, her writing grew as she did, becoming more coherent, as well as riveting. Writing has been a lifelong exercise for Lucy, and she loves the process from the beginning inklings of an idea to the care spent editing interesting tales. She takes particular delight in creating worlds that closely overlap reality with key intriguing differences. The odd, the jarring, and the curious are all themes that often feature prominently in her stories.

The Case of the Green-Dressed Ghost is Lucy's first published novel, and the first in the series, *Dr Ribero's Agency of the Supernatural*. The series unites the realm of the strange with the everyday world. It's a place where chaotic spirits rub shoulders with businessmen, and nothing is quite as it seems.